# SPY CLASSROOM 07

## A Glint in Monika's Eye

D1525089

code name
**GREEN
BUTTERFLY**

code name
**SCARLET
LEVIATHAN**

code name
PANDEMONIUM

code name
FLOWER
GARDEN

A Girl at War

# SPY CLASSROOM 07

## A Glint in Monika's Eye

# Takemachi

ILLUSTRATION BY **Tomari**

YEN ON

New York

# SPY CLASSROOM 07

Translation by Nathaniel Thrasher
Cover art by Tomari

SPY KYOSHITSU Vol.7 <<HYOJIN>> NO MONIKA
©Takemachi, Tomari 2022
First published in Japan in 2022 by KADOKAWA CORPORATION, Tokyo.
English translation rights arranged with KADOKAWA CORPORATION, Tokyo through
TUTTLE-MORI AGENCY, INC., Tokyo.

Yen On
150 West 30th Street
New York, NY 10001

Visit us at yenpress.com
facebook.com/yenpress
twitter.com/yenpress
yenpress.tumblr.com
instagram.com/yenpress

First Yen On Edition: May 2024
Edited by Yen On Editorial: Anna Powers
Designed by Yen Press Design: Andy Swist

Yen On is an imprint of Yen Press, LLC.
The Yen On name and logo are trademarks of Yen Press, LLC.

Library of Congress Cataloging-in-Publication Data
Names: Takemachi, author. | Tomari, Meron, illustrator. | Thrasher, Nathaniel Hiroshi, translator.
Title: Spy classroom / Takemachi ; illustrated by Tomari ; translation by Nathaniel Thrasher.
Other titles: Spy kyoushitsu. English
Description: First Yen On edition. | New York, NY : Yen On, 2021.
Identifiers: LCCN 2021021119 | ISBN 9781975322403 (v. 1 ; trade paperback) | ISBN
9781975322427 (v. 2 ; trade paperback) | ISBN 9781975338824 (v. 3 ; trade paperback) | ISBN
9781975338848 (v. 4 ; trade paperback) | ISBN 9781975343125 (v. 5 ; trade paperback) | ISBN
9781975350284 (v. 6 ; trade paperback) | ISBN 9781975367497 (v. 7 ; trade paperback)
Subjects: CYAC: Spies—Fiction. | Schools—Fiction.
Classification: LCC PZ7.1.T343 Sp 2021 | DDC [Fic]—dc23
LC record available at https://lccn.loc.gov/2021021119

ISBNs: 978-1-9753-6749-7 (paperback)
        978-1-9753-6750-3 (ebook)

10 9 8 7 6 5 4 3 2 1

LSC-C

Printed in the United States of America

# C O N T E N T S

Character Profiles  ii

Prologue
Nightmare  1

Chapter 1
Scarlet
Leviathan ①  7

Chapter 2
Glint ①  23

Chapter 3
Scarlet
Leviathan ②  41

Chapter 4
Glint ②  55

Chapter 5
Scarlet
Leviathan ③  71

Chapter 6
Glint ③  85

Chapter 7
Scarlet
Leviathan ④  105

Chapter 8
Glint ④  121

Chapter 9
Glint and Scarlet
Leviathan  137

Chapter 10
Traitor  159

Epilogue
The Girl and
the World  183

Next Mission  193

Afterword  201

SPY CLASSROOM
Specialized lessons for an impossible mission
Code name: Glint

# CHARACTER PROFILES

Bonfire

# Klaus

Lamplight's founder and the Greatest Spy in the World.

Flower Garden

# Lily

A naive girl from the backcountry.

Daughter Dearest

# Grete

A quiet girl and the daughter of a major politician.

Pandemonium

# Sybilla

A brave girl and the daughter of a gangster.

Glint

# Monika

An arrogant girl born into a family of artists.

Dreamspeaker

# Thea

An elegant girl and the only child of a major newspaper company's president.

Meadow
# Sara

A timid girl whose
parents run a
small restaurant.

Forgetter
# Annette

A simple girl with no
memories. Her origins
are unknown.

Fool
# Erna

An unlucky girl who
frequently gets into
accidents. Also, a
former aristocrat.

## Team Avian

Flock
# Vindo

Glide
# Qulle

South Wind
# Queneau

Cloud Drift
# Lan

Lander
# Vics

Feather
# Pharma

# Prologue

## Nightmare

The tragedy began at dawn.

It took place in the Kashard Doll Workshop, a brickwork building with two stories and a basement tucked away in a corner of the Fend Commonwealth's capital of Hurough. It was an unremarkable building, the kind you could find just about anywhere in the city. The locals assumed it was a quiet little studio full of doll makers, but they couldn't have been more wrong. In truth, it was the headquarters of Belias, a counterintelligence unit that worked for the Commonwealth's CIM intelligence agency. That was where they worked to capture spies who had infiltrated their nation.

It was four in the morning when the tragedy struck. At the time, the building contained four members of the spy team Lamplight and two members of Belias. Lamplight had just extorted Belias into handing over their intel, and its members were reading through Belias's files as quickly as they could.

The first person to sense that something was amiss was "Daughter Dearest" Grete—a redheaded girl with slender limbs and a glasslike frailty about her. As she perused the files in the reception area on the first floor, she spotted the attacker standing in the entrance. The assailant was someone she knew well, so Grete called out to them. A moment later, she saw the flash of a blade. The attack came so suddenly that she was helpless to react, and she lost consciousness.

\* \* \*

Over in the first-floor hallway, "Fool" Erna—a short blond girl with the exquisite beauty of a doll—was the next to notice. From the corridor, she saw Grete collapse, then looked back and forth in horror between Grete's attacker and the bright-red blood pooling under Grete's body. The assailant sent a fierce kick aimed at Erna's stomach, but Erna used her characteristically quick wits to keep the damage to a minimum and fled up to the second floor.

The main reason Erna was able to make it to the second floor safely was because "Dreamspeaker" Thea—an elegant dark-haired girl with curves in all the right places—arrived in the hallway. Thea tried to flee the moment she saw Erna get kicked, but the attacker pinned her down with ease. "Why are you doing this…?" Thea groaned as she lay slumped on the ground. She put up a decent fight, but the assailant eventually smashed their knife into her right arm, breaking it and leaving her with a serious wound.

All the while, Belias's boss watched the tragedy play out alongside one of her agents. The boss in question was "Puppeteer" Amelie—a woman with dark bags under her eyes who was dressed in a Gothic outfit. Unable to comprehend what was happening, all Amelie could do was observe the events as they unfolded.

At one point, she thought she spotted another girl aside from the attacker, one with large scars on her shoulders, but she never got a clear look. She felt as though she'd seen the girl somewhere before, but immediately after the notion crossed her mind, Monika punched her in passing and sent the thought back into the depths of her memories.

As soon as Erna rushed up to the second floor, "Forgetter" Annette—a girl with messily tied-up ash-pink hair and a large bandage over her left eye—readied her weapon, and when the attacker finally made her way to the second-floor workspace, the two of them squared off. Annette fought with her special bombs, and the ensuing flames started making their way through the Kashard Doll Workshop.

However, her efforts were useless against the assailant. Annette suffered heavy wounds when the attacker kicked her bombs back at her, as did Erna behind her. Erna passed out and began bleeding from her head, and although Annette tried to protect her teammate, the assailant struck her hard in the flank with their daggers. Annette's broken ribs punctured her organs, and after vomiting up blood, she passed out as well.

That was when the two girls who'd started outside the building arrived. One was "Flower Garden" Lily—a silver-haired girl with an adorably childish face and an ample bosom—and the other was "Pandemonium" Sybilla—a white-haired girl with striking eyes and a toned build. The two of them witnessed the daggers strike Annette, and they froze in disbelief at the sight.

As the fire spread, the attacker let out a quiet "I'm sorry," then left the Kashard Doll Workshop alongside the girl with scars on her shoulders.

Such was the tragedy brought about by the girl who betrayed Lamplight— "Glint" Monika.

The Kashard Doll Workshop painted the Hurough sky red as it burned.

The rain that had been falling since the night prior washed away the filth that hung so prominently over Hurough, revealing the moon sitting above the fog-smothered city. A moment later, though, it was over, and fat clouds rolled in and covered the moon right back up. The sun had yet to rise over Hurough, and the flames from the workshop climbed high into the sky.

In the end, that fire never reached the surrounding buildings. It got put out before it had a chance to. However, all those who'd been watching knew that the true chaos had only just begun.

"Sturm! Und! Drang!" Over on a nearby rooftop, a girl stood with her arms spread wide. "Gee, Scarlet Leviathan, great going! That was awesome. You really gave them hell!"

She had an alluring body with long, slender limbs, but due to her jagged teeth, smiling made her look sadistic, like she was laughing at someone else's misfortune. Her sleeveless dress left her scarred shoulders bare. "Sturm und Drang!" she shouted delightedly into the chilly air.

The girl's name was Green Butterfly, and she was a member of the Galgad spy team Serpent. With the skillful steps of a practiced dancer, she spun back and forth atop the roof.

Meanwhile, the cerulean-haired girl beside her simply stood there placidly. Aside from her asymmetric hairdo, she had few notable features to speak of. That girl's name was "Glint" Monika—that, or Scarlet Leviathan. "Well, *someone's* enjoying herself," she muttered curtly as she stared at the burning workshop.

Green Butterfly stopped in her tracks and shot Monika a provocative, toothy grin. "I'm just impressed, that's all. We were in and out in a blink, and you even found time to burn the place down. I meant it as a compliment."

"Oh. Thanks, I guess."

"Still, in a perfect world, I bet you could've gotten away with beating another of 'em within an inch of their life." Green Butterfly squinted at her. "Gee, you don't...still have reservations, do you?"

The air crackled with hostility.

Monika averted her gaze from the workshop and drew one of her knives. Its blade was wet and crimson with her teammates' blood. She gently wiped the knife clean as she gave her answer.

"Reservations? Nah. Not me."

Her tone was as dispassionate as could be.

The corner of Green Butterfly's mouth curled upward.

"We accomplished our objective, right? I put a couple of them out of commission, and I took a hostage." Once Monika was done cleaning her knife, she stowed it back in its sheath. "Lily and Sybilla came back. If Klaus had ended up being with them, the situation would have gotten dicey in a hurry. The getting was good. You got any problems with that?"

This time, it was Monika's turn to shoot a probing look at her counterpart.

After a pregnant pause, Green Butterfly clapped her hands together. "Perfection." A crisp round of applause echoed out over the early-morning cityscape. "Gee, Scarlet Leviathan, that's right. That's perfect. That's great, that's great, that's fantastic! I just knew I made the right call with you."

"I don't know why the hell you keep throwing 'gee' into every third sentence..."

"'Cause G is for Green Butterfly, duh."

"...but more importantly, I can't get used to this 'Scarlet Leviathan' code name." Monika furrowed her brow. "Couldn't you have gone with something more normal?"

Leviathans were fictional creatures resembling massive blue snakes that were often mentioned in the same breath as dragons. That was a pretty substantial leap from the flies, spiders, ants, and butterflies that previous Serpent members had introduced themselves as.

Green Butterfly spun her way across the roof over to Monika's back with a dancer's grace. "I wanted to give you a name befitting my new partner, see."

"Huh?"

"You and me, we're about to bring forth the greatest nightmare ever. It'll be like a dance, the way we take each other's hands and plunge the foolish masses into a deep darkness. For a big job like that, you need a big name." Green Butterfly let out a laugh, then slung her arm around Monika's shoulder. "You ever hear the one about the two spy women who took the world by storm?"

"What're you talking about?"

"'Hearth' Veronika. And 'Firewalker' Gerde."

Monika recognized the pair of names Green Butterfly whispered in her ear. She'd heard them from Klaus. Those two had been members of the team that preceded Lamplight—Inferno.

"The two of them put Inferno's name on the map. On every map. With a killer, a gamer, and a soothsayer in tow, they led the Galgad Empire straight to ruin. They might've been our enemies, but there's no denying they were the Finest Spies in the World." Green Butterfly flashed her jagged teeth. "But then they kicked the bucket."

"Yeah," Monika replied succinctly. "I heard. Hearth died over in the United States of Mouzaia, and the last anyone heard from Firewalker, she was right here in Fend." With some consternation, she reached over and touched Green Butterfly's shoulder. There was a scar that looked almost like a lightning bolt. The fissure ran all the way down from her shoulder to her elbow, and it had a matching partner on the other side. "...Tell me, did Firewalker give you these?"

"Gee, clever guess." Green Butterfly gave her a perverse smile. "And it's bang on the money." She reached for Monika's abdomen and gently stroked it. "And just between you and me, I'm the one who put her down."

"Damn. I hear she was supposed to be one badass old lady, too."

"All that past greatness couldn't save her from becoming a senile old hag. I'm telling you, it was pathetic. Wounding me took everything she had left, and in the end, she died begging for her life. Gee, what an idiot."

Green Butterfly continued touching Monika with visible delight. The way her fingers moved was downright tender as she fondled everything from Monika's abs to her thighs to her breasts. Monika furrowed her brow in displeasure, but Green Butterfly paid her no heed.

"The next ones to dance across this world are gonna be us."

As she caressed Monika, she smiled. Then she glared out at the streets of Hurough and let out a delighted cry.

"Now panic, O wretched masses! Burn this endless nightmare as deep in your eye sockets as it'll go!"

Monika stared silently in the same direction as Green Butterfly. Her gaze was fixed, yet there was a dimness in her eyes that made it impossible to tell what exactly she was looking at.

"I'll do my part," she eventually said. "All you need me to do is destroy the world, right? As a filthy, wretched traitor."

With that, the day broke.

The Fend Commonwealth's long nightmare was about to begin.

# Chapter 1

# Scarlet Leviathan ①

The world was awash in pain.

Ten years had passed since the end of the Great War, the largest war in human history. Seeing its horrors had driven the world's politicians to turn to spy work rather than military might as their preferred way of influencing other countries.

Lamplight was a spy team that fought on behalf of the Din Republic. It comprised eight former academy washouts, as well as "Bonfire" Klaus, the single strongest spy in the Republic.

After hearing that their close friends in Avian had been taken out, Lamplight rushed to the Fend Commonwealth to get to the bottom of things. After conducting their investigation, they discovered that the culprit was Belias, a counterintelligence team working for the Fend Commonwealth's CIM intelligence agency. After capturing Belias alive, Lamplight pumped them for information.

That was when they learned that the Galgad Empire's Serpent team was lying in wait in the Fend Commonwealth. The only reason Belias had attacked Avian was because Serpent had fed the CIM some bad intel. Upon learning that, the girls swore vengeance against Serpent. Before they even had a chance to plan their next move, though, they found themselves in a horrible situation.

One of Lamplight's core members, "Glint" Monika, had turned traitor.

◇◇◇

Klaus hadn't been present to see Monika defecting, so the first thing he had to do was get the facts straight.

Out in front of the Kashard Doll Workshop, the firefighters were stopping Lily and Sybilla as the duo tried to charge back into the building. Beside them, a paramedic was wrapping a bandage around Erna's head. Farther back, another group of grim-faced medics was carrying Thea and Annette off to the hospital.

Klaus wasted no time in stealing a firefighter's uniform so he could go investigate the scene inside. Then he got in touch with the medical team and checked in on the wounded girls' statuses.

- Erna had a cut on the side of her head.
- Thea's right arm was injured.
- Annette had damage to her ribs and organs. From what Klaus was able to learn, she needed immediate surgery.

The good news was that none of their injuries were life-threatening. The latter two were going to undergo surgery at the hospital, but the girls had all infiltrated Fend with proper cover identities like restaurant workers and tourists, so they would be treated like any other patients.

Klaus then took his remaining subordinates and relocated to a nearby apartment they'd rented for the mission to use as Lamplight's base of operations. Worry was etched deep on the girls' faces, so he told them, "I want everyone to take a deep breath," then set to work brewing enough tea for the group.

Lily, Sybilla, and Erna sat down on the sofa, and Klaus set a teacup in front of each of them and added a splash of brandy for aroma. After giving them a chance to gulp down a mouthful, he asked for the details.

Monika had betrayed them.

The news shocked Klaus as much as anyone, but he didn't let it shake him. As the team's boss, he held a sense of duty to keep his head clear.

"Take all your emotions and shut them off for a bit. Think of it like you're flipping a circuit breaker," he said after getting the gist of the situation. "Now, I'll go through each part one at a time to make sure I have it all right. First, we're certain that Monika attacked her own teammates?"

Lily and Sybilla nodded. Erna had fallen unconscious for a bit after getting attacked herself, and she gave a pained reply in the affirmative. "...We're certain."

Klaus dispassionately continued asking his questions. "Now, you all saw Grete face down in a pool of blood, yes?"

Lily, Sybilla, and Erna nodded.

"When you did, none of you checked if she was still alive?"

The girls nodded again. "There was no way someone could have survived losing that much blood," Lily replied in a voice stripped of emotion. "I decided that treating her was less important than looking for people we could still save."

It sounded heartless, but it was the rational call to make. In emergencies like these, Lily's mental fortitude really shined.

"But then," Lily said softly, "the fire spread, and there was nothing we could do. We couldn't even retrieve her corpse—"

"There was no corpse."

"Huh?"

"I searched the building, but I didn't see any corpses that could have been hers. If what you saw was true, then there would have been no point in moving her. We can assume that Monika and her partner had some reason for taking her. There's a chance she's still alive."

It was possible that they needed Grete's corpse for something, of course, but it was difficult to imagine what that might be. It was much more likely that they needed her disguise skills, her intellect, or something in that vein.

Color returned to his three subordinates' faces, and they exhaled in delighted relief. "Thank fuckin' God..." and "Yeep...," Sybilla and Erna choked out with tears in their eyes.

Grete's fate had been weighing heavily on them. That was why they'd been trying so frantically to get back in the building.

"However, that does nothing to change how volatile the situation is," Klaus said to center their focus again. Then he began organizing his information. If nothing else, he now knew the details of what had happened. Monika had turned against them, Grete was missing, Annette was badly wounded, and Thea was injured. Lamplight was down a full half of its members.

Once he had that all sorted, he turned his thoughts to the future.

"I have no idea what Serpent was trying to accomplish," he said. "If all they wanted was to get Monika on their side, there was no need for them to make so much noise about it. When you get an enemy spy to turn traitor, the standard play is to have them leak information over a long period of time rather than doing anything too conspicuous."

There was something decidedly half-baked about the attack. If Monika's goal was merely to kidnap Grete, then surely there was a more covert way she could have done it. A spy with her talents could have carried out the abduction, then met back up with the others looking as innocent as could be.

"I can explain that," said Lily.

"Hmm?"

"There's no way she could have fooled you over a protracted time frame, Teach. She would have known better than to even try."

Sybilla and Erna nodded emphatically. "There's only one way for us to fool you. It's to avoid havin' any direct conversations."

"That's right. If she talked with you even a little, you would have seen right through her. It's impossible for us to keep secrets from you for long."

Now that—that made sense. Against the likes of the girls, Klaus could root out just about anything they tried to keep from him. As a matter of fact, he'd noticed that something seemed off about Monika during their strategy meeting just before they attacked Belias.

*...? That's right, I did sense that Monika didn't seem like herself back then.* A feeling of unease overtook him... *Why didn't I think to follow up on that?*

He'd been devoting his full attention to Avian at the time, but had he really not spared a second thought for how out of sorts his subordinate seemed?

He was filled with regret, but more than that, he was deeply baffled. How could he have let that happen? It made him uncomfortable in a way he couldn't quite explain, but there would be time to worry about that later.

"You're right. You girls can't deceive me for any meaningful length of time. In that case, we can safely deduce that Monika's betrayal was engineered over a short time period."

Lily clapped her hands together. "Ah, you're right."

"Sometime after we arrived in the Commonwealth, Serpent reached out to Monika. That's going to be our assumption going forward."

According to the girls' eyewitness accounts, Monika had been accompanied by a girl called Green Butterfly. Green Butterfly had been waiting for them in Fend, and there was a chance she was the one who'd instigated Monika's treachery.

"It all started right here in Fend," Klaus concluded. Ever since they got to the Fend Commonwealth, everything had smelled a bit fishy.

*Prince Darryn's assassination probably ties into all this...as does the Avian takedown... Serpent isn't just doing these things at random. They have an objective, that much is clear.*

One night prior, the man next in line to the Fend Commonwealth throne had been assassinated. By morning, the news had spread across the nation and plunged the country into a state of unrest.

*What is Serpent plotting here?*

Klaus knew of two major operations Serpent had carried out previously. There was the Blue Fly op, where Klaus's old mentor Guido had led Inferno to ruin, and there was the Purple Ant op where, over in Mitario, Serpent had dealt a serious blow to the intelligence agencies of the world by slaughtering their operatives in droves. Klaus and the girls had taken down the two perpetrators, but in both cases, they'd only been able to do so after the Serpent members had already completed their objectives.

By killing off notable spies, Serpent had created an environment where it was easier for them to make covert moves across the world, and on top of that, they'd also assassinated Prince Darryn. Klaus still needed loads of information, but fortunately for him, he knew just how to get it.

"Amelie," he said to the woman who'd been there in the room that whole time, "tell me the inside story about the situation in Fend. That's an order."

Aside from the Lamplight members, there was one other person in the apartment as well: "Puppeteer" Amelie, a woman whose Gothic outfit and dark bags under her eyes made her seem almost like a witch. She stood beside the couch looking decidedly uncomfortable.

"Talk fast, or I start killing your agents one by one."

Klaus delivered his threat calmly. Lamplight had successfully captured twenty-five of Amelie's subordinates, and aside from the aide-de-camp they were holding in a separate location, they had the rest of her agents locked up in a construction site's admin cabin just outside the city. All Klaus had to do was give the order on his radio, and their lives would be forfeited.

Amelie gave her head a feeble shake. "You want me to talk, but I have no idea what you want me to tell you. Monika, was it? Her betrayal makes no more sense to me than it does to you."

"Give me an overview on all the intelligence the CIM has. I'll tell you when I hear something I want more details on."

"I'm not going to reveal state secrets to you. No amount of threats will change that."

"Tell me the parts you can talk about, then."

When Klaus curtly delivered Amelie her orders, she went ahead and joined the girls on the couch. Sybilla sent him a pointed glance, so Klaus begrudgingly poured Amelie a cup of tea as well. As far as he was concerned, enemy spies were under no obligation to show each other such hospitality.

Amelie didn't so much as glance at it.

"Go ahead and start with things you think of as common knowledge," Klaus said. "I can't go into any details, but there are some gaps in what the girls know."

The girls had all been academy washouts, and Sybilla, in particular, had received terrible grades.

Amelie blinked, and a brief flash of puzzlement crossed her face. "......?" When she saw how earnestly the Lamplight girls were looking at her, though, she pulled herself together and gave them a small nod. "Very well," she replied simply. She raised her voice an octave like a professor standing at a lectern. "Then allow me to illuminate you, dear guests, and explain everything from the structure of the world to the state of my fair nation."

"Meadow" Sara shivered and pulled her newsboy cap tighter over her head.

While Amelie was describing the way things were in the Fend Commonwealth, Sara was off away from her team, desperately trying to keep her fingers warm as the heat drained from them.

"Oh, it's so cold..."

It was early morning, and the chill in the air was worse than ever.

An abandoned construction site sat on a small mountain near Hurough where people had once drawn up plans to build a resort. A large swath of the mountain had been cleared, and rows of heavy equipment rested in a corner waiting for the day when construction would resume. That was the site where Lamplight had carried out their daring plan to capture all of Belias alive. Under Klaus's leadership, Sybilla and Grete had fought hard to make the plan a success.

That construction site was home to a two-story admin cabin, and that was where a certain brown-haired girl was watching over the captives. She had the eyes of a small woodland creature and could rarely be found without her trademark newsboy cap—"Meadow" Sara. She let out foggy breaths as she walked down the hallway looking for some sort of jacket to wear.

"Thou'rt shivering up a storm. Art thou all right?" someone called over to her.

That someone was a girl who wore her dark-red hair tied back in a ponytail—"Cloud Drift" Lan. Lan was Avian's sole surviving member, and she was still recovering from the injuries she'd suffered all over her body. She'd popped back to the apartment for a bit to get some shut-eye, but after her short nap, she came right on back.

"Oh, no, I'm okay. I'm just not used to it," Sara replied, frowning in discomfort. "I've never had to confine people for long periods of time before, and it's kind of hard on me..."

That was Lamplight's first time ever taking such harsh measures. They had over twenty people sleeping in a single locked room with their wrists and ankles bound. Lamplight had given them first aid for the wounds Klaus and the girls dealt them, but the treatment was far from sufficient. The Belias agents were hardened spies, but even so, Sara could hear moans of pain coming from the room every so often. For someone as kindhearted as her, it was hard to listen to.

"How long are we going to have to keep Belias locked up for, I wonder...?"

"Indefinitely, of course," Lan replied without a moment's hesitation. "Our task is to keep them confined until we have need of them. If we run into problems, we need but end their lives, then use the construction equipment to bury them. Being discovered is no option at all."

"Oh dear... I—I guess you're right."

"I have not forgiven Belias for their deed. Fooled or not, the fact doth remain that they slew my brethren." Lan bristled and shot a look over at the locked room. "Were it up to me...I would have slain five or so of their number already."

That was when Sara noticed the gun in Lan's hand. She knew Lan was holding it so she'd be able to react immediately if an emergency broke out, but that didn't make it any less ominous.

Belias had been involved in Avian's deaths. It was hard to imagine a group that Lan would despise more.

Right as Sara began legitimately panicking at Lan's ruthless energy, the ponytailed girl's expression completely changed. "...Rather, that is what I would say, were I a different person altogether."

"Huh?"

Lan crossed her arms with a cheerful laugh. "In truth, I have no love for wet work. 'Twould be more in character for me to let down my guard and go play cards with the prisoners."

"Is that something you've actually done?!"

"Oh, the scoldings Brother Vindo gave me."

"I—I think that's a pretty reasonable reaction…"

"But now I have no comrades left to rebuke me." Lan let out a sad sigh, then squinted as she looked out the window. Off in the distance, she could see the morning sun rising over Hurough's streets.

Sara gasped a little when she remembered what had just happened down there.

Lan laid a gentle hand on her back. "Is it the situation with Monika that makes you shiver so?"

"Yeah…" Sara nodded. "It must be some sort of misunderstanding. Miss Monika would never…"

She trailed off. Over the radio, they'd heard about what Monika did. Sara didn't want to believe it. It was clear from Lily's and Sybilla's voices just how serious they were, but the whole situation was so unthinkable that it made her head spin.

"If I recall correctly, you and she were teacher and pupil?"

"That's right…"

"Well, our task now is to wait here and trust in Sir Klaus."

Sara gave Lan's attempt at consolation an unenthusiastic nod. There had been so many tragedies as of late, and she was helpless to do anything about them.

"Do you know what it was that caused the world to go so wrong?"

Amelie's elocution was excellent; she began her speech with a hook before delving into the explanation proper.

"The Industrial Revolution and the imperialism it fueled granted us Western-Central nations too much power. We started by racing to colonize Tolfa as quickly as we could, and before long, we turned our sights to the Far East. Then, once we held the majority of the world in our hands, we finally turned our sights homeward and waged a war with one another."

Sybilla finished that thought. "You mean the Great War."

"That I do, young lady," Amelie said with a nod. "When the Fend

Commonwealth– and Lylat Kingdom–led Allies came to blows with the Galgad Empire–led Axis powers, it was the largest war in human history."

The war in question had started fourteen years ago. It began as a series of sporadic skirmishes, but the war front grew over time in both scope and intensity. As science marched on, it gave birth to one new weapon after another. At around the two-year mark, the Galgad Empire was intent on invading the Lylat Kingdom, and with Din sitting in its way, it wasted no time in occupying the Republic. It had been ten years since the war's conclusion, and the eleventh anniversary was right around the corner.

Klaus had experienced the war firsthand. He didn't remember many specifics, but he had vague memories rattling around in his head of standing aghast as a boy in a town that had been leveled by bombs.

"The Allies may have won the war, but we suffered tremendous losses in the process. There were new weapons such as tanks, airplanes, submarines, and poison gas that were far too effective at killing, there were advances in transportation technology that allowed nations to engage in unprecedented levels of warfare... It was hell, and not a single person who witnessed it would dispute that description."

Sybilla, Lily, and Erna didn't say a word. All of them were recalling the things they'd gone through in their childhoods. The vast majority of Lamplight's members had suffered, either directly from the war or from the period of unrest that had followed it.

"...It was Inferno that helped end the war, right?" Lily asked.

"That it was." A smile spread across Amelie's face. "Inferno was a group of the best spies there were, Hearth chief among them, and together they stole military secrets from the Galgad Empire and delivered them to the Allies. If not for their efforts, it likely would have taken another three years for the war to come to its close."

"Th-that's kind of incredible..."

"There's a good reason why people in our line of work referred to Hearth as the Finest Spy in the World." Amelie shot a glance over at Klaus. "Though, note that in his case, the title of Greatest Spy in the World is entirely self-proclaimed."

"It's a fact is what it is," Klaus replied.

He wasn't sure why Amelie had decided to throw in that remark, but while he wanted to protest that it was his mentor "Torchlight" Guido who'd given him the moniker, he also realized that Guido had already been planning on betraying Inferno at the time, so his feelings about the situation were a bit mixed. However, he wasn't about to tell her all that.

It was time to end the sidebar and get the discussion back on track.

"That all lines up with my understandings," he said. "Tell me about the situation in Fend after the war."

"There were three major ways the world changed in the war's wake," Amelie said, resuming her speech. "The first was the rise of the United States of Mouzaia. Selling supplies during the war allowed them to flourish, and with the heavy wounds the other Western-Central nations suffered, it wasn't long before the United States overtook us all. As of right now, they've overtaken the Commonwealth and become the strongest nation in the world."

The girls had visited Mouzaia, and they all remembered how Mitario had been absolutely packed with skyscrapers. The fact that Mouzaia had been hosting a long-term economic conference was just one more testament to how the world had come to revolve around it.

"The second was the collaborative policies enacted by the world's nations. They all agreed to work together to bring about peace and ensure that war never broke out again. And they signed peace treaties to that same effect."

That one was indisputable, too. Just about every nation in the world had engaged in an armament reduction, and as small as the change was, they had started chipping away at their defense budgets, too.

"And the final change..."

Amelie's voice was calm and sure.

"...was how the world went opaque."

It was a decidedly abstract turn of phrase, and the girls weren't sure what she meant. Klaus sensed what Amelie was getting at, but he stayed quiet and let her finish.

"Nations began devoting their resources to their intelligence agencies rather than their militaries. They had been no strangers to the use of espionage, but now they were pouring far more resources into their spy programs than ever before. It's made it far more difficult to tell who's fighting whom and what's even going on in the world these days."

In short, the era of spies was upon them. The Din Republic had responded to that fact by taking Inferno as well as the best of the best from their Military and Naval Intelligence Departments and creating the Foreign

Intelligence Office. As the Great War had shown them, the coming era was going to be dominated by information.

Now the nations of the world were sending spies beyond each other's borders and fighting shadow wars. Conflict took place quietly, out of sight, behind closed doors, and in complicated ways—making war opaque. When it came to the battle for intelligence, there wasn't a single person in the entire world who could state with any confidence which nation held the advantage. For any operative who thought their homeland was an unassailable monolith, it was only a matter of time before they found the ground crumbling beneath their feet.

"Of course, figuring that out is what we intelligence agencies are for," Amelie added. "The way I see it, the situation is thus—at the moment, the Fend Commonwealth is in a state of considerable turmoil."

The girls' faces hardened. At last, they were getting to the heart of the matter.

"There are a large number of spies within our borders interacting as they please. And while it pains me to admit it, there may very well be a traitor lurking within Hide, the highest body in the CIM," Amelie said with a look of revulsion.

"That's likely the case, yes," Klaus replied. There could be little doubt of it. Back when Prince Darryn's life was under attack, the CIM had erroneously identified Avian as the culprits and ordered Belias to take them down. Afterward, they'd wasted all their effort in a meaningless manhunt for Lan and ultimately failed to stop the crown prince from getting assassinated.

The CIM was rotting from within.

"How could that have happened?" Lily asked sympathetically.

"In all likelihood, the traitor is a Neo-Imperialist. Here in Fend, the belief that we ought to work together with the Galgad Empire has picked up a considerable amount of support."

The girls found that hard to believe. "Sorry, what?" Sybilla cried. "Hold the fuckin' phone. How does that make any sense? In the war, you guys were enemies—"

"Indeed we were, and we have every reason to hold them in contempt. But with how strong the United States has become, that belief has started to shift. People have begun asking if it's really safe to let the United States remain unchecked," Amelie said, reining her in. "My nation is divided between two ideologies. There are those who hold the conventional view that we should work together with the United States to keep an eye on

Galgad. People call them right-wing conservatives and moderates, but by and large, they're simply referred to as Anti-Imperialists. Then there's the newer idea that we should join forces with Galgad to keep an eye on the United States. Reformists, liberals... The simplest term for them is Neo-Imperialists. These two pro- and anti-Imperial sentiments have divided both Parliament and the populace at large. I never imagined the same thing might be happening within the CIM itself, but now..."

The Din Republic had gotten directly invaded by Galgad, but Fend saw things a little differently than they did. The Commonwealth had been the strongest nation in the world for a long time leading up to the war, and many of its people weren't pleased about the way they'd been shunted down to second place. The question was, was their next big enemy going to be Galgad or Mouzaia? That was the issue that had split the nation in two.

"By all rights, the CIM should fall on the Anti-Imperialist side of things. We haven't forgotten the wounds they dealt us. However, there must be those who feel threatened by the way the United States continues to grow in strength."

"B-but that just gives Galgad a million openings to exploit..."

Lily had hit the nail right on the head. No matter how impregnable an intelligence organization was normally, it would be trivial for a foe to make headway on them in conditions such as those.

"That it does," Amelie agreed sadly. "And now we have a traitor among our ranks."

"The CIM I knew was an exceptionally well-run organization." During Klaus's time on Inferno, he'd both fought against and worked beside the CIM a number of different times. Their extreme competence had allowed them to make a fool of him on more than one occasion. "And they had a number of excellent teams. What's Retias doing?"

"They got wiped out in Mitario." Amelie bit down on her lip in frustration. "As did their replacements."

So they, too, had fallen to the far-reaching spy killings that made up Purple Ant's massacre. Many of the world's nations had suffered heavy losses to that man, and by the sound of it, the Fend Commonwealth was no exception.

"I—I have a question." After listening in earnest silence to the discussion, Erna spoke up. "Was Prince Darryn an Anti-Imperialist?"

"He was a member of the royal family; he never commented publicly on their political views. He was a great man, and he spoke of seeking peace with all nations."

Klaus glared at Amelie. There was a slight note of falsehood in her voice, and he wasn't about to let her get away with dodging the question. He intended to make her divulge everything she could, even state secrets.

Amelie let out a small sigh. "...However, rumor had it that he held no love for the Galgad Empire."

She didn't know any specifics, but word was that Prince Darryn had been close with the army's staunchly Anti-Imperialist leadership. It all more or less lined up. Darryn had been an Anti-Imperialist symbol, and by the look of it, it was the efforts of a Neo-Imperialist that had allowed an Imperial spy to carry out this tragic assassination.

The question was, who was an ally, and who was an enemy? Figuring that out in the Fend Commonwealth was about as tricky a task as they came. Galgad spies had wormed their way deep into the nation's core.

"To be perfectly frank, I'm at a bit of a loss. Up until I saw you all and 'Cloud Drift' Lan with my own eyes, I simply assumed that Hide and the CIM were Anti-Imperialist bastions. I trusted them implicitly..." Amelie's final words fell from her mouth like a sigh. "...But now the world is impossible to see. Everything before me lies in darkness."

◇◇◇

Once they were finished listening to Amelie's explanation, Klaus ordered the girls to get some rest. It was clear that they wanted to start searching for Monika immediately, but he was having none of that. They'd been working nonstop since the night prior, and Klaus wasn't about to let them run themselves ragged.

That left Klaus and Amelie in the living room. Once they were alone, Amelie crossed her legs in displeasure. "Might I ask you to release my subordinates now?"

"I still need them. Depending on how things play out, I might ask you to leverage your authority."

"If you let them go, there's a chance the CIM will be willing to lend you its full support."

"........."

It was an attractive proposition. Lamplight needed to start out by tracking down Monika's position. For jobs like that, it was hard to imagine a more useful ally than a local intelligence agency highly familiar with the lay of the land. With Belias operating at full capacity, not even a single alley cat would be able to escape their watchful eyes. That would go a long way toward rooting out Serpent.

However, Klaus refused to bite. "That's not an option. As things stand, I can't trust your people."

There was almost certainly a Neo-Imperialist among the CIM's upper ranks. Teaming up with them would leave him open to information leaks.

That fact wasn't lost on Amelie. "Very well," she said with a nod. "Just know that if you keep us locked up for too long, my superiors will start to get suspicious. If that happens, you can be certain that they'll discover what you've done."

"Consider it your job to keep them in the dark. If you fail, your people die."

"...Even then, that will keep them at bay for two weeks at the very most."

"Understood. I'll make sure to have the situation resolved before then."

After they finished their exchange, Amelie slumped her shoulders ever so slightly. Her face hung heavy with fatigue, and even her makeup was starting to flake off. At that point, she finally reached for the teacup sitting before her. It had long since gone cold, but she drank down the brandy-flavored tea all the same.

"...I'm tired."

"........."

"Our actions are founded in absolute righteousness. We are always just, and we do not err." The corner of her mouth curled upward self-mockingly. "That was what drove me, and I trusted Hide. The thought that one of them might have assisted in the assassination... It came as quite a shock."

It was hard to say if she was acting or being genuine. Her expression had been like an iron mask at first, but between the doubts she harbored about her superiors and the losses she'd suffered to Lamplight, it was possible she was actually shaken.

She quietly set down her teacup. "Bonfire."

"What?"

"Those are some good agents you have under your command."

"...Where's this coming from? Trying to be snide about how one of them just betrayed me?"

"I mean it. Those three—Sybilla, Lily, and Erna. Being able to get right to work in the midst of all this is a strength if ever there was one. It makes me want to know what kind of training you've been putting them through."

"You're right." Klaus was thrown a little off-guard by the unexpected praise. Sure enough, the girls were incredible at switching gears. In no time at all, they'd turned their focus forward and begun evaluating their next options. "You're absolutely right, Amelie. Those magnificent girls do me proud," he said confidently. "That's why I need to get her back. She may have left, but she's still my student."

Once he took a short breather, Klaus planned on heading straight out into the city to search for his top pupil, the tortured one who hid her true thoughts like her life depended on it.

He needed answers.

Why had "Glint" Monika turned her talents against Lamplight?

# Chapter 2

# Glint ①

The tiniest things in people's lives could send them into the pits of despair and torment the deepest parts of their hearts. Things like waking up in the morning and feeling the way the sunlight warmed their bed. Things like noticing the smell of fresh-baked bread on their way home from a shopping trip and setting off in search of a new bakery. Things like freaking out as the wind buffeted the windows on a rainy day and rubbing their shoulders to ward off the chill. Things like realizing that the ginkgo tree in front of the station had changed color and seeing a shower of yellow leaves flutter down on them. They were just normal, everyday occurrences, yet they filled her heart with a striking sense of grief.

Sharing these things brought joy. That was why people did it so much. Children bragged to their parents about being praised in school, women joined up with their coworkers in coffee shops to gripe about their bosses, the elderly visited parks to show off the sweaters their sons bought them, and men gathered in bars to shout at the bartender about their local politicians. There wasn't any special meaning to it. Just being able to share their emotions brought happiness to the people involved.

And that was what the girl was so scared of.

*Am I going to die without ever getting to share my emotions with anyone?* she wondered.

\*   \*   \*

Such was the despair that filled the thoughts of the six-year-old who would one day go by the alias Monika.

That was where her story began.

The girl was born into a family of artists, and she spent her childhood immersed in music, dance, theater, painting, and sculpture. Her father was a painter, her mother was a violinist, and all their friends who visited were artists as well.

Her parents' philosophy was to expose their children to a variety of disciplines while they were young so they could find a field that really spoke to them, and they put it into practice in the way that only the affluent could. The girl's brother and sister were a good bit older than her, and they'd tried out countless art forms as well.

Before she was old enough to really remember it, the whole family had moved to the United States of Mouzaia. They wanted to get as far away from the Great War as they could, and while the war was plunging the Western-Central nations into turmoil, things in the United States were as peaceful as could be. As a matter of fact, the increased demand for supplies like food and clothes meant that the United States were prospering. The girl saw her parents grimace when they heard news of the tragedies befalling the Western-Central region, but they had no desire to return.

Even after the war ended, her family decided to remain in Mouzaia.

"I'm giving the modernist style a shot," her father said cheerfully one day as they were enjoying a dinner their housemaid had prepared for them. "This painting will be of a man and his wife kissing. There's a restaurant in Mitario that's going to display it."

"I have a concert coming up," her mother said with a gentle expression. "It's themed around a classic play. You've heard of it, right? The one about the forbidden love of a man and a woman…"

The girl's siblings joined in the small talk and discussed the art forms they were trying out. For them, bringing up their family's respective pursuits of beauty was a surefire way to get the conversation flowing. And it went without saying that the girl's parents had ushered her toward the art world, as well.

"Go on, dear, try painting like Dad."

"Go on, dear, trying playing like Mom."

The girl wasn't particularly interested, but she did as she was told.

Whenever she picked up a new pursuit, she improved at a breakneck pace. Her specialty was mimicry. She knew that all she had to do was copy someone's technique—her father's, her mother's, or their friend's. No matter the field, be it piano, sculpture, oil painting, saxophone, or water-colors, she learned far faster than any other child could have dreamed of.

However, it was never enough to earn her family's approval.

"This still life is excellent. Your brushstrokes are so delicate and precise." Her father would always start out by praising her, but it was never long before disappointment clouded his face. "But your landscapes and portraits—well, there's some work to be done. Even if you're going for a realistic style, that doesn't mean you can just paint the world exactly as it is. Picking and choosing what parts to leave out will change the impression the piece gives. I know they say that all art springs from imitation, but still..."

Her father, her mother, and the instructors they hired always ended their reviews in the same way.

"It's technically proficient, but...it has no soul."

Every time the girl heard those words, her heart shriveled a little bit more. However, she asked her question all the same. "How do you give it...'soul'?"

Her father's and mother's answers were the same: ""With love.""

"Someday, you'll understand. When you meet your soulmate, your world will fill up with color. Everything will be so beautiful for you; you'll see."

"That's simply how men and women are. Say, are there any cute boys at school?"

"Oh, shut up," the girl snapped under her breath. Her parents gave her a quizzical look, to which she brusquely replied, "It's nothing," and quietly turned away.

She never really fit in with her family. Her parents had thrown them-selves into artistic endeavors even as their hometown burned in the war, their dinners together were filled with discussions of beauty day in and day out, and her siblings followed in their parents' footsteps like it was the most natural thing in the world.

On top of all that, she felt a strange sense of discord whenever they started preaching about love.

She held her tongue to keep the peace when they were all together, and she spent as much time as she could on her own. That left her with more time than she knew what to do with and nothing to fill the hours except playing catch with herself against her bedroom wall.

Time flowed on, and the girl turned twelve without ever figuring out the cause of all her woe.

At twelve years old, the girl returned to the Din Republic.

By attending a regular school, she learned about the Great War's horrors—about how repugnant Galgad's invasion had been, and about the unique brand of terror that came with watching another nation's army stroll down Main Street like they owned the place. Little by little, she came to understand just how many people had suffered in the atrocity that was the Great War.

However, the fact that she'd avoided experiencing it firsthand created a rift between her and her schoolmates. In the minds of children, running away when your country was in trouble was a grave crime. And the jealousy she earned for her outstanding grades and athleticism didn't help matters, either.

After school, she cooped herself up in the studio her father had rented. She was tired of art, but she didn't have anywhere else to go.

Her father's apprentices often frequented the studio and paid her father a usage fee for the space. Turnover there was frequent.

One spring day, a few months after she turned thirteen, she spotted a strange man. Between his well-defined features and his attractive blond hair, he looked like he was probably popular with the ladies. By all accounts, he was very agreeable. Whenever he talked with people, he made sure to give them a merry smile and some witty banter. However, there was always a faint coldness lurking in his eyes, almost like he could see right through them. She would guess he was somewhere in his midtwenties.

*…Where'd he come from?*

The man gave off a floral aroma. The girl recognized that smell, and she decided to think of him as the lavender man.

It all seemed a little odd to her, and as she was staring at him, he called over to her and gave her a carefree grin. Any sense of caution she had went right out the window. It was just the two of them in the studio, and before she knew it, she was spilling her guts to him about the discord she felt with her parents.

The lavender man wasted no time in rejecting her parents' values. "Look, all that stuff about romance between men and women being the be-all and end-all is a load of bull. Your old man doesn't know what he's talking about."

The girl found herself taken back. "Are you sure it's okay for you to say that? Isn't he your teacher?"

"That doesn't make what he's saying any less stupid," the lavender man replied, his smile just as easygoing as before. "History proves that there's more to life than just men and women falling in love with each other. Plenty of the best artists ever were rumored to have been homosexual."

"Yeah, I've heard that."

"In fact, some cultures see homosexuals as their most esteemed members."

The young man seemed oddly fixated on the point.

A question crossed the girl's mind. "And now?"

"Hmm?"

"If people used to be fine with it, what about now?"

On hearing the question, the man's expression immediately twisted in sorrow. He quickly covered his face with his hand, and by the time he lowered it, his happy-go-lucky smile had returned. "Now it's a mental illness," he said, "and a crime. It's a crime to sleep with someone of the same sex."

"...That seems extreme. Why?"

"'Cause everyone's too wrapped up in taking care of themselves." The man shrugged. "When people have their hands full just getting through the day, they don't have room in their heads to think about what'll make other people happy. They've got their own problems to deal with. It's not just here in this country, either. The whole region's still shot up from the war. Plus, the Western-Central nations are still milking their colonies dry."

The man's tone was light, and he began strolling through the studio. Over in one corner, there was an oil painting on a massive size 100 canvas. He himself had brought it in, and it was clear how fervently it had been painted. There was black all across the canvas, swallowing up a number of screaming children.

"It's fear," said the lavender man. "As long it keeps running rampant, nobody's gonna spare a second thought for minorities. War orphans, families of people in jail, people with physical deformities, sexual assault victims, homosexuals, children suffering from poverty, children being abused, the mentally ill... Nobody cares about them."

He stared intently at his painting.

"Nobody can save them."

His murmur echoed with sadness.

For whatever reason, those words tore into the girl's heart. The young man's voice was simply that grim. She was struck by an urge to cry, but she knew that to give in to it would be to admit that what he was saying was true, so instead she let the pain wash over her in silence.

As she stood there, the man went on. "By the way, there's a guy named Crood who paints here, right?"

"Huh?"

"Here's a prophecy for you—tomorrow, he's going to be arrested," he said as nonchalantly as if he were talking about the weather.

The next day, the police arrested the man in question, just like the lavender man said they would. He was taken in for committing a sex crime—namely, sleeping with another man. It had been consensual, but that didn't matter in the eyes of the law.

Crood Colas had been a student of the girl's father, and because of how much time he'd spent in the studio, the incident became something of a local scandal. The girl sometimes saw women chatting about it by the roadside. "Oh, that's so scary," they would say, and "I wonder if he went after my husband, too?"

All his pieces in the studio were immediately discarded.

The girl had known him relatively well. He was an earnest young man who'd devoted himself to his painting and often shared his sweets with her.

The way she stared at the empty spot where his paintings once hung caused her father a great deal of worry. "He didn't put any nasty ideas into your head, did he? Are you all right?"

"...I'm fine."

"Oh, good. That's a load off your old man's back. Make sure you fall in love with a nice boy, you hear? Speaking of which, has anyone caught your eye?"

The girl said nothing.

Eventually, her father took a hint, let out a sigh, and took a look at the canvas sitting before Monika. As always, he sounded so wistful. "Your music and art are all function and no form," he said. "It's technically precise, but it never pops."

That day, though, he took things a step further.

"Perhaps your true calling lies in some other field."

"Sure looks that way," the girl replied without missing a beat. "I can see there's no place for me here."


The lavender man never returned to the studio, but there were a number of things he'd told the girl when he left.

*"Crood was helping an Imperial spy, you know. He would slip ammo in with his art and send it around the world. They found out he was gay and used it to blackmail him into doing whatever they said. In the end, though, they tossed him aside, and tomorrow, he's going to be arrested."*

The deeds he was describing were so far removed from the girl's life that she had no idea what to make of it.

*"I just wanted to stop by to go through his stuff before the cops come and mess it all up,"* the lavender man continued, then sauntered over to Crood's canvas and deftly disassembled it, taking great care not to damage the painting. Inside the wooden frame, there was a sheet of parchment sealed in a tube.

The girl sensed that the man belonged to some underworld group or intelligence organization or something, but the very notion seemed utterly foreign to her.

All of a sudden, the man turned to her.

*"Say, want to come over to my side of the world?"*

When she looked at him in surprise, he handed her something resembling a business card.

*"Here's a prophecy for you—when you do, you'll have that fateful meeting you've been waiting for,"* he declared. *"The Din Republic's intelligence agency is called the Foreign Intelligence Office. If you're interested, head to the spy academy at that address. They're looking for talented kids like you right now."*

The girl couldn't make heads or tails of it. However, she could feel her heart stirring. That card was her ticket, one that would take her far away from that studio and her family. She didn't trust the lavender man, not completely, but she took the card without a moment's hesitation.

The man smiled in delight. *"Magnificent."*

Later down the road, the girl would hear that exact same word from another person's mouth, but by then she would have forgotten the details of her conversation with the lavender man.

With that, the girl discarded her name and identity and all but ran away from home to join the spy academy.

After taking on the name Monika, she distinguished herself in no time at all. She'd been good at observation and imitation since she was a child, and while those talents failed to blossom during her time as an artist, applying mental calculations to anything she saw and flawlessly replicating techniques were useful skills for a spy to have. She was top of her class in marksmanship, and she left the other students in the dust when it came to book learning, too. In just two months after her enrollment, she was already earning the best grades in her academy. People stared at her in jealousy, but her raw talent shut them all up.

Better yet, nobody was preaching inane theories about love.

She felt comfortable there, and she spent her days feeling fulfilled. The more she poured herself into her training, the better she got. She came to believe that being a spy was her calling.

She'd never been happier—right up until she experienced the taste of *pure, unmitigated failure*.

"Wait, for real? This is what passes for top students? Sheesh, what a shocker. You kids are weak as hell!"

The day the various academies' top students were pulled together for a joint training exercise, her pride got shattered into a million pieces.

Technically, it was actually an Inferno recruitment exam, but none of the participants knew that was happening. All Monika understood was the fact that she was no prodigy. It had taken only a single woman to defeat all twenty top students, her included. Monika couldn't even comprehend what the woman had done to them, just that the other students were lying face down on the ground. The woman, whose hair and skin were so white they looked like they'd been bleached, had obliterated them.

That woman was "Flamefanner" Heide.

Monika hadn't known her name at the time, but she'd learned it from Klaus later on.

Facing off against one of the top spies in the world had left Monika's self-worth in tatters. She hadn't been able to do anything but stand there, petrified.

"You can head on back now. Yeah, you, with the blue hair. I heard about you, you know. Getting invited to this exercise after just two months at your academy? You've got promise, kiddo. That's something to be proud of. But with your current skills, you're a total no-go."

Right at the end, Heide singled out Monika and left her with a harsh warning.

"Remember this: In our world, people without fire in their hearts are nothing more than garbage."

There were some heights that no amount of effort would allow her to reach. In Monika's eyes, that had just been made painfully clear.

*What does that even mean, having fire in your heart? I swear, it's like everyone just goes and stands on their own little soapbox.*

It reminded her of those things her parents used to tell her—how her art had no soul.

*...I guess life's just a bitch.*

Starting the next day, Monika began half-assing her training. She couldn't work up any enthusiasm. Apparently, she was lacking something fundamental, just like with her art. How was she supposed to take anything seriously, now that she knew that? Instead, she began cutting classes and spending her days taking the path of least resistance. She didn't even give her best on her exams.

Her academy instructors scolded her constantly, of course, but they weren't able to expel her. She made sure to keep her grades passing, and despite her lack of motivation, she still had talent in spades.

Eventually, they gave Monika a code name: Glint.

Normally, the word was associated with light, like a cold and glistening knife. But a glint only lasts a moment, and long ago, the word also referred to a blade too dull to cut anything. Even Monika herself thought the name was fitting, considering the way she'd been accused of not having any fire in her heart.

The only reason she didn't drop out was because she had nowhere else to go. Either that, or perhaps she had some lingering attachments to the place. Either way, she figured she could take things slow and spend another four or five lazy years there.

It wasn't until she was sixteen that things changed.

Out of the blue, her principal called her in one day. She figured she was in for another tongue-lashing, so she went in with a scowl, but instead, she got handed an envelope.

"I don't quite follow it, myself," the principal explained with a puzzled look on his face, "but there's a new team called Lamplight, and they requested you specifically."

Inside, there was an invitation from Klaus.

Monika would be lying if she said that getting recruited onto Lamplight, a new spy team that specialized in Impossible Missions, didn't excite her. There was no doubt in her mind that the group would be composed of hardened veterans. Surely, one of them must have seen her talent.

However, all she found waiting for her was a group of washouts.

"Teach is out and about right now, so let's go load up his room with as many traps as we can!"

"Hell yeah! That'll give him hell, for sure!"

After drawing up their cockamamie plan, Lily and Sybilla charged straight into Klaus's room.

""AHHHHHH! A bunch of wires caught us as soon as we went in!""

It took them less than ten seconds to bungle it.

That turned out to be a recurring sight, one she got to witness just about every day.

*I swear, this place is like a zoo*, Monika thought in exasperation.

It was shortly after Lamplight's founding, and she was over in Heat Haze Palace's main hall. She was fed up with all of them—with Thea, whose emotional state had crumbled at their repeated failures; with Annette, who spent all her time whipping up bizarre inventions; and with Erna, who kept running straight toward misfortune over and over again. Monika took the training itself seriously, but emotionally, her heart was just as frozen over as it had been back at her academy.

*Well, at least I can always run away if things start looking dicey,* she shrewdly decided. *After all, Klaus can just handle everything on his own. And if there's ever a mission he can't complete, then it's not like I could make a difference in the first place.*

There was one time where she put everything she had into an attack on Klaus, but it ended in a crushing defeat. That brought back memories of the joint training exercise, and she started getting sloppy again.

Running away would have been a reasonable option. As long as she didn't start abusing her spy skills afterward, she was pretty sure that Klaus would look the other way. The fact that he avoided sharing any confidential information with them until just before the mission started was his way of saying that they were free to leave at any time.

After looking at Lily and Sybilla, who'd returned to the main hall battered from head to toe, Monika shot a glance over at Sara, who was anxiously twiddling her fingers beside them. Out of all the team's members, she was the most cowardly by far. Monika always expected her to burst into tears at any moment.

"You might wanna make a break for it," Monika suggested.

"Huh...?"

"You're not cut out to be a spy. Why go putting yourself in peril when you could spend your life somewhere peaceful and quiet instead?"

She felt bad for the timid girl. If she wanted to flee, Monika was prepared to give her some pointers on how to do it.

Sara pulled her cap down low and squeezed herself tight. "I know that, you know... A-and to tell you the truth, I can't count how many times I've thought about running away."

"Then just—"

"B-but lately, I've been feeling a bit braver..."

Sara shot a tentative glance out from beneath her hat's brim.

"What?" Monika said, not understanding what Sara meant.

"It's Miss Lily." A faint smile played at Sara's lips. "When I think about how someone as scatterbrained as her is doing her best, it makes me want to be more optimistic. Miss Lily isn't suited for spy work at all, but she's giving it her all anyway."

Monika shook her head at the vast difference between their two opinions. In Monika's eyes, Lily was nothing but a reckless klutz. Over in her peripheral vision, she could see Lily putting together her next scheme undeterred. Erna, Thea, and Grete had all gathered around her.

Sara let go of her hat and smiled. "When I look at her, it makes me feel like I can be brave, too."

"Oh yeah?" Monika replied with disinterest.

"O-of course, I know I'm a much bigger washout than her, but still!" Sara hurriedly backpedaled, but Monika ignored her.

"There's no way."

"Huh?"

"She's an airhead, that's all. At the rate things are going, she's gonna get herself killed."

As soon as the words left her mouth, she was shocked at how blunt she was being. However, those were her true thoughts. During the time they'd spent living together, Monika had gotten a pretty good handle on each team member's capabilities. Even if you put all seven of the other girls together, they couldn't compare to Monika on her own. Their skills were far inferior to hers.

"On some level, you probably realize it. No matter how hard we work, we'll never be like Klaus. The best we can hope for is becoming half decent, and that'll make us just useful enough until we're thrown away."

Monika wasn't so simple-minded that watching Lily would make her feel brave. Her heart was still as cold as ice.

"At the end of the day, that's all there is to it."

Sara stared at her, completely at a loss for words.

◇◇◇

Monika was pretty sure that people were going to die on the Impossible Mission.

In the end, the only reason she stuck around for the mission was because of how poorly she would have slept at night after leaving. Running away while someone as green as Sara stayed behind would have wounded her pride, and abandoning the mission would mean the death of someone she'd spent a month living with. She didn't want that bad taste in her mouth.

That didn't make for a particularly strong motivator, either. She wanted to leave, but with the amount of deep shit that would leave Lamplight in, she knew it wasn't an option.

As far as retrieving the Abyss Doll bioweapon went, she couldn't have cared less. At that point, the only thing driving Monika was how unpleasant it would be if people she knew died.

Their goal was for everyone to make it back alive, but when they faced off against their foe in the Galgad Empire laboratory, they were reminded of just how tall an order that was going to be.

"Torchlight" Guido, aka Blue Fly, was a combat specialist whose skills surpassed even Klaus's. Back on Inferno, he'd been their strongest fighter. The girls found him waiting for them at the pharmaceutical research lab, and he completely mopped the floor with them. At no point was he actually giving it his all, and he swung his sword around casually with a look of utmost composure on his face. That was all it took for him to deflect their bullets, and he knocked out Monika's teammates one after another with the flat of his blade.

She felt utterly outmatched, more so than she had even against "Flame-fanner" Heide and "Bonfire" Klaus.

Even after tag-teaming him with Sybilla, they couldn't so much as scratch him. Guido wasn't the kind of foe one could best with a few tricks and a clever strategy. They were just built out of fundamentally different stuff. No matter how hard she tried, she couldn't envision a future where they beat him.

They were done for. She was sure of it. They did have the outlandish "eighth girl" tactic they'd prepared in advance, but Monika had little faith it would work on him. Without some way to divert his attention, there was no way for them to even put it into motion.

That was what left her so astounded as she lay face down on the ground.

*"Now, I'm gonna get seriouser than serious. You'll finally get to see what happens when Lily, Din's slumbering wunderkind, finally wakes up."*

Even when faced with an impossibly strong foe, that girl wasn't backing down an inch.

She had no special skills. No talent. If she and Monika went head-to-head, Monika could have beaten her dozens of times in a row without breaking a sweat. All she had was an abnormal physiology and the boldest spirit around.

"I'm code name Flower Garden—and it's time to bloom out of control."

Yet the sight got burned into Monika's heart all the same—the sight of "Flower Garden" Lily putting all of life's radiant splendor on full display.

Once the mission was finished, the girls headed back to Din ahead of Klaus. Then they got on board the predesignated truck and made their way home hidden among its cargo. They knew that they might have pursuers coming for them, so none of them said a word while they were on the road. As they approached the border, they all held their breaths.

It wasn't until they crossed back into Din that the fact that they'd completed the mission really sank in. All eight of them had made it back alive, and they'd successfully retrieved Abyss Doll. Everything they'd set out to do, they'd achieved with flying colors.

The girls let out a cheer from the cramped truck bed. They smiled with joy, exchanged high fives all around, jostled each other's shoulders, and finally struck triumphant poses.

"Your favorite unbeatable spy hottie is coming home, Din!"

Unsurprisingly, the biggest merrymaker of the bunch was Lily. After fist-bumping Sybilla, high-fiving Grete, squeezing Erna's cheeks, and tousling Sara's cap, she came over to Monika. "Great work back there, Monika! That was classic, the way you and Sybilla went in and gave Guido what for!"

The compliment brought Monika no joy. It was plain as day that their MVP back at the Endy Laboratory had been Lily, with Erna as a clear runner-up. "You were pretty impressive yourself," she replied.

"Hmm?"

"Weren't you scared, making those bold bluffs against someone like him? There was nothing stopping him from just killing you."

As a matter of fact, Guido would likely have started offing them one by one if Lily hadn't stood up when she did.

After staring back blankly for a moment, Lily's expression softened. "I'd be lying if I said I wasn't scared at *all*, but honestly, I was pretty calm."

"...How?"

"'Cause Teach believed in us, remember? He was all like, 'You each have boundless potential just waiting to be unlocked.'" Lily smiled like it was no big deal. "It made me feel like maybe it was all right for me to believe in myself."

Monika bit down on her lip a bit. "Even though you're an academy washout?"

"Yeah, of course. I'll have you know: I was born to be a spy."

The words rang utterly alien to Monika. How could Lily say them so brazenly when she was so much weaker than Monika?

The question hung heavy in her mind, only to be interrupted when Lily abruptly wrapped her in an embrace. "And hey! Don't forget—that means you're a magnificent prodigy, too, Monika!"

"........."

It was possible Lily was riding the post-mission high, as she was being downright exuberant. Her hair grazed the tip of Monika's nose as it gently splayed out, and Monika could feel the softness of her figure and the warmth of her body through their clothes.

".........Get off." Monika shoved her hard.

"Huh?"

"You're being a pest. I'm gonna take a nap. I think I'm coming down with something."

Lily stared at her, dumbfounded, and as Monika moved over to the corner of the truck bed and sandwiched herself between some of the cargo, she could hear Lily murmur. "I—I guess that's Monika for you. Always as cool as a cucumber."

Monika pulled her spy uniform's hood over her head and covered her mouth with her hands.

Something weird was happening to her body.

Her mouth was dry. Her heart was racing. Her temperature was elevated. Her body felt hot, and she couldn't stop sweating. She closed her eyes. Lily's voice from a moment ago echoed through her head. She covered her ears with her hands, but the voice kept on going. She bit down on her lip, but not even the pain was enough to make the feeling go away. Her fingertips trembled.

*What's...happening to me?*

All she could do was sit there in bewilderment.

*...This feels like shit.*

There was a change taking place inside her. It was messing her up, and there was nothing she could do about it.

Her parents' quotes played back in her mind like a curse. She despised that ideology of theirs, and she thought she'd discarded it, but now it was eating her alive.

She could tell, on an instinctive level, that that emotion would destroy her someday.

She knew she had to conceal it, and she did everything she possibly could to keep it hidden. She wasn't going to be able to share it with anyone in the world, but that was just something she was going to have to put up with.

*I'll never be able to share this with anyone. When I die, these emotions will die with me.*

There was despair in that conclusion, but the girl quietly began accepting it.

# Chapter 3

# Scarlet Leviathan ②

Queen Clette Station was downright packed.

The station was a brickwork building that had been built a half century prior, and voices carried well there. There was a line of people with suitcases at the ticket window, and upon being told that all the seats had been filled, they began shouting with rage. The long waits were weighing on everyone, and once the clamor of children started up, it didn't stop. There were countless sets of tracks extending out from the station, yet no trains seemed to be coming, and platforms were overflowing with people.

Out in front of the station, there were a number of activists denouncing politicians and the police. The protesters were furious that the authorities had failed to protect Prince Darryn, and the majority of the people who passed by gave them supportive rounds of applause. However, they didn't have a permit for the demonstration, so the cops came charging in midway through, and a fight broke out between them and the citizenry.

The ground in the area was littered with flyers, and Klaus picked up a few of them and looked them over.

*"Defund the police!" "Keep foreigners out!" "Encourage people to report spies!" "The royal assassination was a left-wing plot!"*

There were myriad different ideologies at play, but the common thread behind the flyers plastered across every surface in sight was rage. There were even some up on the station walls and the nearby telephone poles.

Ten days had passed since news broke about Darryn's death. By Klaus's side, Amelie let out a quiet sigh. "This is a madhouse. I never could have imagined my nation would sink this far into chaos."

"You can say that again."

Information about the crown prince's assassination had spread across the entire world.

The people of Fend had cried out in sorrow, but they'd accepted the facts of the matter, at least at first. As time dragged on with no arrests, though, voices of anger at the government's failure started rising up instead. Just like Queen Ribault, Prince Darryn had been loved and adored by the entire nation.

As soon as those voices started coming out, the unrest spread like wildfire. People held protests against the authorities, and for a time, public order went on a sharp decline. Word was that the CIM had been absolutely flooded with tips about foreign nationals who people suspected of being spies. Hurough had become a powder keg, and the citizens stormed the train station in hopes of fleeing to the countryside.

There was one crying girl at the station who'd been separated from her parents. She clutched her pink teddy bear, shouting, "Mommy, where are you?" as the currents of the crowd pushed her this way and that. She looked to be about eight. More than once, she very nearly got clocked by one of the adults' suitcases.

"…Nobody spares a second glance for the crying child, I see," Klaus remarked.

Unwilling to let the situation stand, Amelie took the girl and guided her over to the police box in front of the station. After dropping her off with the officer and returning, she awkwardly offered up an excuse. "One can hardly blame them, I should think. The crown prince was simply that great a man. Small wonder, then, that righteous indignation should rob people of their ability to think rationally." She handed Klaus a newspaper she had bought inside. "Especially with articles like these floating about."

It was the morning edition of the fourth-largest paper in the country, and its headline was emblazoned in fierce letters.

"Was Prince Darryn's Killer a Din Operative? This is absurd. Are they *trying* to start a war?"

He'd heard about the article earlier, but that didn't make it any less appalling to see it for himself. The mass media had been publishing huge amounts of speculation about who the assassin might be. Their recklessness was the main culprit behind the unrest engulfing the nation, but it was also a testament to how deeply the issue had captured the people's interest.

Amelie shook her head. "Naturally, they'll be receiving sanctions for this. We have no interest in going to war with Din, either." Allowing the Great War to repeat itself wasn't an option. The entire world was united in that stance. "More importantly," she went on in a hushed voice, "the only people who know that the killer was a Din spy are CIM agents."

"...That intel isn't even true."

"Be that as it may, this means that the CIM has a leak."

Klaus nodded. The groundless report had been intentionally spread before the truth had time to come out. This was no mere false alarm. "The Neo-Imperialists. Whoever's doing this is in bed with Galgad spies."

"I concur. The unrest has spread too far, too fast. Someone is pulling strings behind the scenes."

Klaus agreed with Amelie's assessment.

Having reaffirmed their understanding of the situation, the two of them hailed a taxi and returned to the apartment.

The two of them had been operating as a pair over the past few days. For Klaus, Amelie's local knowledge and ability to wield the CIM's authority made her a valuable asset, and on top of that, they shared the same objective—tracking down information about Serpent's infiltration of the Commonwealth.

For the moment, their motives were aligned.

They had "Bonfire" Klaus, the Din Republic's strongest spy who could find answers on intuition alone. And they had "Puppeteer" Amelie, the leader of an unassailable intelligence unit that ruled over the Fend Commonwealth. With the two of them working together, there were few cases they couldn't crack. And yet...

When they got back to the apartment, they noticed that the radio was blinking. More accurately, it was a wireless transceiver disguised to look like a radio. The CIM had designed it specifically for spy work. By turning the tuning dial, you could input the password to play back the recordings.

There were five messages saved on the machine.

The first voice to come through was Lily's. *"There was a big fire at the funeral home on Coen Street, Teach. I'm hearing that the owner was from Din, so it was likely a targeted hate crime—"*

The second was Sybilla's. *"The Domin family is meetin' up with other mafia groups, boss. They say they're just talkin' about keepin' the peace while the government's fucking everything up, but people are gettin' jittery."*

Klaus listened through the recordings, and they were all about the same. Each of them detailed some sort of conflict or uprising that had happened in Hurough.

Amelie sighed. "With how chaotic things are—"

"Yeah, we have no idea which incidents Serpent had a hand in."

That about summed it up—the search was going poorly. Even with Klaus and Amelie working together, they had completely failed to locate Monika or track down Serpent. Suspicious deaths and bizarre events were happening with a frequency that normally would have been unthinkable. It was taking everything they had just to stay on top of the rapidly changing situation, so the search had ground to a halt.

The city of Hurough had become an impenetrable morass.

On day one, they'd been optimistic that they would be able to find Monika in no time. The team's motivation was high, and after getting some rest, Lily, Sybilla, and Erna started getting ready to head out into the city.

However, the most gung ho of them all was the girl who'd sneaked out of the hospital—Thea.

"Teach!" she cried as she rushed into the room. Her right arm was swaddled in layer upon layer of bandages. She'd come over the moment they finished stitching her up. "Please, let me head up the investigation! I'll track down Monika, even if I have to haul her back by the scruff of her—"

"Calm down, Thea. Are you okay to be working with your arm like that?"

"How am I supposed to be calm?!" she cried hysterically as she sat herself down on the sofa. She shook her head back and forth, messing up her hair as she did. Beads of sweat trickled down her forehead. "I can't believe it. How could she do something like that to Annette?"

She'd clearly suffered quite a shock. Erna gave her a consoling pat on the back.

Klaus started out by ordering her to take some deep breaths. "How's Annette doing?"

"…The surgery went well. They patched up her injuries, and she's sleeping now."

"Good," Klaus replied with a nod.

"However, her wounds were pretty bad. The doctor said that it'll be a month or two before she's able to walk right."

If anything, they were lucky she'd gotten off that lightly.

After calming down a bit, Thea repeated herself. "Please, Teach. I—"

"Magnificent. All right, you're in charge of the search efforts. Just make sure you don't push yourself."

The fact of the matter was, they were short on people. Thea was excellent at coordinating with the others and giving them practical orders, so having her back in the field was a welcome bit of news.

Klaus raised three fingers. "We're going to split into three groups. On Search Team One, me and Erna are going to gather intel on Serpent. On Search Team Two, Thea's going to lead Sybilla and Lily in trying to find Monika's location. And finally..."

The image of their absent team member—"Meadow" Sara—flitted through his mind. He hadn't talked with her except via radio, but it was clear that her mental state was suffering. The string of emotionally harrowing events they'd been through recently was hitting her hard.

Perhaps she wasn't ready to join in on the search teams just yet.

"...Sara is going to continue keeping an eye on the Belias hostages alongside Lan."

That job demanded just as much vigilance. If one of the hostages escaped and got in touch with the secret Neo-Imperialists, things could get ugly in a hurry. Plus, even without her, they could still borrow her pet dog, Johnny. He was sure to be invaluable in their search efforts.

"Roger that," the girls replied with their lips firmly set, then hurried out into the streets of Hurough.

Given how determined they were, Klaus was sure they'd be able to track down Monika's location in no time, and yet...

The two of them sank into the sofa and made a quick lunch of the sandwiches they'd picked up on their way back. They hadn't had time to do any cooking these days.

"I must say, I was expecting more from you." Amelie carried herself with an unmistakable elegance, holding her sandwich with both hands and leisurely finishing her meal. "So even the mighty Bonfire is powerless in the face of such chaos. And here I was, assuming you would just solve the whole thing and not even be able to explain how you did it."

Klaus coolly deflected the verbal jab. "I'm not some omniscient deity, you know."

His hunches weren't a superpower. It was merely the inferences his accumulated experience allowed him to make. If he was really that all-knowing, he wouldn't have let Avian get annihilated right under his nose.

Considering how Hurough was the biggest quagmire he'd seen in the past decade, his intuition wasn't going to help him much.

Klaus shot Amelie a glare. "Besides, you're in no position to be acting all high-and-mighty. Not after the way we mopped the floor with you."

".........." Amelie's expression twitched with irritation. She'd been feeling down for a bit, but now she was back to firing on all cylinders. "Someone's certainly feeling full of himself. That victory was a fluke, nothing more."

"What, you're suggesting that you weren't operating at full capacity?"

"We absolutely were not. The only reason we lost was because of Hide's misinformation. They had us chasing down false leads, and you took advantage of the opening that provided. If it wasn't for that, you people never would have been able to—"

Her remarks, initially so eloquent, came to sudden halt. She'd realized that she was saying too much.

"Isn't it high time you gave up on Hide?" Klaus said. "It's become abundantly clear that they've allowed a traitor to infiltrate their ranks. Give me their names. I'll do a clean sweep."

"I have my pride as an intelligence operative. I'm not about to sell out the highest ranks of my agency."

"Isn't the whole reason you're working with me because you don't trust Hide anymore?"

"Even so, there are lines I'm unwilling to cross."

In order to demonstrate the depth of her conviction, Amelie pressed her fingertips to her own throat. That was her way of saying that if he wanted to press the issue, then he might as well kill her and her agents off now.

Klaus knew that there was no point arguing further. Belias was an elite intelligence unit. They were prepared to kill themselves if that was the only way to protect their state secrets.

He quietly shook his head and offered her a few words of warning. "You should make sure to question everything you know. About Hide—and about Prince Darryn, too."

"……………"

Amelie bit down on her lip and sank into silence. A moment later, though, her expression lightened, and she let out a hollow laugh. "You're the last person I want telling me that right now."

"What do you mean?"

"One of your own subordinates just turned traitor."

"………………………………………………"

This time, it was Klaus's turn to go silent. Getting betrayed by one of their own teammates was about as unambiguous a failure as a spy could have. He bit down on his tongue to keep Amelie from seeing how upset he was.

*I left too much of their training to Avian lately.*

He knew he was just making excuses, but that didn't mean it hurt any less.

Lamplight had lost to Avian over in the Far East nation of Longchon, and after witnessing the consequences of his poor pedagogy firsthand, Klaus had invited Avian to Heat Haze Palace and created an environment for the two teams to train together. The idea was that Klaus would help Avian hone their skills, and Avian would do the same for the girls.

Klaus stood by that decision, but it had also left him with less time working directly with the girls. Now, just weeks later, one of them had betrayed the team.

*I'm a failure as an instructor.*

He squeezed his fists tight as he wrestled with his feelings of regret. Could all this have been avoided if he'd just spent more time with her?

*And Monika is an especially acute case…*

While he was mentally replaying their conversations, he heard someone call his name.

"Teach!"

He looked over in the direction of the voice and saw Erna. At present, she was handling odd jobs like helping out Sara and Lan and sorting through all the intelligence the team was gathering.

"I have news from Big Sis Thea. There's an eyewitness account of Big Sis Monika being spotted in a mixed-use building downtown, on the west side."

"Got it. Tell her to keep up the good work."

At long last, they had a lead.

Klaus was grateful for what Thea had accomplished. She had been attacking the problem with an uncommon fervor, and now her efforts had paid off.

He headed to the scene of the sighting without a moment's delay.

Out of all the girls on Lamplight, Monika was the one Klaus interacted with the least.

Monika could perhaps be described best as self-sufficient, and Klaus had relied on her a lot since Lamplight's inception. Not only was her talent as a spy head and shoulders above the others, but it also took a lot to throw her off her game.

The fact of the matter was, Klaus spent a huge amount of time cleaning up after his other subordinates' messes. Between Lily's clumsiness, Sybilla's screwups, Erna's misfortune, Annette's eccentricity, and having to comfort the easily demoralized Thea and Sara, he generally had his hands full. Even Grete, who worked hard to avoid adding to his burden, needed him to dote on her from time to time. Klaus wasn't trying to pick favorites or anything, but he ended up spending less time with Monika merely as a matter of course. Failing to give enough attention to one's best students was an issue every teacher in the world grappled with, and it was something he felt very guilty about.

"Hey, Monika."

There was one time, and one time alone, that he tried to get her to open up to him.

It was just after they returned from their mission in Mouzaia, and one afternoon during their time off, Klaus called over to Monika as she walked down the hallway. The two of them were the only ones around, so he figured it was the perfect opportunity.

"What do you want, Klaus? You need something?" she asked, stopping and giving him a quizzical look.

"I just got my hands on some nice tea. What do you say?"

"What do you mean, what do I say?"

"We've never had a chance to have a real heart-to-heart. Why don't we have a nice chat over some tea?"

For a brief moment, Monika's eyes went wide with surprise, and she froze, unsure of how to react. However, it didn't take long for her to reassume her usual cool demeanor. "I appreciate the invite to your little date, but I'm good. I want to get some shut-eye." She gave him a small wave and turned to head to her room.

"Monika," Klaus called after her, "I know about the burden you're carrying—about your secret love."

Monika whirled around on the spot, and Klaus could see panic written all across her face. All at once, her face froze and went as pale as a sheet.

It had never been his goal to scare her. He did his best to make his voice as gentle as possible. "Don't worry; I'm the only one who's noticed. You've done an impressive job of hiding it."

The rest of the girls probably had no idea. The change was subtle, but whenever Monika looked at one specific member of the team, there was a faint tremor deep in her eyes. She put up a confident front, but there was an underpinning of awkwardness and delicate sentiment behind everything she did and said.

Klaus shook his head. "I won't press the issue any further. Just know that if you ever need advice, I'm here for you. Feelings like yours can be a dangerous vulnerability for a spy."

Few things had the power to make people act irrationally like love and lust did. Even men who normally operated on pure logic would completely let their guard down around women they had the hots for, and loads of spies, men and women alike, had been brought low by honey traps.

That was why he was so concerned for her.

"Would you mind looking me in the eye every now and then, Monika?"

The girl had been avoiding him for some time now. It was like she was terrified of having her feelings exposed.

It took Monika a good long while to reply. Instead, she shot him a rude look, as though she was sizing him up. Her lip trembled ever so slightly.

Eventually, she let out a small sigh. "Yeah, no. Sorry, Klaus, but this isn't something I want to talk to you about."

She gave him a forlorn grin and turned away.

"I've gone my whole life without telling anyone my secret, and I'm gonna keep it that way till I go to my grave."

There was a fierce determination in her voice, and it cut Klaus's next question off at the pass.

*You're never planning on telling her how you feel?*

He wanted to ask it, but she'd made it clear what her answer would be.

Her love was going to end in secret. The rejection in her tone was so unambiguous it would have been tactless of him to ask her to elaborate.

With a quiet "Thanks for looking out for me, though," she walked away.

There were definitely traces of Monika in the building Thea had found. Klaus took Erna with him to search the scene.

The building sat in an alley just one road off Hurough's main street in the heart of the city. It was home to a restaurant and a law office.

The aforementioned traces were up on the unoccupied third floor. According to Thea, there were people who'd seen a cerulean-haired girl coming and going from there. At the moment, Thea was scouring the surrounding area.

Originally, this was some sort of office space, and there were marks on the wood floor from where the desks had been. Over in the corner, there was a basket full of food waste. Based on how full it was, Monika had been staying there for at least five days. The building was just a mile from the workshop, so that must have been where she'd gone to lay low.

"This place is a bust," Klaus concluded. "Monika's gone."

At that point, Erna stopped walking loops around the floor and called over to him. "Teach, come look at this." When he did, he found a scrap of what looked like human skin lying on the ground over in the corner. It had holes in just the right places to leave openings for someone's eyes and nose.

"I recognize these materials…," Erna said. Her voice sounded hoarse. "They're the ones Grete uses for her masks."

Nearby, there was a chain thick enough to tie down a person. It was stained with blood.

Klaus had been worried about Grete's condition. More than ten days had passed since she was taken, and he had no idea if she'd received the treatment she needed. Now that he saw where she'd been held, there was no doubt in his mind that her body was breaking down. The realization caused an ugly feeling to rise up within him. He could feel it start to ever so slightly affect his judgment.

However, there was no sense assuming the worst. He switched gears and started thinking through it rationally.

*That's odd… It's not like Monika to leave so much evidence behind.*

It was just a single mask, but still. It felt as though she'd left it there specifically so Klaus and the others would find it.

*...She's up to something.*

The question was, what was she going to do next? She hadn't just attacked the Kashard Doll Workshop. She'd also kidnapped Grete and assaulted Annette and Thea. At some point, she was going to make another move, and Klaus needed to figure out her plan so he could preempt it.

"This is my comeuppance for never truly facing Monika."

He steeled his resolve again.

Then, the next day, the incident and the investigation both progressed in a rather unexpected fashion.

On the eleventh day of the investigation, there was yet another development that shocked the Fend Commonwealth to its core: a second assassination.

The victim was a thirty-four-year-old scientist who worked for the Kevin National Research Institute named Mia Godolphin. She specialized in theoretical physics, and she was the director of the nation's rapidly progressing aviation development program.

One day, after exiting the institute just as she always did, she went missing. Her car had been left untouched in the parking lot. When she didn't come home that night, her husband called the police.

Eventually, her body was found in the river running through Hurough. There was a bullet wound in the side of her head.

The news had been playing constantly on the TV since morning.

As he continued watching from their base to see if there was any new information being reported, Klaus let out a long breath. "What are your bosses at the CIM saying about the case?"

Amelie shook her head in disappointment. Klaus had given her orders to stop by CIM headquarters every now and again so she could lie to them about the Lamplight situation. "Hide's stance is consistent—that Lan is likely behind this assassination, as well. They want me to capture her as quickly as I can. That's all they're saying."

"Incompetents, the lot of them. At the rate they're going, the body count's going to keep rising."

"...I'm afraid it's really not my place to comment," Amelie replied. She sounded frustrated, but she knew that chewing out Hide wasn't going to get them anywhere.

"What can you tell me about Mia Godolphin?"

"She was a scientist working for the state. She was an associate professor at Winston University up until three years ago, when the National Research Institute headhunted her."

"Go back through every document you have on her. There might be some connection between her and the crown prince. If we find something they have in common, that'll tell us what Serpent is after."

"I'm way ahead of you."

The room was piled high with files on every person related to the case. By threatening Amelie, Klaus had been able to get his hands on every piece of information the CIM had, aside from the ones that involved state secrets. They read back through them as quickly as they could.

As they started to get into the thick of it, Erna came running back from the shopping trip they'd sent her on. They'd also told her to buy a copy of every paper for sale at the newsstand in front of the station.

Erna's voice sounded panicked. "Teach!"

"What's wrong?"

"Th-there's a newspaper with a weird article in it."

Time was a scarce resource, so Klaus didn't look up from the document he was reading. "They've all been filled with odd reports these last few days. What does it say?"

"This is way more serious than that!"

Erna raised her voice. The shock in it was plain to hear.

"It has a photo of Prince Darryn and Director Mia's killer!"

Klaus's and Amelie's hands froze. They exchanged a glance.

They reached their verdicts in unison.

"That's impossible." "That simply isn't possible."

It was getting to be a real pain, having to refute misinformation that blatant. Of the two, Amelie seemed particularly indignant. "That's preposterous. Ludicrous. Not even the CIM has a photograph of whoever it was that killed the crown prince. There's no way some little local newspaper could have gotten their hands on anything of the sort." She massaged her temples in annoyance and took the paper from Erna. "We'll have to issue swift sanctions against this kind of slapdash—"

She trailed off midway through her sentence. Her lips gave the faintest of trembles.

"Bonfire." Amelie handed him the paper. "I'm afraid the situation may have just taken quite the turn."

After taking a look at Erna's worried expression, Klaus read the article. The paper was called the *Conmerid Times*. As he recalled, it was a fairly major publication. Inside, there was a pair of photos so large they covered just about an entire spread, styled almost like wanted posters. The quality wasn't great, and it looked like they'd been shot at night, as the images were dark. However, there was definitely a humanoid figure in the middle of each of them.

BREAKING: CROWN PRINCE'S ASSASSIN THE MOST HATED PERSON OF THE CENTURY

The two pictures sitting alongside the inflammatory headline were captioned AT THE SITE OF THE CROWN PRINCE'S ASSASSINATION and AT THE SITE OF THE MIA GODOLPHIN ASSASSINATION. The first was a photo of someone, presumably the killer, fleeing the scene of the crime. However, the second was a much more definitive photo of the killer dragging a corpse that looked an awful lot like Director Mia's. Despite how grainy the image was, it wasn't hard to make out Director Mia's face or the loathing in the killer's eyes.

Klaus gasped.

"Teach," Erna stammered, "the photos are of Big Sis Monika."

That much was unmistakable.

The person in the photos depicting the assassin of the century was none other than their own missing ally.

# Chapter 4

# Glint ②

The first thing Monika did was to assess what exactly was wrong with her. Her temperature was up, as was her heart rate. She needed to understand why.

During Lamplight's second Impossible Mission, the one where they rooted out the assassin Corpse, the team got split into two. Spending a whole month away from Lily gave Monika an opportunity to calmly analyze herself.

As soon as she became aware of the weird ways her body was acting, she began reading every romance novel she could get her hands on. The majority of them were about heterosexual love, but she was still able to find a number of descriptions of the characters undergoing physiological changes.

Once she had that, it was time to run some tests.

After Lily left Heat Haze Palace, Monika headed for Lily's bedroom. The room was full of chemical vials, and the faint smell of herbs wafted through the air.

*I feel like some sort of pervert.*

The thought gave her a little twinge of self-loathing, but she needed to carry out her experiment. She shifted her gaze over the item of furniture sitting in the corner of the room.

*That's the bed Lily sleeps in.*

She let out a small breath and lay down in it. Then, after laying her head on the pillow much the way she imagined the room's owner did, she quietly closed her eyes.

She did a quick check on her body.

Sure enough, her heart was beating out of control, her face was flushed, and she felt unbearably embarrassed. The changes fit the description. If elevated temperature, perspiration, increased blood flow, and becoming feverish were all signs of being in love, then it looked like her hypothesis was right, and her feelings were indeed romantic. Given the preponderance of evidence, she would be naive not to admit it.

She was in love with Lily.

Monika was bewildered by the prospect, but at the same time, she had no choice but to accept it. She'd assumed she would go her whole life without dating a soul, but she never imagined she would go and fall in love with a woman, let alone such a carefree klutz. She'd had no idea she had such bad taste.

Then she heard footsteps coming from the hallway. She took out the notebook she'd kept nearby for just such an occasion and starting pretending to write in it.

The door swung upon, revealing Thea's scowling face. Klaus was forcing them to complete a task before they would be allowed to participate in the Corpse mission, and Thea was none too pleased that Monika had skipped out on the strategy meeting.

"What, you need something?"

Thea glared at her in annoyance. "Well, for starters, what are you doing in Lily's room?"

"Investigating," Monika replied evasively. Technically, she wasn't even lying.

After discovering that she was in love, Monika had just one thing to say about it.

*This sucks. I figure my symptoms'll go away on their own at some point, but I wish they'd hurry it up.*

She decided to do everything in her power to keep her feelings hidden. She could think of plenty of reasons why.

For starters, there was the harsh stance the world at large had about homosexuality. In the modern era, loving someone of the same sex was treated as a crime and a mental illness. Monika had no idea whether her teammates would be repulsed by her, especially considering they had to live under the same roof as her.

Then there was the fact that, as a spy, it could be used against her. If an enemy spy found out, they would be able to blackmail her like that guy from her dad's studio.

Third—and probably the biggest of all—was the way they had no chance of being realized. For that to happen, Lily would have to be gay as well. Considering her behavior, though, there were no signs that was the case.

*I have to keep it a secret from everyone until this weirdness goes away...*
With her mind made up, she continued going about her spy work.

Monika spent the time leading up to her reunion with Lily continuing to sort out her feelings.

Midway through, Thea managed to uncover a part of Monika's love. It was when they were forced to make a decision about how to deal with Annette's mother. Unable to see eye to eye, Monika and Thea ended up fighting it out. Thea ultimately managed to persuade Monika to lend her a hand by peering into her heart, but the experience taught Monika a hard-earned lesson about how difficult it was to keep a secret.

Then Monika discovered Annette's brutal nature. Annette pretended to be pure and innocent, but deep down, she was pure evil and had manipulated the others into helping her assassinate her mother. Monika was the only one who realized what had happened and, in doing so, learned even more about what it meant to hide a part of yourself away.

Aided by what she'd been through on the mission, Monika was able to successfully conceal her feelings. The way she interacted with Lily was exactly the same as ever. When Lily screwed up, Monika continued reading her the riot act, and whenever Lily tried to pester her, Monika responded with violence. It helped her maintain some of the distance between them.

As a spy, she'd learned how to avoid letting her emotions show on her face, and by taking advantage of those skills, she managed to keep everyone aside from Klaus from finding out her secret.

Everyone, with one exception.

Grete constantly threw Monika's emotions into disarray.

Of all the girls on Lamplight, Grete was by far the most proactive in her pursuit of love. Grete had feelings for Klaus, and it was for his sake that she fought so hard on her missions. Rather than hide her love, she made sure Klaus knew exactly where she stood.

It was all so admirable that Monika found her own heart filling up with gloom. She did an impeccable job keeping her feelings hidden during everyday conversations, but when those conversations overlapped with times her emotions were out of whack, she sometimes ended up letting the mask drop.

For example, there was the time the two of them were out shopping.

The team had just wrapped up the Corpse mission, and they were in the middle of getting ready for their next job in the United States of Mouzaia. Monika was in charge of cooking that day, so she and Grete went out to get ingredients.

While they were walking, Grete brought up a new topic. "You know, there's something Lily mentioned while we were working on the Corpse mission."

"Hmm?"

"She told me that you often ask her for massages. I got one myself, and I must say, her technique is really quite incredible. How did you discover that she had such talents?"

During the time she'd spent working undercover in the politician's mansion, Grete had been run ragged. She'd been so sleep-deprived she hadn't been able to think straight. The only thing that had saved her were Lily's massages.

Upon this sudden mention of Lily, Monika replied "Dunno" and dodged the question. She'd asked for the massages as part of her quest to figure out if her feelings were really love, and being reminded of that threw her for a loop. She needed to quickly change the subject.

"Hey, Grete, you mind if I ask you a question back?" The words were out of her mouth before she could stop them. "What does it feel like, being so earnest about love?"

Grete opened her mouth in shock, and Monika found herself bewildered as well. The plan had been to change the subject to something completely unrelated, like work or the weather.

After a brief moment of astonishment, Grete quickly regained control of her face and returned her expression to its usual tranquility. "It feels very, very lovely."

"...Is that so."

"If there's one thing I'm disappointed about, it's that there's little chance my feelings will ever be requited... But even so, my days with the boss have been full of so many little joys."

Ever since the Corpse mission, Grete had started smiling contentedly a lot. Klaus had offered her a few kind words, no doubt.

The faint smile playing at Grete's lips got Monika feeling all mixed up again. "Well, good for you. There wasn't any deeper meaning to the question, by the way. It's just..." Monika bit down on her lip. "...like I told you before, I can't help but get jealous when I see someone else get so earnest about their love."

Grete's lips twitched. It looked as though she had something she was dying to say, but Monika had had just about enough of that conversation. She sped up her pace, practically fleeing from Grete as she speed-walked away.

After admitting to herself that she was in love, Monika began working even harder in her day-to-day training.

She'd assumed that her feelings were just temporary, but in the time she had waited, they refused to go away. Meanwhile, Lily had no intentions of retiring from spy work. Monika didn't want her to die, so if Lily was going to stick with Lamplight and continue to put her life in danger, then Monika was going to need to temper herself like steel. That was also why she started tutoring Sara after they got home from their mission in Mouzaia—she was confident that Sara had room to grow, and she wanted to raise the entire team's skill level.

On top of that, Monika started challenging Klaus more frequently herself.

Unsurprisingly, Klaus picked up on the difference.

"Did something inspire this change of heart?"

Out on the Heat Haze Palace lawn, Monika had just launched a rubber bullet surprise attack from behind on Klaus as he was getting back from a mission. In addition to the gunshots, she'd also woven in a series of strikes using rebounding rubber balls with iron cores.

Klaus dodged all her attacks without breaking a sweat.

"Nah." Having failed spectacularly, Monika strode out in front of Klaus and grinned. "Not much has changed. I just figured it was high time I admitted to myself I was a prodigy, that's all. Makes it pretty easy to get into my training."

"I see."

"That's on your head, for the record. You're the guy who had to go and call me magnificent."

Monika drew her knife and twirled it around in her hand. She had lost faith in her abilities when Flamefanner shattered her pride, but the more she watched Lily and the others give it their all, the sillier she felt for having lost her nerve. Surely, she was more sensible than that band of washouts.

"*...You're a magnificent prodigy, too, Monika!*"

Those happy-go-lucky words were still ringing in her ears.

Klaus squinted at her, looking a little pleased. "Magnificent. That change will serve you well."

Before he had a chance to open his eyes all the way back up, Monika moved quick as a whip and thrust her knife at his collarbone. She had to be prepared to seriously injure him if she wanted to stand a chance at actually taking him down.

Her knife froze in midair.

Klaus had caught it between his thumb and index finger.

"But you're still a long way from being able to beat me."

After snatching away the knife and leaving her unarmed, he tossed it by her feet and strode into the manor.

Wanting to improve meant having to hit wall after wall.

Those walls didn't just come in her training with Klaus, but during the time she spent interacting with Avian, too.

After their mission in Longchon, Avian spent just about every day at Heat Haze Palace during their proverbial honeymoon period.

The time they spent together was raucous and rowdy, but behind the scenes, there was an agenda at play. In exchange for training up Avian, Klaus was having them give pointers to Lamplight in turn. Avian's behavior seemed obnoxious at first glance, but the truth was, they were actually helping the Lamplight girls shore up their sorely lacking fundamentals.

Klaus had gone and devised a whole new sort of classroom—one where he didn't just train them directly, but where the students could teach each other skills and push each other to grow.

Monika immediately figured out what he was up to, and the afternoon Avian all showed up, she stood on the Heat Haze Palace roof and observed the other spy team down in the courtyard. As she watched, she started picking up on what each of their assignments seemed to be. "Lander" Vics's job was to train Sybilla in hand-to-hand combat, "Feather" Pharma's job was to hone Thea's and Grete's negotiation abilities, "South Wind" Queneau's job was to teach Lily and Erna how to conceal themselves, and "Cloud Drift" Lan's job was to show Annette how to restrain people.

A taunting grin spread across Monika's face.

"Wonder who I'm gonna get?"
"That would be me, blue girl."

The reply came from behind her.

She turned around to see a brown-haired man with sharp eyes. He must have just used his body's bizarre springlike flexibility to scale the building by kicking his way up the wall's protrusions. He strode toward her with a cold, condescending expression.

That was "Flock" Vindo—the man who'd once held the top grades out of the entire academy student body and was currently serving as Avian's boss.

"No one else was qualified to keep up with you," he said, positively radiating arrogance.

"Makes sense. That's probably the right call."

Even among Avian's members, Vindo was in a league of his own—so much so that Klaus had appointed him as boss of the entire team. Despite his age, he was already one of the top spies in the entire Republic.

He stood before Monika, not a hint of warmth in his gaze. "As a fellow operative working to protect the Republic, I'm going to get you up to snuff. Consider it an honor."

"Huh?"

Monika crossed her arms and cocked her head in annoyance.

Vindo paid her no heed. "You've got a fair bit of potential. You're, what, sixteen? If you do as I say and train a bit harder, you'll be a decent spy in no—"

Monika cut him off. "Hold the fucking phone, smug boy." Vindo's expression froze. She'd caught him completely off-guard. "Where do you get off, acting all high-and-mighty? You clearly think you're better than me, but I don't recall ever agreeing."

Monika had a good reason for being so combative. Back in Longchon, she and Vindo had only fought head-to-head for a brief moment right at the very end. Together with Erna, Sara, and Sybilla, Monika had successfully detained him in a four-on-one offensive. In short, she'd never gotten a chance to gauge his actual strength.

"Flock" Vindo was Avian's boss, and if you excluded Klaus, he was a strong candidate for the best spy of their generation. Meanwhile, "Glint" Monika was Lamplight's star player who'd been integral to their many successful Impossible Missions. The question was, which of them was a better spy? The answer had yet to be determined.

"I'd show some respect if I were you. I'm a generous gal, so if you do, I don't mind showing you a thing or two."

Vindo furrowed his brow in annoyance at Monika's taunt. "...This is insipid."

He quietly clenched a pair of knives in one hand and began giving off an almost bloodthirsty sort of pressure. There was no need for them to exchange any further words. What they needed was a simple yet definitive way to fight, and that meant that there was just one option on the table—using any methods they had at their disposal to get the other side to say two little words: *I surrender.*

"Come at me," Vindo said. "I'll show you just how far beneath me you are."

The arena was the Heat Haze Palace roof. The time was 2:12 PM. The skies were clear. There was a slight breeze. Seven feet separated them.

The battle began in a flash.

Monika recognized that she would be at a disadvantage in close quarters. As she put some distance between them, she took five mirrors and hurled them across the roof, where they found purchase and stood upright. Vindo ignored them and rushed her down, but Monika's attack was far,

far faster than his knife. She threw one of her rubber balls both to keep Vindo at bay and to ever so slightly shift his gaze.

"I'm code name Glint—now, let's harbor love for as long as we can."

The flash on the camera she had hidden in her hand flared, then bounced across the mirrors to ambush Vindo. Her attack quite literally came at the speed of light.

"——?!"

Vindo was blinded, and Monika slipped by his side and hurled another of her metal-cored rubber balls. It bounced off the roof's chimney and struck Vindo in the side of the head.

She moved to launch a follow-up attack, then froze. Vindo had already regained his footing. With an impressed expression, he rubbed the spot where the ball had hit him, then shot Monika a cool glance. "Light? No, a creep shot." He seemed to be none the worse for wear. He must have used some technique to mitigate the blow. "That's a good trick. Being able to observe a target from any angle is the perfect skill for a spy to have."

"Yeah, thanks."

"Problem is, it's not suited for combat. Once someone finds out about it, it's a useless gimmick."

With that, Vindo did something unthinkable. He *closed his eyes.* Monika was facing him with a weapon in her hand, yet he willingly chose to deprive himself of his vision.

She let out a silent groan. *Gah! You're telling me he can fight like that?!* It didn't take long for her to get her answer.

Vindo launched himself forward, and before Monika knew it, he was right in front of her. He'd moved so fast it was like magic. There was no time for her to react.

"Your mediocre technique isn't going to work on me."

Vindo's attacks came hard and fast, and Monika's dodges were far too slow.


After their fifth clash, Monika fell off the roof.

The good news was that she hit a tree on her way down, and the numerous branches she broke served to keep the damage to a minimum.

However, the landing still knocked the wind out of her. She tried to get back to her feet, but she couldn't muster the strength.

Sara happened to be out in the yard at the time. "Miss Monika?!" she cried, then rushed on over.

Monika exhaled. It wasn't exactly her finest moment.

She'd been well and truly bested.

Vindo had only been using the flats of his knives, but that hadn't stopped him from packing a hell of a lot of power into his hits. Monika wasn't the heaviest person around, and the force from the blows had lifted her straight off her feet and sent her careering ignobly across the roof. After shutting down Monika's technique, Vindo been able to go on the offensive unopposed.

On the fifth such hit, Monika had toppled all the way off the roof. She was out of bounds. "I surrender," she groaned. "What the hell were those moves...?"

It shouldn't have been possible for someone to move so nimbly. It wasn't even his top speed that was the problem, it was how quickly he could switch between accelerating and decelerating. One moment, he was stationary, the next, he was barreling forward at full speed. Monika had been completely unable to keep up with the sharp tempo of his movement.

Vindo descended and calmly looked down at her. "It's a technique I learned from 'Firewalker' Gerde. She was my teacher."

"Wasn't she on Inferno?"

Vindo nodded and recounted his encounter with Gerde. He told her about the old woman he ran into in the Fend Commonwealth who left her brawny muscles exposed for the world to see. He told her about how the old woman had taken him to the wooden apartment building she used as her hideout and how she'd spent several days training him in the basement. And he told her about how, hellish as they'd been, those days had allowed him to inherit some of the old woman's skills.

Beside them, Sara's eyes were as wide as dinner plates.

"...So you knew Inferno, too, huh?" Monika muttered.

"That's right," Vindo replied with a small nod. "And Gerde gave me an order. She told me to back up Klaus. That's why I'm here."

"Seems like a lot of work to go to for some random old lady."

"I owe her a lot. And besides, we come from the same roots. Me, Gerde, and Klaus, too. We're all headed to the same destination," he declared. "Revenge against the Galgad Empire—and against the world."

The raw hostility he was giving off caused Sara to inhale sharply.

Vindo gave Monika an intense stare, then went on in a voice dripping with disdain. "We're fighting on a whole different level than you are."

Monika's life had been filled with setbacks.

Despite being blessed with talent, not even she had been able to avoid defeat. After meeting failure after failure in the world of art, she practically fled to the world of espionage, but once she got there, she ran into Heide, then Klaus, then Guido, then Vindo, and got bested by them at every turn. She didn't feel triumphant all the time, not by a long shot. There were plenty of nights she spent quivering in frustration.

She made sure not to let her teammates realize it, but she spent huge amounts of time trying to find a way to be able to stand up to the strong.

*I've got to revamp my fighting style from the ground up. I can leave stuff like infiltration and negotiation to the others. What they need from me is for me to never lose a fight.*

Day in and day out, she devoted herself diligently to her studies.

*How can I catch up with the powerful? What can I do to enter their world?*

Her heart didn't break like it had back at her academy, and Lily's presence played a huge part in that. Monika wanted to continue showing off her own genius around her, and over time, she gradually stopped believing that her feelings were going to fade.

By staying with Lamplight, Monika could keep on protecting her. She'd made up her mind never to tell Lily how she felt, but that was how she expressed her love.

When news of Avian's deaths came in, Monika felt empty inside.

This was her first encounter with the deaths of people she was close to. An intense feeling of loss pierced her chest. It was overwhelming, being reminded that even spies stronger than her could perish in the line of duty.

*After all that arrogant stuff they said, they went and got taken out like it was nothing,* she thought irreverently as they headed for the Fend Commonwealth.

When they met up with Lan in the admin cabin, she saw her own future reflected in the sobbing girl's figure. She wondered how she would react if she lost her team like that.

As she fell into contemplation, Lily did something she never would have expected. With an inexplicable cry of *"I wanna see some smiles!"* she forced the whole team to link hands together. Then she got serious.

*"We need to make an oath. I don't want anyone else to die here. We're all gonna make it back to Heat Haze Palace, and we're all gonna make it back alive. I need everyone to promise me that."*

It initially came across as childish, but that promise was an important one.

*She never changes, not even at times like these.*

Monika wasn't certain, but there was a chance a smile crept across her face. Lily had the mental fortitude to fix her sights clearly on the future, even when her back was against the wall.

It was that very strength that had made Monika fall for her.

After that, she spent a lot of time working alongside Lan.

Lan was badly injured and couldn't operate at her full capacity, but even so, they were going to need her help if they were going to uncover the mysterious group that attacked Avian. Any time she had to go out into the broader Fend Commonwealth, Monika always went along as her bodyguard. Lan would tell her that she had somewhere she wanted to go, and they would quietly slip out at night so as to remain unseen and ride double atop a large motorcycle.

At one point, Monika asked her if she was all right to be moving around so much with her injuries. Lan gave her a laugh from the back seat. "Bit by bit, my body doth heal. I'm a long way from being the picture of health, but I daresay I've recovered enough to be able to lend a hand. Heh-heh. The moment of my comeback is nigh. Like the undying phoenix, the symbol of Avian and Lamplight's unity, so too shall I rise from the ashes."

Her voice rang with good cheer. Monika got the sense she was putting up a brave front, but she chose not to say that part out loud. "And? Where're we going?" she asked, to which Lan replied, "Verily, Sir Klaus hath given me a task."

The destination Lan led them to was a small village called Immiran to the southeast of Hurough.

"Brother Vindo said something before his death. He said he found Gerde's legacy."

"What's that?"

"I know not. We were attacked just before he was to brief us."

There was a hint of sadness in Lan's voice.

"Firewalker" Gerde had gone missing there in Fend, and Avian's mission was to discover the truth about her final days. What had she been investigating, and why had she been killed?

"What I do know is where he had just been. He was at Dame Gerde's hideout, the one where she once trained him. Brother Vindo spent just about every day visiting it to search for clues."

While the rest of the team had been trying to track down eyewitness accounts and records of Gerde's activity, Vindo had spent several days identifying where her apartment was so he could look through her belongings.

The spot Gerde had been using was in a four-story apartment building built out of shabby, run-down wood. The walls inside were moldy, and their wood grain was untreated and exposed. There were three units per floor, but the building had quite a few vacancies, and light was only visible from two or three windows total. Gerde had paid several years' worth of rent in advance, so her unit had yet to be cleared out.

When the two of them went to the apartment up on the third floor, they found both the living room and the bedroom absolutely littered with beer bottles and cigarette butts. Vindo had clearly searched the place from top to bottom, as the floor and wallpaper were in tatters.

"Brother Vindo found something... But perhaps he took it with him?"

"What did Klaus say?"

"'Granny G was bad at hiding classified documents. It won't be hard to find.'"

"That's not a great look for a spy."

Monika and Lan glanced around the room.

"It's not here." "I tend to concur."

Nothing was jumping out at them. They thought about checking the other units, but they hadn't prepped for that, so it would be trouble if any of the other residents caught them. They decided to come back another day disguised as contractors and left.

Losing Avian was a tragedy, but aside from that, their scheme in Fend was just another mission for Monika. None of the details changed what she needed to do—keep a cool head, use her talents to their fullest, and keep Lily safe. She continued making the best moves she could find that would prevent her teammates from getting wounded.

That was supposed to be all there was to it.

However, she soon learned that she'd been too optimistic.

By the end of their search, they'd identified the group that attacked Avian as a team called Belias.

After laying a series of traps, Klaus announced that he and Sybilla were going to go infiltrate Belias and investigate them from within. The rest of the team's job was to back them up.

While Klaus and the others headed for the dance party being held at Heron Manor, Monika was stationed alone over at Belias's base, the Kashard Doll Workshop. Thea was being held hostage inside, and the plan was that she would send Monika a distress signal if she got into hot water.

Up on the roof of a nearby building, Monika surrendered herself to the passing of time.

Then she sensed someone's presence on the corner of the roof; they must have jumped from the next building over. The person landed nimbly, with visible confidence.

"Who's there?"

Monika already had her gun at the ready. If she wanted to, it would take her a fraction of a second to pull the trigger.

By the look of it, the interloper was a girl whose age wasn't far from Monika's. It was too dark to make out all her features, but her pointed teeth gleaming in the night's faint light suggested cruelty, like she reveled in mocking others.

"Gee-hee-hee," her counterpart laughed gratingly. "So we finally meet."

"I asked for your *name*, you moron."

"Green Butterfly." The girl grinned. "That's my code name."

At that point, Monika still had no idea who she was dealing with. However, every instinct she had was picking up on the unsettling malevolence she carried herself with.

Green Butterfly extended her index finger Monika's way and smiled sadistically. "It's a pleasure to make your acquaintance, Monika. I'm here from Serpent to bring you a flawless little slice of despair."

That moment marked the beginning of Monika's nightmare.

# Chapter 5

# Scarlet Leviathan ③

There was a crowd gathered in front of the *Conmerid Times* main office.

The office was an impressive eight-story building right in the heart of Hurough. It was noticeably taller than the buildings around it, and its walls were a beautiful age-worn gray. Due to its frosted windows, it was impossible to see inside. Out in front, it had a set of imposing stone pillars that seemed to inherently reject any who might approach.

According to Amelie, the newspaper had remained in print for over a hundred years. Politically speaking, they had a centrist lean and had yet to throw in with either the Neo-Imperialists or the Anti-Imperialists.

Now there was a large group of citizens hurling angry shouts at the building. There were so many of them they were spilling into the street and obstructing the flow of traffic. The cars unfortunate enough to pass by laid on their horns, but they were no match for the mob's zeal. The people gathered all wanted to know the same things. "Was that article true?" they bellowed, and "Where did those photos come from?"

From their positions hidden among the crowd, Klaus and Erna shared their thoughts.

"They're practically rioting."

"Y-yeah. It's a little scary."

Their goal went without saying—to get some details from the reporter who'd taken those photos of Monika.

◇◇◇

"........It doesn't make sense."

Upon seeing the pictures, a deep furrow spread across Amelie's brow. The paper had devoted its entire front page to reporting that they'd found the culprit behind Prince Darryn's and Director Mia's assassinations. The image quality on the photos wasn't great, but the person in them was unmistakably Monika.

She shot a skeptical look over at Klaus. "Bonfire, please do be honest with me. Where was Monika the night Prince Darryn was assassinated?"

"I had her watch over the Kashard Doll Workshop. Those were the only orders I gave her."

"But you have no way of proving that." The suspicion in her eyes deepened. "Actually, strictly speaking, you don't even know yourself. You were at Heron Manor at the time, so you weren't observing her actions."

She'd had him there, in fact. Klaus and Sybilla had spent the time leading up to Darryn's death under Belias's watchful eye. With Thea taken prisoner, the two of them had been doing exactly what Belias told them to. He had no way of knowing what Monika had really been up to during that period.

Amelie went on. "Would it have been possible for 'Glint' Monika to assassinate the crown prince?"

"No. She couldn't have gotten past his guards."

"That's a lie, and you know it," Amelie replied sharply. "I've seen her work with my own eyes. She stands head and shoulders above the rest of Lamplight's members. With proper backup, she could very well have overcome them."

"If you already made up your mind, then don't ask the question."

Amelie's analytical abilities were frustratingly on point. She was right; Monika had the skills of an elite spy. If she had help from someone on the inside, someone who could leak intel on the security detail, then she would have been entirely capable of carrying out the killing. And kidnapping a single scientist would have been child's play.

"Please don't tell me that you actually *believe* this nonsense about Monika killing the crown prince," Klaus said with a hint of censure in his voice.

"I'm considering it as a possibility, nothing more," Amelie replied with a wave of her hand. "Naturally, I find the report dubious in the extreme. I have no intention of just accepting it at its word."

"I would hope not."

"But I can't very well ignore it, now, can I? That *is* Monika in those photographs, of that there can be no doubt. The question is, how will CIM leadership react to the situation?"

It called to mind the way Avian had gotten killed. CIM personnel had a habit of blindly following their superiors' instructions. If Hide ended up giving the order for them to eliminate Monika...

"In any case, the sooner we interrogate that reporter, the better." Klaus rose to his feet. "Wherever this intel is coming from, that's where we'll find Monika."

As they continued standing in front of the *Conmerid Times* headquarters, they spotted Sybilla and rendezvoused with her in a back alley behind the building. She had information she wanted to pass along about what had happened in the underworld following the article's release.

"Thea's been workin' her ass off," Sybilla whispered as they hid behind a nearby building so nobody would spot them. "She's gotten in touch with every mafia group in the region, and she's been pumping them for all the intel they've got. Meanwhile, she's been givin' me and Lily instructions, too. I dunno if anyone else coulda pulled off the kind of multitasking she's been up to."

"I certainly doubt it," Klaus agreed.

Pharma had been the Avian member in charge of undercover ops, and after getting some pointers from her, Thea's and Grete's ability to infiltrate hostile organizations had improved dramatically. Grete still hesitated to join groups with lots of men in them, so the fact that Thea was willing to worm her way into just about anywhere was a huge asset. On top of that, she also had the ability to sense people's desires by looking them in the eyes. Taking advantage of that talent allowed her to form ties with all sorts of different organizations, and she was the one who'd gathered most of the intel in Sybilla's report.

"First off, here's what's been goin' on these last couple days. Apparently, all the mafia groups are colluding for the moment and puttin' together a new armed group. Their goal is to slaughter any spies who threaten their nation."

"So we have organized crime pretending to be a militia?"

"Yeah, basically. Everyone loves the royals, even the gangsters."

"I guess that's true. Besides, it's not uncommon for power to gather in the hands of unsavory groups when trust in the government falls."

Tension was mounting, and it was mounting quickly.

Sybilla frowned. "From what we've seen, the report from this morning is makin' 'em join ranks even faster."

"Noted. Someone could well be pulling the strings. Keep up the investigation. We're going to go to the paper and find out the what's really going on with that article."

"...You make it sound so damn easy. But hey, maybe it is for you," Sybilla remarked. Then, with a quiet "Anyhow, leave the other stuff to me," she left.

With that, Klaus and Erna headed back to the front of the building.

Observing the gathered crowd made it clear just how many walks of life were represented in the shouting voices—average joes, reporters from other papers, and people who looked like they operated on the shady side of the law. There was even a television crew just off to the side with a male reporter talking in front of a big camera. Every person in the nation wanted to know the truth behind that article.

"How's Conmerid responding to all this?" Klaus asked a man who appeared to be a journalist from another publication and was staring up at the headquarters. "I have some questions I'd like to ask the reporter."

The journalist shrugged. "I'd take a look over there before you start getting your hopes up, friend." He pointed at the building's entrance, which was sealed up tight. "They're refusing to announce who their source is. The police came by, and they wouldn't even let *them* in. All the employees are holed up inside."

"Sounds like they're keeping a tight lid on things."

"The police don't have any evidence the article is fake, so they can't even make any arrests. The only people who could hope to make any headway are—" Then, upon seeing the cars driving up by the side of the crowd, the journalist cut himself off midsentence. "Ah, speak of the devil."

There were two cars, both of them shiny and black, and eight brawny men and women got out of them. All of them were dressed in unsettling black coats.

"There's the CIM, right on schedule," said the journalist with a hint of amusement in his voice.

"...And their authority supersedes all human rights."

"Yeah, that reporter's done for. That team there is called Vanajin, and word on the street is they don't pull their punches. They're probably here to accuse the reporter of being a spy and drag 'em off to an interrogation room."

Klaus thanked the reporter for the information and stepped away. Theirs was an age of spies, and intelligence agencies had far more power in investigative matters than the police did. They could force their way onto other people's property, and they were no stranger to inhumane acts like abducting people without evidence or a warrant. Given the way Klaus dealt with traitors to his own nation, he was in no real position to judge them.

Belias wasn't the only counterintelligence team working the case anymore.

The Vanajin operatives pinned the security guard's arms behind his back and began trying to force their way into the building. It wouldn't be long before they got inside and abducted whatever reporter knew the full story.

"Yeep..." Erna frowned worriedly and bit down on her lip.

Klaus gently patted her back. "You want to do everything you can to save Monika?"

"Yeah. Of course." Erna gave him a determined nod. "There was something off about Big Sis Monika right before she betrayed us. I noticed it, but...I wasn't able to do anything to help her!"

"Got it. In that case, let's do this. We can't afford to trust the CIM, and I'll be damned if I let them snatch a key source of intel out from under us." Klaus stooped down to meet Erna's eyeline. "This tactic is going to be risky. That's why I chose you as my accomplice this time around."

There was a crowd gathered behind the *Conmerid Times* building, too. Their plan was that if anyone tried to go in or come out the back exit, they would catch them and press them for information about the article's source. When the back entrance went unused, though, they were left with nothing to do but stare up aimlessly at the building.

All the entrances and exits were barred shut, the windows were sealed up tight, and with the CIM out front, going in through there wasn't an option, either.

Klaus and Erna wasted no time and headed for the next building over, a five-story structure owned by an insurance company. There was a guard out front, but Klaus flashed him the special token he'd stolen from Belias and fed him a quick lie: "We're with the CIM." The guard stared at them in shock, and the two of them slipped on past him, went up to the second floor, and tracked down the window at the end of the hallway. Klaus opened it up. He'd spotted it from down on the street, and sure enough, it was directly across from one of the *Conmerid Times* windows.

Klaus stepped back and tapped Erna on the shoulder. "We're jumping."

"Yeep?!"

Ignoring her alarm, Klaus took a running start and hurled himself out the window.

There were fifteen feet between the two buildings, and Klaus smashed his way into the *Conmerid Times* building through its glass window. Shards scattered around him as he stuck the landing.

The second floor was apparently home to the paper's editorial department. The room had twelve desks packed end to end, each of them piled high with documents, as well as seven employees, all of whom stared at Klaus in a slack-jawed daze. The man standing right next to where he'd landed dropped the entire stack of papers he was holding.

"My apologies. I misremembered where the entrance was." Klaus gave them a small, apologetic bow. "While I have you, though, would you mind telling me who wrote that headline article? Where are they?"

"W-we don't know!" the man beside him yelped. "It just showed up in the paper out of the blue. Peons like us don't get consulted about these things. And besides, who even are you—?"

Klaus took out the list he'd prepared and shoved it in the man's face. "All you have to do is point at someone who might be able to give me answers. Do that, and no more harm will come to you."

The man's gaze darted around. "I—I can't, I mean, I just…"

"Raymond, the editor in chief? Much appreciated."

"Huh?"

"The direction your eyes moved told me everything I needed to know. Don't worry; I won't tell him how I figured it out."

After bulldozing his way through the conversation, Klaus raced out of the editorial department. As he did, a shout of "Yeep!" sounded out from behind him as Erna successfully made the jump as well.

With her in tow, he headed into the hallway and found the elevator. He pushed the button, then used the nearby stairs to go down to the first floor while he waited for the elevator to arrive.

When he ran a quick spot check on the entrance, he found that the eight

CIM members had already made it past the guards. Standing at their vanguard was the blond man with dark skin and a saber hanging from his waist. He grabbed one of the employees and stared her down as he pressed her for information. "We're from the CIM. Where's Raymond?"

The employee averted her gaze. "Oh, no, I'm afraid I really can't—"

On hearing that, the man grabbed her by the collar and hoisted her up with one hand. "If you think you have the right to remain silent, think again. You're about to earn yourself a one-way trip to the gallows."

"_____"

"We are always just, and we do not err. You really want to defy me, 'Armorer' Meredith, when my orders come straight from the Crown? You may be one of the Crown's subjects, but that won't save you if you choose to oppose us. I'll weep with contrition as I tear off your fingers."

He grabbed one of the woman's fingers, and she let out a feeble croak. "H-he's on the seventh floor..."

Meredith cast the woman to the floor, and the CIM squad headed deeper into the building.

There was no time to waste. Klaus knew that if he ran into them, things could get messy in a hurry. After returning to the second floor, he boarded the elevator as it arrived and headed for the seventh floor alongside Erna. When they got off, he made sure to stick a knife between its doors to render it inoperable.

The seventh floor was home to a room labeled OFFICE OF THE EDITOR IN CHIEF, and after ordering Erna to wait in the wings, Klaus headed in without so much as knocking.

Inside, there was a man by the window holding a cup in one hand. He took a sip from it, clearly relishing its taste, and cast his gaze out the window at the crowd gathered below.

"Ah, that was fast," the man murmured as he calmly turned around. He was in his midforties, sporting a stubbly five-o'clock shadow, a worn-out jacket, and an unconcerned grin.

That was Raymond Appleton, the paper's editor in chief. He was apparently the mastermind behind the article featuring the photos of Monika, and judging by the reactions from the second-floor editors, he'd done so by leveraging his authority.

"Hmm? Wait, are you not with the CIM?" After looking at Klaus, Raymond stroked his stubble in delight. "Well, that's interesting. Who are you, then? Some foreign spy, maybe?"

"I see no reason to answer your questions."

"Nor I yours," Raymond replied with a shrug. "I assume you're here about the article, but I'm afraid there's nothing I'm willing to tell you. Not even if it costs me my life."

"You seem quite set in your conviction."

"How astute. But honestly, I've got my pride as a journalist to consider. It's our job to keep this nation on the right path. If you're going to kill me, then get on with it. If nothing else, it'll lend credence to the article."

"And you're fine taking your family down with you?"

"Don't have one. Don't even have any friends."

Raymond didn't so much as flinch at Klaus's threat; he had real nerve. He took another sip from his cup as though to demonstrate how confident he was.

In Klaus's experience, people who were operating out of conviction were a royal pain in the ass. Standard-issue blackmail and bribery didn't tend to work on them. Klaus could hold the man at gunpoint, and he doubted Raymond would shed so much as a drop of sweat.

"I'd give up if I were you. Won't be long before the CIM gets here." Raymond let out an amused laugh. "I can't imagine that'd be good news for you. Don't worry, though. I'm not going to give them my source, either. They can torture me all they like; it won't do them any good."

From the sound of things, the CIM had figured out that the elevator wasn't running and had started ascending the stairs. The sound of footsteps from outside the room was gradually getting louder.

They had less than two minutes.

"Oh, so it's a matter of pride." Klaus shook his head. "In that case, there's no point trying to talk you out of it."

"That's right. I don't know what country you're spying for, but this'll make a great topic for my next article—"

"I did get you a parting gift. Cute, isn't she?"

Klaus snapped his fingers, and Erna came in looking as adorable and blond as ever. She gave Raymond an expressionless bow, then went and stood beside him as Klaus took out a glove and put it on.

Then he drew his revolver and shot her.

Blood splattered across the editor in chief's room.

Erna let out a hoarse "How unlucky..." and coughed up blood as she collapsed to the floor. There was no vitality to the fall. She was already dead, it seemed.

"Wha—?"

Raymond's jaw hung open in disbelief.

The smell of gunpowder smoke still lingered on the revolver, and Klaus tossed it at Raymond's chest. After making sure that Raymond had instinctively caught it, he nodded in satisfaction. "Good-bye, now. It is a shame I won't be able to stick around to see how you explain this one to the CIM. I imagine they'll arrest you as a suspect in the girl's murder," he said tauntingly. "I wonder how many people will believe your article after that little tidbit comes to light?"

Raymond hurriedly let go of the gun and approached Erna with a look of horror on his face. He reached out with trembling fingertips, but before he could touch her, his foot reached the blood spreading across the floor. "Eek!" he shrieked as he reeled backward. Journalists like him didn't come across dead bodies that often.

"D-did you seriously just...?"

"Now that they've heard the gunshot, the CIM's going to come running. Thirty seconds. That's how long you have before nobody even wants to think about that article you poured your heart and soul into. They'll write it off as the deranged ravings of a homicidal lunatic."

"......!!"

"You'll lose everything. Your reputation as a journalist, the respect of your peers, and your status."

After coldly laying out the facts, Klaus turned and left Raymond in the room with the prone girl. Getting out would be simple. All he had to do was jump from the roof to the next building over.

The CIM's footsteps were thundering up the stairs.

Raymond began sweating profusely, and Klaus noticed. Right as the spy was about to leave, Raymond grabbed his arm. His expression was one of pure anguish. "Please, take me with you," he begged.

Klaus ran up to the roof and brought Raymond over to the apartment he'd rented in advance.

Raymond was sweating from every pore in his body—maybe it was the time he'd just spent clinging to Klaus as he jumped from roof to roof. He collapsed limply into the dining chair and didn't move for a good long while. Klaus offered him some water, and after chugging it down, Raymond let out a big sigh and cradled his head in his hands. "...You know, now that I think about it, I probably didn't actually need to run for it. It's not like my fingerprints were on the trigger... But even so, that woulda been a hard situation to talk myself out of..."

He'd had enough time that he was starting to think rationally again. Any civilian would have panicked after seeing a dead body like that, so it was hard to blame him for his hasty decision.

"Regardless, fleeing was the right call. CIM interrogations are far more brutal than you could possibly imagine. No amount of conviction would be enough to get you through one of those."

Klaus thought back to the torture devices he'd seen lined up in the Belias headquarters. He doubted there was a person alive who could withstand implements such as those.

"You sure about that?" Raymond said skeptically.

"I'm telling you that for your own good. Your actions were rooted in a desire to serve your nation. Our positions and ideals might differ, but I can't hate you for that. I have no intention of causing you any more harm than I already have."

Raymond scratched his head awkwardly. "That's a cold comfort, coming from a murderer."

"You haven't realized yet?"

"Huh?"

"I didn't actually kill her. She was faking it."

Right as Klaus explained the situation, there was a knock on the door. Klaus opened it up and revealed Erna, who'd just changed into a clean outfit.

"I'm back, Teach."

"AHHHHHHHHHHHH!" Raymond let out a shout that wasn't far from being a genuine scream as he crumpled to his knees. Seeing her must have come as a real blow. "Seriously? How did I not notice...?" he groaned.

Again, though, it wasn't really his fault. Erna had an uncanny knack for pretending to run into mishaps and disasters. It would have been all but impossible for an untrained eye to see through her acting. Her put-up jobs made for a powerful liecraft, one that took full advantage of her adorable looks.

"You did well," Klaus told Erna. He handed her the slice of cake he'd been keeping in the fridge, then stood before Raymond. "Don't worry. The CIM will assume you've been kidnapped, so your article's credibility will be unaffected. If anything, this'll make it that much more believable."

"W-well, that's good news."

"The problem is, that doesn't exactly serve my interests," Klaus went on threateningly. "Depending on how things play out, I may need you to retract it."

"Wh-who even are you people...?"

"Talk. Where did you get those photos from? Did you take them yourself?"

"........."

Raymond averted his gaze. Desperate to change the topic, he glanced around the apartment and sighed. "You mind if I smoke?"

Klaus glanced over at Erna. A look of displeasure flitted across her face, but she clenched her fists and nodded. She was willing to put up with it.

Klaus handed a lighter over to Raymond, who pulled a metal case out of his pocket and popped a cigarette in his mouth. He lit it, took a long drag, and exhaled a big cloud of smoke. "I keep telling you, I can't give up my source."

"Mm-hmm."

"But you—you intrigue me. With the right conditions, I could be convinced to let a few details slip. And if you don't want to play ball, then go ahead and give me an honorable death right here and now." Still holding the cigarette in his mouth, Raymond raised his hands in a show of surrender.

"Name your price," Klaus replied. "You have things you want other than just your safety?"

"Of course I do." A sarcastic grin spread across Raymond's face. "Give me your information. What's going on here in Fend?"

That was Raymond's sense of duty as a journalist talking. The look in his eyes had changed to that of a consummate professional.

Klaus had no issues with that. Getting in good with a local news source was the oldest move in the espionage playbook. "Have you heard of a group called Serpent?"

"...Hmm?"

"They're a spy team from the Galgad Empire. You heard about that mass murder over in the United States, right? The official story is that some nutjob called Lillian Hepburn did it, but the truth is, that was Serpent's handiwork." Klaus paused for a beat, then went on. "They were involved in Prince Darryn's assassination."

"Do you have any proof?"

"The intel is solid. I got it from a friend in the CIM. Have you heard of her? Her name's 'Puppeteer' Amelie, head of the Belias team. The two of us are good buddies. We've even been living under the same roof lately." As he laid out a story that was mostly true with a few lies mixed in, Klaus handed Raymond a few CIM-signed files he'd looted from the burned-down Kashard Doll Workshop. "That's all I can tell you. Now it's your turn to talk."

Raymond gave Klaus an intense stare to try to figure out if he could trust him. He shot a couple of glances over at Erna, too, and spent a long time mulling things over. The smell of the smoke he was exhaling permeated the room, and Erna pinched her nose in disgust.

Eventually, he lowered his voice. "Not a word of this to anyone, okay?"

"My source for the article...was a girl. She was beautiful like you wouldn't believe."

"Can you describe her?"

"I didn't get a good look at her, just a brief glimpse of her face. She's the one who gave me the photos."

A look spread across Erna's face as though something had just dawned on her. "Teach, could that be—?"

Klaus said nothing.

Aside from members of their own team, there was only one spy hiding in the Fend Commonwealth who could be reasonably be described as a "girl." With his final breaths, Vindo had left them a message about the people who'd led Avian to ruin, and one of them was a girl with exposed scars from a wound running down her shoulders—Green Butterfly. Nothing was certain yet, but that could very well have been who Raymond was talking about.

As Erna pensively murmured, "We finally got a lead on Serpent," Raymond went on with audible delight. "That girl's going to be the leader of a new institution." He'd burned through his first cigarette in record time, and he snatched away Erna's empty cake plate in place of an ashtray to stamp out his butt. "She's building an anti-government coalition here in Fend and has named herself the leader. We can trust the current administration about as far as we can throw them. Even we can tell how deep traitors and turncoats have wormed their way into the system. If we want to protect Her Majesty's great nation, we need a new group to do it."

Hearing that reminded Klaus of something. "...I've heard that the mafia and other armed groups have been joining forces recently. Is that what that's about?"

"What, you already knew? If you want to get pedantic, it isn't just mafia groups. A bunch of journalists like me have signed on as well." A crooked smile played at Raymond's lips. "The group is called the Fires of War."

Klaus had never heard the name before.

Raymond took out his cigarette case again and plucked out a fresh cig. "That's as much as I can tell you. If you want more information than that, then it's your turn to—"

"Hold on."

"Hmm?"

Klaus gave Raymond a harsh stare. "Tell me—did the girl give you that cigarette case?"

"Huh? How'd you know?" Raymond asked with a confused tilt of the head, to which Klaus gave a very simple answer.

"Because there's a homing device stuck to the bottom of it."

The other side had read them like a book.

Raymond stared blankly at the silver cigarette case, and Klaus grabbed it out of his hand. It was longer than it needed to be. Klaus crushed the end with his finger and retrieved the device from within.

Erna rose to her feet, her nose twitching like mad. "Teach!"

"I know."

The window shattered as something came flying inside.

It was a hand grenade.

Klaus's body moved on pure instinct. He grabbed Raymond by the collar and dashed to the back of the room. Then he flipped up the dining table to use as a makeshift shield. Raymond wasn't quite on the same page yet, and he let out a confused "Huh?" as Klaus crammed him behind the table, squeezed Erna's shoulder tight, and braced himself.

An explosion rang out.

When dealing with grenades, it wasn't the explosion itself that would kill you, but rather the ensuing shrapnel. As long as you avoided getting hit by the shards, you could emerge completely unscathed. On the other hand, one wrong move could easily prove fatal.

The explosion blasted out the entire window frame, giving them a clear view of the building across the way and of the person standing imposingly atop its roof.

"What...?" Raymond gasped.

It was no wonder he recognized the figure. There were a pair of photos of her seared into his memory.

Klaus wiped the dust off his jacket and walked over to the window. "So you finally show your face."

The girl standing on the opposite building had cerulean hair and cold, ruthless eyes. She was the one who'd attacked them, that much was clear.

Erna looked like she was about to cry, and she slumped against the wall as though her legs had just gone limp. Through trembling lips, she choked out a few words—the name of the enemy who'd just tried to kill them.

"Big Sis Monika...?"

Monika practically radiated hostility as she stood there. She looked down at them motionlessly, probing them with her gaze. In her hand, she was clutching her pistol.

# Chapter 6

# Glint ③

*"It's a pleasure to make your acquaintance, Monika. I'm here from Serpent to bring you a flawless little slice of despair."*

When the strange girl appeared out of nowhere, Monika acted fast. She squeezed her pistol's trigger and began firing with no questions asked. It was odd that girl had gone out of her way to introduce herself, but Monika had no interest in figuring out what her intentions were. The name she'd given had immediately identified her as a foe. Those people had become Lamplight's sworn enemies the moment they plunged the Din Republic into chaos.

Monika needed to defeat her. Then, once she rendered the girl incapable of fighting back, she could force her to give up information through merciless interrogation. That was the only way Lamplight was interested in interacting with Serpent.

"Gee, wow."

Green Butterfly's moves were deft. Double-action revolvers were designed for quick-draw firing, yet she dodged the bullets Monika shot at her shoulders with just the smallest of movements. She didn't do anything bold or flashy; she just twisted her body a little, and the bullets soared on past her.

"No! Quarter! Given! Those are the vibes we're working with, huh?" Green Butterfly said with a confident grin. "Ah-ha-ha, so *assertive*. But like, would it kill you to have some common courtesy?"

"You people don't deserve courtesy."

Monika had no intention of letting the exchange drag on any longer than it needed to. Everything about Green Butterfly's behavior seemed designed to rile her up, and she didn't care for it one bit. She wanted out of this conversation, pronto.

Monika recognized that Green Butterfly was just going to keep on dodging her shots if she stayed at that range, so she decided to close in on her. Keeping a close eye on her foe's reaction, she shifted her right foot forward.

"Hey, Monika."

Right as she was about to charge, Green Butterfly gave her a mocking smile.

"You're in love, aren't you?"

Monika froze in place. She gave Green Butterfly a look, trying desperately to conceal her panic. "What're you talking about...?"

"I know it's true, y'know. We've got a guy on our team who's supergood at making nasty little guesses like that." Green Butterfly began slowly twirling her arms. It was almost like she was dancing. With her long, slender limbs, she certainly had the physique for it. "He loves weakness more than strength, he prefers flaws to virtues, and his life is chaotic rather than ordered. He's got the worst personality around. He's a coward. He's a loser. And on top of all that, he's got no taste. You'll never meet anyone less impressive."

"........."

With her finger still fast on the trigger, Monika decided to listen to what Green Butterfly was saying. If her opponent was so cocky she was willing to give up intel on Serpent of her own volition, Monika certainly wasn't about to stop her.

When she heard the next thing that came out of Green Butterfly's mouth, though, she realized she'd made a grave mistake.

"It's 'Flower Garden' Lily you're in love with, right?"

By the time Monika came to her senses, she'd already pulled the trigger. However, the bullet she'd fired straight at Green Butterfly's skull got intercepted by an unexpected third party. All of a sudden, a man came in from the side with something resembling a shield and blocked it. Monika switched to her knife so she could go in for a follow-up attack, but a group of men and women rushed in and planted themselves between her and Green Butterfly.

"Ooh, perfect," Green Butterfly said behind her new bodyguards. "Gee-hee-hee, that reaction! I love it. Makes me feel like I totally hit the nail on the head, huh?"

Her six protectors were dressed in black, and Monika could tell just from looking at them that they were no amateurs. Their bodies had been well trained. The one thing they all had in common were their lifeless, lightless eyes.

Seeing them reminded her of something. "Wait, are those—?!"

"They're Worker Ants—mercenaries, courtesy of Purple Ant. But this isn't your first time tangling with them, is it?"

Monika knew all too well how much of a threat Worker Ants could be. In order to faithfully carry out their king's orders, they trained around the clock and immediately killed themselves when they lost. They were soldiers that Purple Ant—one of Serpent's members—created through psychological domination. Apparently, there were still Worker Ants under his control and serving Serpent across the world.

"Just so you know, we captured your king," Monika told them.

Green Butterfly smiled. "Gee, nice try. But if you think that'd be enough to break Purple Ant's control, think again."

Sure enough, the Worker Ants' expressions were just as hopeless as before. They were never going to believe a word that came out of Monika's mouth.

Monika steadied her breathing. At least now she knew that Serpent was involved in the current situation. That allowed her to make a number of deductions. "So you people were the ones who got Avian taken out," she said. "That pretty much lines up with what I figured. You manipulated Belias from behind the scenes to crush Avian, and now you're lurking around their base to keep an eye on our investigation."

Green Butterfly smiled just the way she had when she exposed Monika's love. "Gee, you figured that out fast. You really *are* good at this!"

It pained Monika to discover that she'd been none the wiser to Serpent's surveillance, but it made sense. Most people couldn't sense the very presence of others the way Klaus could. If Serpent had been staying away from Klaus and only observing the girls, then it was no wonder that they'd gone undetected. Plus, she now knew that Serpent had someone whose ability to sniff out the subtleties of people's emotions was on par with Klaus's.

Green Butterfly ordered her Worker Ants to stand down for a moment, then took a step forward. "We got down to thinking, and we realized that, gee, Bonfire's a real problem. He's just going to keep getting in our way. But there's something else we figured out—that we've got no shot at killing him."

"Hey, it takes a big person to admit that." Monika was surprised she seemed to be taking it so well, and Green Butterfly nodded amicably.

"Yeah, well, the facts are the facts. I mean, the guy beat Purple Ant. It takes an absurdly good spy to do that. Ha-ha, it's kind of messed up, if you think about it. There were leagues of spies on that mission for half a year, and he went and finished it in a couple days. And it's the same deal here. It barely took him any time at all to figure out that Belias were the ones who took out Avian."

".........."

"But the thing is, he isn't omnipotent." Green Butterfly's expression grew sterner. "The key thing is that some missions take him a couple days to finish. If we hit him with multiple of those at once and make things so chaotic that no one can tell what'll happen next, we can slow him down as much as we like."

"...How're you planning on doing that?"

Green Butterfly laid one of her long fingers atop her lips. "Tonight, Prince Darryn is going to be assassinated."

"——!!"

"We gotta keep the initiative. By the time Bonfire beats Belias, we'll have made a whole new problem for him to deal with."

That was deranged. Monika couldn't for the life of her figure out what Serpent was thinking. If they went and murdered a member of the Fend royalty, they would have no way of controlling the madness that ensued.

"Why...?" Monika gasped.

"Ooh, can't tell you that. But what I'll say is that there's a reason why someone would want the prince to get shot. When Bonfire starts digging into it, he'll fall even further behind us."

"No, that's not the part I'm asking about!" Monika shouted. There was a bad feeling stirring inside her. Her instincts were sending out warning signs so loud she couldn't help but raise her voice. "What are you telling *me* for?"

".........."

"If some foreign royal dies, it's no skin off my back. But if you go through with this, you'll cause a war between Fend and Galgad. You seriously want to see your nation get crushed into dust?"

Monika was at odds with the Empire's spies, but that didn't mean she saw its entire citizenry as her enemies, too. She had no desire to see war break out, not even between two foreign countries. Din might end up getting caught up in the conflict as well, but more importantly, there was no moral framework she could get behind that allowed her to derive joy from the death of innocent civilians.

Green Butterfly let out an unconcerned laugh. "It's fine. It's like, gee, that's not even a problem. We'll just pin the assassination on a spy from Din. No one'll ever believe that Galgad had anything to do with it."

"...You're gonna make Avian take the fall, huh?" Monika bit her lip. "I get it. That's why the CIM had Belias attack—"

"Naaaah."

"Huh?"

"We're not pinning Prince Darryn's assassination on Avian. That was the original plan, sure, but then we decided to move on to a new scapegoat."

Green Butterfly tilted her head.

"It's 'Flower Garden' Lily. She'll take the blame for Prince Darryn's death."

It took Monika a good long while to comprehend what she'd just heard. How was a girl with such shoddy skills supposed to have committed a crime that grave?

"...That's absurd."

"That's how it's going to be. Remember how our false intel got the CIM to hunt down Avian?"

She wasn't lying. Lamplight's investigation had made it clear that the CIM unit Belias were the ones who'd attacked Avian, a team that had had no intentions whatsoever of causing the Commonwealth any harm.

If Green Butterfly wanted to, she might well be able to do it—both assassinate Prince Darryn, heir to the Fend Commonwealth throne, and pin the crime of the century on "Flower Garden" Lily.

Monika began sweating from every pore. She wanted desperately to kill the girl standing across from her as quickly as she possibly could, but that wasn't feasible. There was no guarantee that Green Butterfly was the only Serpent member in the region.

"Even if you pull it off...," she said, scraping together a rebuttal, "...Klaus'll protect her."

Giving that answer was akin to abandoning her pride and putting everything on Klaus's shoulders. She clenched her fists in shame, but the fact of the matter was that she was confident he could overcome any challenge. When things got ugly, relying on him was the ultimate tool Lamplight had in their arsenal.

"That's pretty sad," Green Butterfly replied. She shook her head as though to say she hadn't expected any better. "Look, Monika, I know you're freaking out, but you gotta reeeally think things through. This whole time, Bonfire's been working his butt off to avoid having to duke it out with the CIM. Why is that, huh? If he wanted to, he could rip through every last Belias member like it was nothing. Gee, I wonder why he doesn't just do that?"

She had a point. Klaus had been actively avoiding picking a fight with the full CIM. That was why Lamplight was specifically prepping to capture the entirety of Belias without letting any of the other CIM teams realize what had happened.

Green Butterfly smiled. "It's obvious, isn't it? It's because in a fight between the Din Republic's and Fend Commonwealth's intelligence agencies, the Republic would get annihilated."

".........."

The theory held water. The Fend Commonwealth had controlled countries around the world and possessed the second-largest economy in the globe, whereas the Din Republic was tiny and rural. The gap in their national strengths and the amount of personnel and resources they could devote to their intelligence organizations were too great for even Klaus to overcome on his own. As such, Lamplight had been forced to do everything in their power to avoid sparking an all-out conflict with the CIM.

"Bonfire's a dyed-in-the-wool patriot, you know. The guy loved Inferno like family, and the Republic's a symbol of what that family fought to protect. He feels like he's got a duty to inherit their mission," Green Butterfly said. "He *can't* save his subordinate, not when it puts tens of millions of his countrymen at risk."

The words weighed heavy on Monika. It was all too easy to imagine that horrible future coming to pass.

What would happen if the Fend Commonwealth ordered the Din Republic to hand "Flower Garden" Lily over to them?

What would happen if C, Klaus's boss at the Foreign Intelligence Office, ordered Klaus to give Lily up?

What if refusing to do so ran the risk of starting a war between the two nations?

Monika didn't know. She had no idea if Klaus would still protect Lily, even in the face of all that. As a spy, the man had a cold, unfeeling side. He needed it in order to protect his country.

"...I'll ask you again," she said feebly. "......Why are you telling me all this?"

"Oh, gee, I think you've probably figured it out."

Green Butterfly extended her hand and spoke in a voice so deep it lingered in Monika's ears.

**"If you join Serpent, we can guarantee 'Flower Garden' Lily's life."**

Monika had no immediate response to that. She couldn't agree, nor could she refuse. All she could do was stand there with her lips sealed tight and groan in agony at the trap she'd been caught in.

Green Butterfly went on to tell her a few other things, each and every one of them more than sufficient to send yet another shock through Monika's heart. By the time she was finished, her voice rang with delight. "I've got one last special present for you. Wanna see something cool?"

She snapped her fingers. The noise rang out crisp and clear.

All of a sudden, gunshots sounded out from all directions.

The cacophony surrounded them as the shots echoed out into the night. Countless bullets, far more than just ten or twenty, all flew up into the air at once. Screams rose from across the city.

Even for a show of force, there was no need for Green Butterfly to have gone that far. With that many shots fired, the cops and the CIM would begin investigating at once. For a spy, there was all downside and no upside.

However, Green Butterfly was as calm as ever. "There's nothing for me to be scared of. None of them can touch me. Not Fend's police, or its CIM, or its government. I can hide my followers all across the city and command them freely with just a twitch of my finger." She let out a sadistic laugh. "I can do *anything*—and there isn't a person out there who can catch me."

After Green Butterfly left, a torrential rain began falling and made it hard to see. Monika decided to put lookout duty on hold and head back to the base. Lamplight had rented out two units in a Hurough apartment building, and the girls took turns using it as a crash pad.

When Monika returned, she found Erna and Lan there.

"Welcome back," Erna said from the kitchen with a smile. "I was just about to make some food."

Over in the living room, Lan gave her a wave. "Thou didst well to endure in such rain, Dame Monika."

Lan offered her a towel, and Monika dried off her hair and took a seat on the opposite sofa. After she gave her report about what had been going on inside the Belias base, Lan's eyebrows softened in contrition. "I feel as though I should apologize, the way I've been leaving all the work to Lamplight."

"Having you operating out in the open would cause more problems than it's worth."

"True that. I spent today taking a nice long nap." Lan crossed her arms, looking strangely proud of the fact.

Monika couldn't bring herself to snap at her. She looked up at the ceiling and said nothing.

"Hmm? Dame Monika?" Lan tilted her head. "I daresay thou seemest out of sorts. I had expected you to cry *Quit lazing about!* and level a punch at my stomach."

".........."

She must have been very worn down for Lan to see through her that easily. The offer Green Butterfly made was really eating away at her.

Monika buried her face in her hands and spent a few seconds deep in thought. It wasn't like she could just tell them what was going on—not with the bug Green Butterfly had planted on her.

The bug was attached to her collar, and it meant that Green Butterfly could hear everything that was going on. If the feed ever cut out, or if

Monika's voice so much as cracked, Green Butterfly had made it clear that she would immediately give the false intel on Lily to the CIM. She had reservations about communicating with them in writing, too. If Erna or Lan made the slightest misstep, that would be that.

For now, she had no choice but to play it off.

"Just worrying about something unimportant, that's all."

Lan peered over at her in fascination. "Goodness, how unlike you."

"By the way, you ever resent us?" Monika asked.

"Hmm?"

"If Klaus had become Avian's boss, Avian might've survived. You ever think about that?"

"………"

The thought had been on Monika's mind a lot. Avian had once fought with Lamplight in an attempt to install Klaus as their boss, and at the end of their showdown, Avian had emerged victorious. However, they'd recognized Lamplight's talents and relinquished their right to take Klaus from them.

Had that really been the right call?

If Klaus had become Avian's boss, the whole tragedy might have been averted.

Lan had been smiling through the rest of the conversation, but on hearing that, her expression darkened. "Prithee, do not insult me." Her voice brimmed with anger. "When we chose not to take Sir Klaus, 'twas a decision borne of conviction. The call we made was to have Avian and Lamplight protect our nation on two fronts. I bear no regrets."

"…Got it."

"'Tis not a matter of fault or blame. Post-hoc thinking is naught but folly."

Lan waved her hand to say that the conversation was over, then leaned back and placed her weight on the sofa's backrest. There was no bravado or false courage in her expression. She hadn't gotten over losing Avian, not completely, but she'd at least gotten her feelings in order.

There was nothing Monika could say to that.

*…But, Lan, would you be able to stay that unfazed if you knew the truth?*

She hung her head so as to avoid letting Lan see her bite down on her lip.

*Green Butterfly told me. About the* traitor *in Avian's ranks.*

The fact was, Green Butterfly had made contact with Avian, too.

Serpent had carefully observed them and taken full advantage of their weakness.

Moments earlier, when Green Butterfly was proposing that Monika betray her team, she gave her an all-knowing laugh. *"Gee, I wonder if I can guess what you're thinking right now?"* She grinned like she could see right through Monika. *"You're planning on pretending to turn traitor for a bit, then gathering intel on Serpent from within."*

She was right on the money. It was your standard double agent scenario—a tactic so basic that there had been whole lectures on it back at Monika's academy. The idea was that you made it look like you'd switched sides by passing along some unimportant information to curry favor with the other side. When Green Butterfly made her offer to Monika, that was the very first idea that had passed through Monika's head.

*"Ha-ha, you smart spies all think the same way. It's so stupid."* Green Butterfly slumped her shoulders in annoyance. *"There was an idiot like that on Avian, too—'Glide' Qulle."*

Monika gulped when she heard the familiar name. That was Avian's strategist, a girl with glasses and a jade green ponytail.

*"I made her a similar offer, and at first, I got her on board. She had these biiig old tears in her eyes, and her little fists were trembling in frustration when she agreed to betray her country. She was the one who told me your names and what you all looked like."*

Now that was unexpected. Qulle had the pride of an elite spy. She should have dutifully carried out her mission. Monika wouldn't have taken her for a traitor.

She asked Green Butterfly what she'd offered her.

*"I promised to spare all of Avian."* A noble request. *"She was a clever one. She figured out faster than anyone that the Commonwealth was rotten to the core, and she knew that submitting to Serpent was the only way for them to survive. Gee, what a great girl. I was going to use her until she broke in my quest to kill Bonfire."* Green Butterfly let out a melancholy sigh before spitting out her next words. *"But at the eleventh hour, she was stupid enough to turn on us."*

Monika thought back to the photos she'd seen of Avian's corpses. Qulle had died having the back of her neck hacked up by some strange bladed instrument. Rather than getting killed by Belias, she'd had her life personally taken by one of Serpent's members.

Not even one of her generation's most elite members had been able to escape Green Butterfly's trap.

*"She really underestimated me, and Avian got wiped out because of it. She died without achieving a single one of her goals."*

The moral of the story was, going for any sort of half-cocked betrayal was a bad move. Mere moments ago, Green Butterfly had given Monika a glimpse of her power. She had countless resources stationed around Fend, and Monika had no way of knowing where her stooges might be lurking.

*"Don't go disappointing me, now, Monika."*

It was uncanny, being able to feel her options narrow in real time.

As she thought back to her conversation with Green Butterfly, she heard her name. "Big Sis Monika?"

Erna came over to her, still holding a potato, and peered at Monika with worry swimming in her eyes.

"You really don't seem like yourself right now. I think you should get some rest in the other room."

"...Yeah, maybe I'll do that."

"The plan is, Teach is going to be here in about an hour. You can go ahead and sleep until then."

"........."

What Erna told her next sent a wave of alarm through her. Erna had just gotten word via the wireless that it wouldn't be long before Klaus and Sybilla got back from their op with Belias. Once they did, there was going to be a team meeting, and Monika was naturally going to be expected to attend.

*...That's gonna put me face-to-face with Klaus.*

She felt a stifling tightness in her chest. She couldn't even keep Erna and Lan from noticing how shaken up she was.

Lan did a big, delighted stretch. "I see. Then perhaps I'd best bathe while the opportunity yet remains," she declared before heading off to the bathroom.

"Yeah, I'm gonna go get some sleep," Monika said, slowly rising to her feet.

"You know," Erna said kindly, "I was just in the middle of making some soup. Would you like some once it's done?"

Monika's reply was curt. "I'm good."

"You must really be tired. If things are too hard on you, you could always talk to Teach about—"

"Oh, shut up. Get off my back already!"

Before she knew it, she was raising her voice. When she turned around, she saw that Erna's eyes were wide and pained. Erna's breath was caught in her throat, and she was shrinking back as though in terror.

"...Sorry, I'm just exhausted." Monika averted her gaze. "But don't tell Klaus about this. I can still work just fine. I don't want him getting worried over nothing."

"O-okay," Erna replied, then gave her a quick bow and scurried back to the kitchen in fright.

Monika realized how awful what she'd just done was, but she didn't have the capacity to worry about that right now.

The coming meeting with Klaus was going to determine her very destiny.

"*I can't.*"

Monika replied to Green Butterfly's repeated threats with the honest truth.

"*It's not an issue of being willing or unwilling. Me turning traitor literally won't work.*"

"*Gee, why's that?*"

"*Because sooner or later, Lamplight's gonna have a meeting. If I don't show up, it'll look suspicious, and if I do, I'll run into Klaus. As soon as we're in the same room, he'll see that something's up with me.*"

Monika knew all too well how difficult fooling Klaus was, and at the moment, she was pretty darn shaken. There was no way she could possibly get through a twenty-odd-minute meeting without him catching wind of that fact. He was going to sense that something was up, and once he pressed her, she would be forced to tell him everything.

"*Are you really going to force me to decide if I'm going to turn traitor here and now, even in the face of that?*"

"*And if I did, hypothetically, what would you say?*"

"I'd say no, obviously. You've got nothing to back up anything you've told me. Hell, I'm beginning to wonder if Prince Darryn is even really gonna die."

"Oh, what fragile hopes you cling to. Eh, I guess you'll understand soon enough." Green Butterfly gave her a breezy wave, then shook her head in annoyance. "Go ahead and attend that meeting. And once you're there, I guess I'll just need you to bring your A game."

Monika had no idea how to respond to Green Butterfly's flagrant carelessness. It made her want to explain how good Klaus's intuition was, but it wasn't as though she could just go leaking intel to the enemy.

"Make sure you fool him," Green Butterfly said menacingly. "Unless you want 'Flower Garden' Lily to die, that is."

There was a coldness to her voice, and that alone pierced Monika clean through.

After stepping away from Erna and Lan, Monika headed to the vanity and worked on her face.

It took her far longer than ever before to get her expression under control. She worked to loosen up her facial muscles over and over, making sure she looked the same as ever. None of her feigned emotions could appear off.

She hadn't made up her mind about turning traitor yet, but for the moment, she had little choice but to do as Green Butterfly said. She took her emotional turbulence and hid it deep down inside.

A short while later, she heard the telltale sounds of Sybilla getting back. After tightening up her expression one last time, she put some pep in her step and headed back over to the room from earlier. Lan was being obnoxious again, so Monika gave her an ax kick and a cry of "Can it!" to make a show of how chipper she was.

Once she was finished, she got Sybilla to share her latest intel so she could assess the situation. That was how she learned that the CIM was going after Avian as suspects in a failed assassination attempt on Prince Darryn, and how just then, someone had shot the crown prince and taken his life.

She didn't let it show on her face, but a wave of despair crashed over her.

...That settles it, then. Green Butterfly wasn't bluffing.

All of a sudden, the rest of Green Butterfly's threats seemed dramatically more credible.

"By the way, where's Lily?" she asked, making sure to keep her tone 100 percent business.

"Huh? She's keepin' hidden in Heron Manor. Why?" Sybilla replied like it was no big deal.

Sure enough, Lily was staying out of sight at the dance hall, just the way they'd drawn it up. The plan had been to have her poison one of the Belias aides from under a table so that Grete could swap places with them. That part had already gone off without a hitch, but apparently, she was still down there.

"And she was under the table when Prince Darryn got killed, too?"

"Well yeah, duh."

"Makes sense," Monika replied cheerfully. She had to suppress the urge to curse under her breath.

Lily had no alibi. Her whole job had been to make sure nobody from Belias knew she was there, and that meant she had no one but her Lamplight teammates to vouch for her whereabouts. Monika felt a pang of regret. When Green Butterfly had told her to turn traitor, one of the first things she'd considered was rushing straight over to rescue Lily. However, there hadn't been enough time.

Then there was a knock on the door, and in came Klaus. "I'm back," he said succinctly as he came in alongside Thea.

It was time for Monika to renew her resolve. She couldn't let him catch on to her, no matter what. If Klaus found out about the bug hidden in her collar, Green Butterfly would discard her without a second's thought, and Lily's life would be in grave danger.

She needed to devote her full efforts into fooling Klaus. She had no other options, and she put everything she had, all her talent as a spy, into making sure her agitation didn't show. She couldn't let the mask slip, not even for a moment.

Before too long, the meeting got started. There were six of them: Klaus, Monika, Thea, Erna, Sybilla, and Lan. Klaus began by laying out what he'd gathered by working alongside Belias as well as the intel Thea had managed to extract while in captivity. All the while, Monika remained composed. Luckily for her, Klaus showed no signs of noticing that anything was wrong with her.

*But like...*

An emotion stirred from deep, deep inside her heart, crying out in a voice too quiet to manifest in her actions.

She turned her gaze over to Klaus. He wore a stern expression as he described how they were going to approach Belias going forward.

*...I want* him *to notice.*

It was a contradictory wish, but as soon as she became aware of it, it began surging within her. She continued putting her all into her performance, but she couldn't make those pathetic feelings go away.

*What the hell. Klaus is supposed to be able to see everything; that's his whole deal!*

She wanted him to see her. She wanted him to rescue her. She was being swallowed up by something vast and unfathomable, and she wanted him to free her.

It was the impossibly optimistic wish of a coddled little girl, yet it refused to go away. Even as she devoted all her attention to keeping up her deceptive act, there was still a part of her that was praying for Klaus to see right through her and save her from Green Butterfly. There was no one else for her to rely on.

Every second Klaus spent talking about the plan, she wanted to shout at him that it wasn't what mattered right now.

*Why don't you notice? Why can't you hear me?!*

The feeling echoed, loud and intense.

*Why?! All this time, you've been able to see through every lie I told you, no matter how much I put into selling it!*

The meeting came and went, and she spent its whole duration having to fight back the violent screams raging in her heart. In the end, Klaus never sensed her anguish. All he did was comfort her teammates and spur them on with promises of revenge. Not once did he cast any special looks her way.

As soon as the meeting ended, Monika immediately left.

Not even the mighty Klaus could see everything. It was obvious, in retrospect, and it was hardly his fault. If anything, it had been asking too much for him to keep tabs on each and every one of his agents' mental states in a mission as messy and protracted as theirs. At the end of the day, Klaus was no god.

Throughout the whole meeting, he'd intimated how important it was for them to avoid an all-out conflict against the CIM. Sure enough, not even he wanted to go to war with them.

Klaus was just a man, and realizing that broke something precious in Monika.

◇◇◇

From atop the roof, Monika quietly looked down at the sleeping city.

The battle against Belias had ended without fuss or fanfare. Belias had fallen for Grete's scheme hook, line, and sinker, and all the traps Lamplight had set around Sybilla had worked like a charm. They'd successfully captured all the Belias members up at the construction site in the mountains.

The time limit Green Butterfly had given her was up.

Klaus was about to get the truth out of Belias and make his next move, and Green Butterfly needed to throw the situation into chaos before that happened. Her goal was to prevent Klaus from ever getting his feet under him.

Monika waited atop the building next to the Kashard Doll Workshop, and before she knew it, Green Butterfly was standing behind her.

"You want to know why I wanted you as my partner?" Her voice came out of nowhere. "It's 'cause we have so much in common."

Monika offered her no reply, and Green Butterfly went on.

"I've seen firsthand just how *heartless* this world can be, and it made me realize that, gee, I need to make a statement. **I need to show those ignorant masses a nightmare they won't soon forget.** That was when I first started going by Green Butterfly. And when I spotted you, I could feel it. You're just like me. You want to take your feelings and scream them at the top of your lungs."

There was a strange kindness to her voice. It usually sounded so mocking, but there was none of that now. Instead, it was warm, like she was talking to a friend.

"Y'know, even if you don't betray Lamplight, 'Flower Garden' Lily will probably be fine. This is Bonfire we're talking about, after all."

"True."

"I'd say there's a fifty or sixty percent chance she makes it."

Those numbers sounded about right. Knowing Klaus, there was a probability he could actually emerge victorious from a head-on fight with the CIM. The odds weren't even that bad.

"But that means," Monika said, "there's a forty or fifty percent chance she dies."

She'd played it out in her head more times than she could count—her, going to Klaus and begging him for help. Him, bringing his full talents to bear and saving them like he had so many times before. Him, overcoming any and all obstacles in their path.

However, she had no proof that things would play out that way.

If Monika defied Serpent, there was a fifty-fifty chance Lily would die.

If Monika betrayed Lamplight, Lily would definitely live.

As soon as she laid out the two options, she already had her answer.

"I've got three questions," Monika said.

"Go for it."

"First, why wasn't Klaus able to see through my acting?"

Green Butterfly grinned in delight. "Hmm? Gee, maybe it was 'cause you're just *such* a good actor."

"That wouldn't be enough to fool someone like him. What did you do?"

There were still a lot of mysteries surrounding Serpent, but the one thing she knew for sure was that its members had unimaginably powerful talents. The way Purple Ant had been able to psychologically dominate hundreds of people was evidence of that, as was the mystery individual who'd been able to sniff out Monika's love. It was safe to assume that Green Butterfly had some sort of special skill, too.

Green Butterfly offered her a shrug and a smirk. "Oh, gee, I don't think we're at the point where I can start giving away my personal details just yet."

"Fair enough. That rules out question two, then."

She wanted to know what Serpent was trying to accomplish. What could be worth assassinating Prince Darryn and sowing the seeds of war? However, there was no way Green Butterfly was going to tell her that. She needed Monika to demonstrate her conviction first, it seemed.

"Third, what would you have me do?"

"C'mon, I think you've figured that out already."

Monika sucked in a small breath at Green Butterfly's provocative tone. She knew full well what Green Butterfly wanted from her. There was only one task she could imagine Serpent coming after her for.

Question: How do you kill an invincible spy who's defeated any enemy he's come across?

Answer: It's obvious. *You attack him with someone who isn't his enemy.*

Green Butterfly twirled her hair around her fingers, strode over to

Monika, and coiled that hair around Monika's neck as innocently as a little girl playing house. "For starters, though, could you go attack your team for me? I want to see your resolve." She stepped away, and the hair unwound itself. "Destroy it all—and if, in the end, you get *the big one*, then 'Flower Garden' Lily gets to live."

Before Monika gave her answer, she closed her eyes.

Memories of her time in Heat Haze Palace floated up in the darkness.

There was her first time meeting Klaus, who marched to the beat of his own drum so adamantly it had filled her with exasperation. There was how surprised she'd been when Erna had been late to their very first meeting. There were the times she'd been jealous of Grete's romantic earnestness, the times she'd competed with the physically gifted Sybilla, and the times Annette's eccentricity had left her at a total loss. There were the times she'd tutored Sara, who started out cowardly but gradually grew more ambitious, and there were the times she found herself in contention with Thea over their differing views on espionage.

And then there was Lily, always doing her best to encourage the others no matter how tough things got.

What was she going to choose, and what was she going to cast away? The world wasn't so kind a place as to let her have everything she wanted.

"Fine."

She needed to say it, loud and clear.

The path ahead of her was a thorny one, but walking it was the only way to stay true to her ideals.

"I'll kill 'Bonfire' Klaus."

With that, the tragedy commenced.

# Chapter 7

# Scarlet Leviathan ④

Monika stood atop the opposite building and looked at them coldly for a while, but eventually, she turned and left. Her reason for being there was gone.

"Monika...," Klaus murmured.

Panicked voices were rising up from outside on account of the explosion. There had been a lot of similar blasts and gunshots in Hurough over the last few days. Scared cries echoed up from the street wondering if there had been yet another murder.

Given the situation, they didn't have the luxury of carefully thinking things over.

"Erna, get all the intel you can out of him. I'm going after Monika."

Klaus cast a brief glance at Erna, who gave him a dependable nod, and Raymond, who was cowering against the wall, before leaping through the blown-out window. Behind him, he heard a pair of disoriented voices say "I— I'm no good with strangers, but I guess I'll just have to do my best" and "Wait, you're going to leave me with this little girl...?" but he had no time to deal with them. Monika couldn't have gotten far yet.

Klaus assumed she was traveling via the rooftops. She was on a de facto wanted list if not a literal one, so she couldn't exactly afford to be seen on public streets. As such, he took to the rooftops as well, bounding from one building to the next.

It didn't take him long to spot Monika. She was a few hundred feet away from him, but that was still close enough for him to tail her. Her destination was away from the heart of the city, over in an area with fewer buildings and people.

She made no efforts to shake him.

*She's luring me after her. That much is obvious.*

That was the only reason she would have showed herself so blatantly. In all likelihood, she was leading him into a trap.

*That said, falling back isn't an option... She probably factored that into her calculations.*

The two of them had completed countless missions together. She knew his personality like the back of her hand.

Eventually, Monika picked a building and headed inside it.

The building in question was a large church with a pair of steeples and a gleaming gold cross at each end. There must not have been anyone maintaining it anymore, as its walls and roof were noticeably dirty and stained. Klaus followed after Monika and headed right in the front door.

Inside, the building was an impressive piece of architecture. The nave running right through its center was flanked on each side by a long aisle, and the transept running through the middle cut the church into the shape of a cross. Its ceiling was high, held up by decorated arches, and there were six oratories lined up alongside the wall.

However, the church was no longer in active use, and it had fallen into disrepair. The sanctuary was notably home not just to pews, but to desks, as well. Also notable was the out-of-place aroma—the smell of gunpowder. Someone had brought some serious weaponry in there.

Klaus marched straight down the nave. "What's the deal with the church?"

"It used to be a school."

Monika smiled proudly as she gave her reply from beneath a glittering piece of stained glass. She'd made the arrogant choice to stand atop the dais.

"Hurough's one of the most overcrowded places in the world," she explained without hesitation from atop the cracked wooden dais. "Agricultural tech got a big jump start about a century back, and it put a bunch of farmers out of work. All those people who lost their jobs ended up moving to the city and toiling away in factories. And kids were no exception. Up until they passed the Factory Act and banned child labor, peasant kids didn't have time to do any book learning," she said quietly. "The priest started a school right here in the church for 'em. Kids from the underclass used to come here to learn how to read and write."

So a Sunday school. Now that Klaus looked, he could see traces from pen marks on the long desks in the sanctuary. That said, the building was no more a functioning school than it was a functioning church anymore.

Monika flung a taunt his way. "Come on and school me, Klaus."

Klaus continued advancing until, eventually, he was directly in front of the podium. There was less than thirty feet between them. Klaus could close that in an instant. Just this once, though, the distance felt impossibly far.

"Let me ask you this straight," he said. "Why did you betray Lamplight? I assume you didn't have a choice."

His voice carried well through the church. There was even a faint echo.

Monika squinted at him. "Well, if I had to describe it…" Her lips curled into a self-mocking grin.

"…then I guess it's 'cause you didn't really see me."

It sounded like there was a faint sadness in her voice, but perhaps he was just hearing what he wanted to. He had hoped for more of an explanation, but Monika didn't seem keen on giving one. The hostility she was emanating swelled. It felt as though the room was slowly being drained of air.

Monika drew the pistol from the holster hidden on her hip. "That's all I can say. But hey, you're a spy, aren't you?"

"True enough." Klaus drew his knife. "Information exists to be taken, not given."

Klaus knew that they were past the point of peacefully talking things out. Hoping for that would have been a waste of time. Monika had clearly steeled her resolve before waiting for him there, and all he could do now was answer her with all the power he had at his disposal and crush her.

He sucked in a small breath. "Monika, if you're going to surrender, do it fast. It pains me to have to attack my own student."

"Someone sure took his condescending pills today. You really don't think there's any chance you'll lose, do you?"

"Not in a million years."

"Arrogant much? I gotta say, Klaus, you get a lot meaner when you're staring down an opponent."

"If anything, this is more who I really am."

"Damn, and you're normally such a softy."

"When I'm dealing with my students, sure."

"Oh yeah? Y'know, Klaus, this could be the chance we've been waiting for. How about we share how we *really* feel about each other, all that stuff we've never been able to say? That way, we'll be able to go into this with our heads clear."

"That's not a bad idea. Thinking back, you and I haven't spent much time being frank with each other."

It was a very Monika thing to suggest.

The two of them spoke in unison.

"Hey there, you dog shit excuse for a teacher, where does Inferno's errand boy get off calling himself the World's Strongest? Avian's instructions were two thousand times easier to follow than yours, you know. Have you ever considered that maybe you're just incompetent?"

"All that venom, and for what? You can play cocky and arrogant all you want, but it'll never cover up just how lonely you are. You're an immature little contrarian, and I'm going to come beat that personality of yours into shape."

With that, the fight kicked off.

Monika fired a shot at Klaus and leaped backward at practically the same time. There were wires hung from the arch above the sanctuary, allowing her to put quite a bit of distance between herself and Klaus.

Klaus dodged the bullet and clutched his knife as he waited for Monika to make her next move.

*Looks like she's not planning on coming at me head-on.*

Klaus's close-quarters capabilities were unparalleled. Monika knew that, so it made perfect sense that she would want to fight from afar. If Klaus wanted to close the gap, he doubted she would make it easy for him. This was going to devolve into a firefight.

However, that posed a major issue.

For Klaus, using his gun wasn't an option.

It was the same reason he never used his gun in their training exercises, either. Unlike knives, guns didn't allow their wielder to hold back. Try as you might to indirectly attack someone by shooting the objects around them, there was always the risk of the bullets striking them instead, and Klaus was unwilling to use any method that put Monika's life in danger.

Naturally, that was going to make things a whole lot harder for him. He had no way to attack from range, leaving his opponent free to fire at him unopposed. Against someone as overwhelmingly talented as Monika, that handicap was downright debilitating.

However, Klaus couldn't use his gun—not if he wanted to reclaim his pride as her teacher!

There wasn't a teacher alive who pointed guns at their students. That wasn't something Klaus needed to be taught. For him, it was simply common sense.

*The problem is, Monika won't hesitate to take full advantage of my mercy.*

He didn't think it was underhanded of her. Klaus himself was the one who'd taught her how to exploit a target's kindness, and he would've been disappointed if she didn't heed his lessons. Chivalry and sportsmanship were of no use to spies.

After ascending too high for Klaus to reach her, she stepped over onto one of the sanctuary's pillars. By standing with her foot perched on its sculpted protrusion, she was free to point both her hands at Klaus. She made right angles with her thumbs and index fingers, then put them together to form a quadrilateral like a child pretending to play with a camera.

"Angle... Distance... Focal point... Rebounds... Speed... Timing..."

After muttering to herself, she spoke softly.

"I'm code name Scarlet Leviathan—now, let's harbor love for as long as we can."

Klaus heard a *click* from above him to the right.

He ducked, largely on reflex, and a moment later, a gunshot roared out as a bullet flew over his head and shattered the desktop beside him into pieces.

The bullet hadn't come from Monika.

Klaus looked over and spotted something fastened to the top of one of the church's thick pillars.

*Is that what I think it is?*

Sure enough, there was a gun there with a metal fixing keeping it bound to the pillar.

*Ah. So she did set up some guns.*

To Klaus, the revelation didn't come as much of a surprise. He'd been expecting firearms to come into play since the moment he walked into the church and smelled gunpowder.

He looked closer at the rifle and spotted a little cogwheel built into it. That was the component that had made the clicking sound.

*It's on a time delay. Looks like it's set to fire once every few minutes.*

Once he finished his analysis, he turned his gaze back over to Monika. "So that's your plan. I have to say: I'm surprised. You really think that's going to be enough to beat me?"

"Yeah, I do."

As Monika calmly gave her reply, another nasty *click* rang out. This time, it was from the dais straight ahead. Klaus could see a gun barrel wedged between its cracked boards.

"_____!"

He parried the bullet and sent it flying behind him with his knife.

"Nice catch." Monika grinned. "But there's more where that came from."

There were a pair of *clicks* one after another, each from a different direction.

Klaus gave up on tracking the bullets with his eyes. He leaped to the right on instinct alone, and a bullet practically grazed his shoulder before slamming into one of the sanctuary's pillars.

"…Again?"

Based on where the bullet hole was in the pillar, Klaus could deduce where the gun was. It was hard to see, but he could just barely make it out stuck to the sanctuary wall. Its barrel was pointed directly at the spot Klaus had just been standing in.

*That's odd. Monika never had a chance to move it.*

After all, she hadn't moved from her spot on the pillar.

*How could a gun she set up in advance have shot at me so accurately?*

Upon carefully surveying the church, Klaus discovered the answer to his own question. He hadn't noticed back when he first entered the building. Monika must have cleverly calculated it so they would be out of his line of sight, masking them in shadow by adjusting the building's lighting. Now that his perspective had shifted over, though, they were plain to see.

There were more than just three or four guns stationed around the sanctuary.

"Angle... Distance... Focal point... Rebounds... Speed... Timing..."

Klaus looked at Monika as she continued muttering her incantation. "Don't tell me you did what I think you did."

Monika gave him a quiet nod.

"I've got two hundred and eighty-four guns all set up on timers in here."

The gun hadn't been aimed at Klaus at all. It was just happenstance. Each of the 284 guns was aimed in a random direction, and Klaus had simply wandered into one or two of their lines of fire. And if Monika was telling the truth, then those 284 guns were all—

"There isn't a spot in the sanctuary where human life is safe."

As Monika made her declaration, the leaden storm began.

*Click, click, click,* they went, too many clicks to possibly keep track of, and the bullets started flying. The church's desks and chairs exploded into splinters one after another, stripping the sanctuary of places to take cover. The destruction was downright tempestuous. Bullets went soaring in every direction conceivable, transforming the space into a killing field and filling the church with the incessant echoes of gunshots.

Klaus immediately devoted every ounce of his attention toward staying alive.

The vast majority of the bullets flew off in completely the wrong direction, but every few seconds, one or two shots would invariably come soaring straight toward him. The only recourse available to him was to detect them all so he could avoid them by the skin of his teeth. He twisted his body to allow a bullet to fly right past the tip of his nose. A moment later, he twisted his hips to dodge a shot that would have sunk right into his foot.

Sometimes, he had no choice but to deflect the bullets with his knife. One shot nearly slammed directly into his left shoulder, and he swatted it with his knife to change its trajectory. Parrying bullets was a talent exclusive to first-rate spies, but the fact of the matter was that it was a defensive skill of last resort. Klaus tried to avoid using it whenever he could, as each bullet he blocked caused more and more damage to his wrists, and the most he could do in rapid succession was four times per hand. Eight total parries was his hard limit.

The tempest of shots continued for some time, and the bullets kept on flying. Monika hadn't been kidding—there wasn't a single safe spot anywhere in the sanctuary.

"Are you trying to get yourself killed?" Klaus asked during a brief lull in the gunfire, to which Monika replied, "'Course not."

"Don't you worry about me," she said. *"I can see every single bullet."*

What Klaus witnessed next made him doubt his very eyes.

Without warning, Monika hopped off the pillar and landed down on the ground. Klaus had assumed that the pillar's peak she was perched on was the one spot in the room the guns weren't aimed at, but a bullet went flying straight at it and obliterated the pillar's decoration.

Below, in the gunshot-riddled hellscape that was the sanctuary, Monika began walking with an air of complete nonchalance, and not so much as a single bullet went flying her way.

She really could see them all. She knew the guns' positions, their angles, their shot cadences—everything.

*I did know about her special "creepshot" talent, but this...*

Back when he first scouted her, her academy instructor had told him how Monika could use reflective surfaces like mirrors to steal glances at anything within a given space. However, that was just one technique in her arsenal, not the full scope of her talents. This was her true power—*the raw calculation ability to be able to anticipate everything that would happen within that same space.*

"You gonna come at me, Klaus?"

Despite her taunting smirk, Klaus was hardly in any position to charge her. A bullet flew at him from his blind spot, and he reacted to it on pure intuition, swatting it away with his knife just before it hit him.

That marked his fourth right-handed parry, and he felt the numbness in his wrist. He wouldn't be able to use it for the time being. He swapped his knife over to his left hand.

Klaus began getting ever so slightly concerned.

*It's a pain, not being able to sense her hostility.*

If there had been humans firing those bullets, this whole thing would have been miles easier. Then he could have used the gunners' tics to predict the trajectories and timings of their shots. With skills like Klaus's, it would have been child's play to casually lead their aim astray while closing the gap so he could trounce them. Against mechanical foes, though, all of his vast experience was for naught.

It was a method designed specifically to combat him.

Now, given enough time, he could simply memorize the position of every last gun in the sanctuary. However...

*...Monika can move around freely, and that means she can shift their angles.*

Monika was still a good distance from Klaus, and one after another, she went over to the guns and used a tool to adjust their metal fittings and alter their trajectories. She only moved each barrel a fraction of an inch, but that was enough to make a big difference in where their bullets flew.

There were 284 guns, each with a constantly shifting aim and firing cadence. Getting a bead on every last one of them while surviving the storm of bullets was a feat that was beyond even Klaus.

On the fifteenth time he tried to close in on Monika only to have a bullet fly in and cut him off, he found himself forced to use the knife in his left hand to parry an eighth shot. He swapped the knife back to his right. He had no idea how much longer his wrists were going to hold up.

Monika ran across the sanctuary, grabbed hold of the wires attached to the frontal arch, and used them to hoist herself into the air.

"All right, time out."

Suddenly, the bullets stopped. The silence in the church was deafening.

Klaus wondered what she needed the time for, but when he looked up and saw her by the ceiling, it all made sense. Up on the arch, she was panting with oceans of sweat pouring down her forehead. After catching her breath, she gave him a self-deprecating grin.

Monika was exhausted, and for good reason. Even knowing where all the bullets were going, running through them must have been unimaginably stressful.

That said, Klaus was in no hurry to take advantage of the opening she'd presented. He, too, had lost a great deal of energy and stamina, not to mention the fact that he had no idea when the bullet storm would start up again.

"Classic Monika," he said. "I'm impressed you were able to gather so many guns so quickly. I take it you had help from the Fires of War?"

"Oh wow, you've already dug that far?"

"You're really giving me a run for my money here. Of all the people I've fought lately, you're giving me the hardest time of them all."

Klaus meant every word of it. Corpse, Purple Ant, and Belias didn't hold a candle to her. Anyone who tried coming at him with raw force didn't even qualify as a threat, but Monika had hit him with one devastatingly effective ploy after another. It had been a long time since he'd met an opponent who'd pushed him so far.

"You've got it backward," Monika said with an exasperated laugh. "You're just making things harder for yourself all on your own. Why not just run?"

"Oh, and you'd just let me go?"

"Not a chance. But if you really put your mind to it, I'm sure you could come up with a way to escape the church."

"...Probably, yes."

Monika's Bullet Zone technique had a number of flaws, one of which was that as soon as you left the area the guns were set up in, the technique was neutralized. Here, Klaus could simply have left the church. Doing so would have been far easier than continuing to fight amid the leaden storm.

"And I bet you've already figured out how to beat me," Monika went on. "You can just change the angles of the guns yourself. Sooner or later, one of those bullets I didn't account for will hit me."

That there was another flaw. If Monika could redirect the guns' aim, then surely Klaus could do the exact same thing.

"Why aren't you?" she asked.

"I don't feel like it."

"...How very like you."

"That's the way I feel, so that's the way it is. I don't want to run away from you, not now. And doing something as dangerous as messing with the guns is out of the question." If he was up against a Galgad spy, he would have taken either option without hesitation. Here, though, his value system refused to give him the green light. "Gun to my head, I guess it's because I'm your teacher."

Over the course of Klaus's life, he'd had six people he would describe as teachers. There was his very first mentor who taught him how to fight, "Torchlight" Guido, as well as "Hearth" Veronika, who taught him the proper mindset for a spy to have. Then there was "Firewalker" Gerde, who taught him how to snipe; "Soot" Lukas, who taught him how to work with his hands, "Scapulimancer" Wille, who taught him how to negotiate; and

"Flamefanner" Heide, who taught him technical skills like art and cooking.

Klaus was sure that any of them would have made the same choice.

"I'll admit that I'm not the best teacher ever. I would be lying if I said I always kept a proper eye on you, and my lessons never went quite the way I wanted them to. But as your instructor, I still have my pride." He set his gaze straight on her. "Not once have I ever fled from you girls. I've always come and faced you head-on."

"Yeah. Yeah, you have," Monika murmured, then leaped backward as though fleeing from Klaus's gaze. "Are you gonna die for me, then?"

The storm of bullets resumed.

The array of guns planted in the church all began firing again in unison. There were countless bullets flying in every direction, and dodging them all in such close quarters would have been a nigh-on Herculean feat.

Klaus stretched his nerves as tight as they would go and wrenched his body right before the shots landed. It felt like there were far more bullets in the air than there had been earlier. Monika must have set them up that way. By the time the guns ran out of ammo, one of their bodies would be lying on the floor.

Monika had put everything she had into her scheme—into her timed bullet zone. If Klaus wanted to break through it, he was going to need an equal level of resolve.

"Sorry, Monika. I can't afford to die here."

He locked his gaze on her and spoke loud and true.

"And by the way—how much longer should I keep playing along with this game?"

As Monika moved through the air on her wires, she gasped.

The option Klaus had taken was the simplest one imaginable—a direct, full-speed charge. There had been seventy feet between them, and Klaus dashed straight at her without giving her a chance to respond.

Monika had been completely blindsided. Her reaction was delayed.

*This isn't the kind of thing you could see coming.*

He could tell what she was thinking.

*You know where all the bullets are, and because of that, you never anticipated someone being stupid enough* to plunge straight into their path.

Monika tried to reverse course in midair, but she was too slow. Klaus grabbed her by the throat and, still running at full speed, smashed her back into the sanctuary's stained-glass window and sent the both of them soaring out of the church.

He'd successfully escaped the guns' range.

The stained glass lay in four colors: red, blue, yellow, and green, all gleaming in the sun's light.

"How...?" Monika groaned in disbelief as shards toppled down around her like raindrops.

Once Klaus landed on the ground, he let go of Monika's neck. She crumpled to the ground and let out an agonized cough. Klaus had put some serious pressure on her throat.

She shot him a harsh glare. "How'd you come straight at me without getting hit?"

"What do you mean?" Klaus patted his left thigh. "I got hit just fine."

"What?"

Monika stared at him in shock. Fresh blood was gushing from Klaus's left leg. A silver bullet had struck him in the femur. It hadn't passed through, either. It was still lodged there in his flesh.

"I figured I would take a few shots. I made sure to protect my vitals, but still."

"_____!!"

Klaus had determined that as long as he kept his head and important organs safe, he was at no risk of suffering a fatal wound. In the end, he'd gotten hit three times—grazed on the right shoulder and right hand, and a direct hit to the left thigh.

He fished the bullet out of his leg with his fingernails, then used his knife to cut a strip off his shirt to bandage the wound with. Luckily, there was nothing wrong with his bone—Guido's technique for catching bullets in one's muscles had paid off. That said, he still wouldn't be running any marathons anytime soon.

It had been a good long while since he'd suffered an injury that meaningful.

"Are you outta your mind?" Monika's lips quivered as she lay there on the ground. "You could've just ran. Either that, or if you'd been ready to kill me, you could've—"

"I believe I've already addressed those points."

".........."

Monika's eyes went wide.

There was a storehouse out behind the church, a brick structure where they kept the tools they used for special events. Klaus and Monika were in the clearing between the storehouse and the church proper. There was nobody else around.

At long last, they were finally in a spot to have a real conversation.

Klaus knelt before Monika as she crouched on the ground in pain. "I've more or less figured out why you betrayed us, you know."

Monika bit her lip and looked up at him. "Go ahead, then. Guess."

"It was for Lily, right? Someone on Serpent came to you and threatened to pin the blame for Prince Darryn's assassination on her. Go on, tell me I'm wrong."

It would take more than your average motive to get Monika to turn traitor, and if it was simply Lily's life that was in danger, then Monika would have gone and consulted him on the spot. It had to be a problem that demanded delicate political decision-making. As soon as Klaus considered what had happened to Avian, it hadn't been hard to come up with a theory.

Monika let out a long breath, confirming his suspicions. "And if they did, what would you do?"

"Crush the CIM," Klaus replied instantly. "It wouldn't matter if they were manipulated by Serpent or not. Anyone who comes after my people gets put down."

Klaus was no fool, and he knew full well the consequences of making that choice. There was a real danger that doing so would put his homeland in danger. That said, there were plenty of ways to skin a cat. Klaus had no intention of avoiding a fight if the price of doing so was having to hand over Lily. Furthermore, he was confident that the rest of Lamplight would stand by that decision.

"........"

Monika hung her head and went silent.

Klaus softly laid his hand atop her head. "Come on home, Monika. Come back to Lamplight."

They could work out the details later. First things first, he needed to bring her back. If things kept on the way they were going, Serpent was going to swallow her whole.

"Sorry, Klaus." Monika lifted her head and gently brushed away his hand. "That's not happening."

* * *

It was such a rare sight that Klaus's thoughts ground to a halt.

There was a calm smile on Monika's face. She looked happy, yet at the same time, like she was on the verge of tears. The stained-glass shards lit up her face with their warped reflections.

Klaus knew that smile. It was the smile of someone who'd given up.

Unsettling thoughts began rising to the forefront of his mind. Thoughts of an extreme plan that only she was capable of pulling off, a plan she seemed all too liable to put into motion.

"Please tell me you aren't—"

"Would you look at that. Our eyes finally met. Problem is, it's too late now."

He needed to stop. He needed to capture her, even if he had to break both her legs to do it.

However, Monika made her move first.

"You might know how I think, but that there's a two-way street," she said mockingly as she pointed above the church. Up on the roof, there was a person tied to the cross with their eyes blindfolded and a gag shoved in their mouth. Klaus hadn't seen them when he went in. They'd been carefully angled and hidden from view.

There on the cross, *Grete had been crucified.*

What's more, the cross was slowly tilting. Its base was broken, and it was about to send Grete toppling seventy-odd feet to the ground.

"You'd better save her. You saw where I was keeping her, right? She's not in good shape." Monika's voice was ice cold. "She won't survive the fall."

Klaus had no time to muse on the fact that he finally knew what she'd needed the hostage for. He turned his back on Monika and ran as fast as his legs would carry him. There had been a deep truthfulness in Monika's tone. Grete's life was in very real danger.

Monika's sad voice reached him from behind. "Bye, Klaus. I hope you two take care."

Klaus dashed up the church's wall, wincing in pain as his wound deepened, then leaped out into the air and severed the rope tying Grete in place. As he did, he caught her and held her tight.

As soon as they landed, and Klaus removed the gag and blindfold, Grete let out a feeble "Boss...," limply clutched at his arm, and buried her face in his chest.

The good news was that her life wasn't in any imminent danger now. As relief flooded through Klaus at that realization, he turned and looked over his shoulder.

Monika had already disappeared from sight.

Grete had lost a lot of weight, and her body was weakened and limp. Her life had been in constant danger, so she hadn't had a moment of proper rest that whole time. She clung desperately to Klaus's arm, unwilling to let go. It made her seem heartbreakingly childish.

The fact that Monika had been willing to put her through all that showed Klaus just how firm her resolve was. He had no idea what to say.

"Teach!" "Boss!" "Teach."

Eventually, the other girls began pouring into the church. Erna must have gotten in touch with them. She, Lily, and Sybilla rushed in, and after gawking in shock at Klaus's wounds, they spotted Grete and let out big sighs of relief.

"Where's Thea?" Klaus asked.

"She said she was in the middle of an infiltration," Lily answered.

*Yep, sure enough*, he thought. It looked like his deduction was right on the money.

"What happened to Big Sis Monika...?" Erna asked anxiously.

"She got away," Klaus said. The girls' expressions froze, like they couldn't believe their ears. "I'm sorry."

"No, no." Lily waved her hands. "If you couldn't do it, then that's not your fault."

"No, that's not what I'm talking about. I'm ashamed to admit it, but I overlooked it as a possibility." The moment Monika gave him that resigned smile, the full situation had become clear to him. "Perhaps I should be happy she's grown so much. You girls never fail to surprise me."

Lily gave him a quizzical look. "Huh? What is it you figured out, Teach?"

"Monika isn't the only traitor in our ranks."

The girls knew that if they wanted to fool their teacher, the best thing to do was to avoid direct contact with him. They'd told him once that that was their SOP. Knowing that, Klaus should have immediately grown suspicious when one of them started actively trying to avoid him. After all, there was someone who'd done exactly that—someone who'd been working just fine, yet who'd delegated all her reports to Klaus to the others while she continued pulling strings in the city's underworld.

The girls stared at him in disbelief as Klaus dropped the bombshell.

"Thea's betrayed Lamplight as well."

# Chapter 8

# Glint ④

In front of her, she could see the Kashard Doll Workshop.

There were only a handful of people inside—Grete, Erna, Annette, Thea, Amelie, and Lotus Doll. The rest of Belias's members had all been captured, and the Lamplight girls had just started going through Belias's files.

The point had come where Monika needed to attack her own team.

"Gee, Scarlet Leviathan, you mind getting started?" Green Butterfly asked her, her voice eager and delighted. For all the glee in her voice, though, there was an unspoken threat to her demeanor that told Monika she had little choice in the matter. Green Butterfly made sure to put a special emphasis on "Scarlet Leviathan," the new moniker she'd just given her.

Monika exhaled and tightened her grip on her gun.

"Oh, and you don't have to kill anyone," Green Butterfly told her with a little wave. The condition worked out in Monika's favor. She did find it odd, though, and Green gave her a grim smile. "If you killed any of your teammates, Bonfire wouldn't hesitate to return the favor. That wouldn't do anyone any good."

Ah, that made sense. Monika wasn't surprised that Serpent knew so much about Klaus's personality. "You're really preying on his weaknesses for all they're worth, huh?"

"Exactly. We want to send him down the rabbit hole. All the way to rock bottom."

On its own, Monika betraying the team wouldn't be enough for Klaus to be willing to kill her. The man was a softy through and through. The way Monika had heard it, he hadn't even been able to bring himself to kill his own traitorous mentor. If Monika killed one of the other girls, though, Klaus would pass judgment on her without mercy. Serpent's plan was to have her walk that narrow tightrope for as long as she could in order to wear Klaus out and squeeze their odds of winning up by whatever tiny percent they could.

"That said, I still wanna make sure you're in all the way," Green Butterfly said with a cruel smile. She had no intention of letting Monika get away with half-assing her attack. "Could you beat, gee, at least one of 'em half to death for me?"

Monika gave her a wordless nod. She'd already made her peace with that.

"Also, it'd be great if you took someone hostage, too. Make it someone dainty, someone who'll give Bonfire a good scare."

"You really know how to push the man's buttons, don't you?"

"It's one of my absolute favorite things to do," Green Butterfly whispered in her ear. "If you defy us, 'Flower Garden' Lily is a goner. Remember, we've got eyes on her around the clock."

Green Butterfly was going to join Monika on her raid, so she wouldn't be able to pull any cheap tricks. The listening device was still attached to Monika's body, and considering Green Butterfly's doubtlessly keen eyes, fooling her would be nigh impossible.

This was a test.

"Show me you mean it," Green Butterfly said. The point of the attack was to see if Monika was truly willing to betray Lamplight. Monika couldn't afford to make a single misstep, not if she wanted to win Green Butterfly's trust.

It was time for her to pull off the ultimate con.

"Go on, Scarlet Leviathan," Green Butterfly urged her. "Go carve a pitch-black nightmare right into the foolish masses!"

The command was succinct, and Monika leaped off the building's roof. After landing in front of the Kashard Doll Workshop, she charged straight through the entrance. Green Butterfly followed along right behind her.

Monika drew her knife, spun it in her hand, and clutched it tight. Grete was standing in the reception area directly in front of her holding a set of files. She turned around and gave Monika a puzzled look. "Monika...?" she asked. "Where were you? And why are you holding that—?"

Monika didn't give her time to finish her sentence. She bounded forward and smashed her dagger's handle into Grete's chest, hard. As soon as Grete limply keeled forward, Monika took the vial of blood she'd prepared in advance, pressed it against her back, and wedged it into her armpit.

Blood poured from the vial and stuck to the blade of Monika's dagger. *Not you...!*

Monika clicked her tongue to push down the feelings of revulsion rising up within her.

Grete lost consciousness without so much as crying out in confusion. She collapsed on her side with the vial of blood meant for transfusion still tucked in her armpit. Its contents pooled around her, as if her back had been sliced wide open.

Monika's fabrication earned her a disapproving smirk from Green Butterfly. "Gee, that was weak. Still, I guess she would be a pain to kidnap if you roughed her up too bad. Seeing that much blood'll be enough to give Bonfire something to puzzle over, at least." Her voice turned threatening. "But I'm gonna need you to attack the next one for real, 'kay?"

Monika didn't reply. One way or another, her actions would speak for her.

Then she heard the sound of something falling over by the reception area's entrance. It was Erna. She'd just dropped the documents she was holding and was looking back and forth in horror at Grete, who was collapsed in a pool of blood, and Monika, who was standing beside her with a dripping knife.

"Big Sis Monika?"

She looked like she might burst into tears at any moment.

Monika raced forward and closed the distance to her in a flash. Erna drew her gun a beat too late, and Monika smacked it out of her hand with her knife, looming before her now-unarmed opponent. Erna went pale and stared up at her with an expression steeped in despair.

*Not you, either!!*

She kicked Erna's abdomen. Spittle flew from Erna's mouth, splattering across Monika's legs in tepid droplets as the younger girl's body went hurtling backward like a rag doll. However, Erna instinctively jumped back as the hit landed, blunting the blow. She quickly rose to her feet and fled down the hallway. As she did, Monika caught a fleeting glimpse of her expression. It was colored with fear, like she'd just seen a monster she couldn't make heads or tails of.

Monika gripped her blade and gave chase. Her right hand still buzzed slightly with the sensation of hitting Grete, and her left leg with the sensation of kicking Erna. A pounding noise echoed in her head. The sound was like metal crushing metal, and it refused to stop. A wave of nausea rose up from within her, and she wished so badly she could just give in to it.

"Gee, can't let her get away," Green Butterfly said with a look of absolute rapture on her face. "Better hurry up and go after her."

Monika dashed down the hallway.

By betraying her allies—by taking the memories they'd built up together and shattering them with her own two hands—she was destroying herself, nothing less. As she crumbled, there was a horrible ringing in her ears, and the color drained from her vision. However, she'd prepared herself for all that. If she was going to stay true to the conviction she'd decided to uphold, then she had no choice but to walk the path of carnage.

Then a hysterical cry tore through the air.

"MONIKA!!"

Thea was standing in the middle of the first-floor hallway. Her voice was raised, and the rage in her eyes was incandescent.

"What did you do to Erna?! Where is that blood from?!"

Green Butterfly gave Monika a cold "Shut her up."

Before the order even came, Monika was already on the move. She squeezed her knife and leaped.

Thea tried to flee, but she tripped over her own legs. She tumbled ignobly to the ground. Monika planted her foot down hard on Thea's stomach, then moved forward until she was sitting astride her and looked down at the agonized expression on Thea's face. She swung her knife down at her throat.

Right before the knife's tip reached her neck, Thea reached up and grabbed Monika's wrists. "Monika...why...?" she asked through tears.

With Monika trying to bring down the knife and Thea trying to hold her in place, it became a simple contest of strength. That left them at a deadlock, but only for a brief instant. When it came to raw power, Monika had her beat.

Little by little, the blade inched ever closer to Thea's throat.

"Why are you doing this...?"

Thea kept asking questions that Monika had no way of answering. She could feel Green Butterfly's gaze on her back.

Monika couldn't say a word. She couldn't even beg Thea to save her.

She could try using sign language or some sort of code, but if Green Butterfly spotted the slightest hint of the gestures those would require, her trust in Monika would vanish. Then she would give up on the traitor-Monika plan and lie to the CIM in a way that entrapped Lily.

Monika couldn't reveal a single iota of her real intentions. All she could do was what she was ordered to. That was the nightmare Green Butterfly had engineered. That was the scheme she'd trapped the girl called Scarlet Leviathan in.

*And yet*, Monika thought fervently as she put more strength into the knife, *there's one person on Lamplight.*

Ever since she started her raid, she'd been searching for them, and every time she attacked one of her allies, she silently screamed, "Not you."

As Monika loomed over Thea's body, she looked her in the eye.

*One person who can* sense my desires without us needing to exchange a word!!

There was only one way to beat Serpent and their exhaustive intel on the Din Republic's spies. Academy washouts were the one group who never got their unique talents leaked, and gambling on that was the one thread that could lead her out of that nightmare.

If there was one thing the Lamplight girls knew, it was about "Dreamspeaker" Thea's special skill—*her ability to sense people's desires by looking them in the eye!*

Monika could tell that Thea hadn't hesitated to use it. Her eyes were open wide. Considering the position they were in, it was the obvious thing for Thea to do.

Thea's expression softened ever so slightly.

*"Ah, so that's what's going on."*

The words echoed in Monika's head out of nowhere. It was like some sort of auditory hallucination, yet as she looked in Thea's eyes, the voice streamed in all on its own. Perhaps she had Thea's exceptional conversational skills to thank. Either that or maybe it was the fruit of all the time they'd spent training together.

Thea's gaze spoke with eloquence. *"You know, Monika, my power doesn't let me see every last thing in a person's heart. I don't know what it is you're suffering through, not all of it. All I can see is one small part."*

She put more strength into her fingers.

*"The fact that for the sake of your love, you're trying to fight a powerful enemy all on your own."*

It worked. Thea had successfully deciphered Monika's distress.

Nothing changed in their positions, and they both kept jostling for control. There was no reason for Green Butterfly to believe Monika was doing anything to Thea but trying to kill her.

*"You helped me once when I betrayed the team."*

Thea was referring to the incident involving Annette's mother. Thea and Monika had fought and locked eyes then, too. What they were doing now was a re-creation of that.

*"This time, I'll betray Lamplight with you. Being Dreamspeaker means saving everyone, even my enemies."*

It was a ludicrously optimistic way to be, but right now Monika couldn't bring herself to laugh at Thea.

They didn't have much time left. They were sharing information far faster than they would have been able to verbally, but if they spent too much time staring at each other, Green Butterfly was liable to get suspicious.

Sensing Monika's concerns, Thea guided her with her gaze. *"Go ahead and break my arm. You need to sell your story, right?"* There was a joking tone to the way she narrowed her eyes. *"Try not to leave a scar, though."*

Monika drew back a bit, flipped her dagger around, and broke Thea's upper arm through her clothes. Then she sent Thea flying with as hard a kick to the flank as she could muster.

Thea went tumbling across the floor, ultimately clutching her right arm in agony and cowering in the corner.

"Ooh, I love it." There was no change to the pleasure in Green Butterfly's demeanor. She was none the wiser to the wordless chat Monika and Thea had just exchanged. Even so, though, the threats kept coming undeterred. "But gee, it really is high time you beat someone half to death for me."

That was Monika's assignment—to beat at least one person half to death. There was no way Monika was going to be able to con her way out of it.

She'd long since decided who she was going to go after.

*Honestly, this might be a good opportunity. No sense letting it go to waste.*

Monika headed straight down the hallway. Her target was up on the second floor.

*I'm the only one who can do this, and this is the only time for it.*

Over by the staircase leading upstairs, Amelie and Lotus Doll were standing frozen with their eyes wide. "Why are you doing this...?" Amelie stammered.

"You're in my way," Monika growled, then charged at them. The two of them weren't on her prescribed list of targets, but considering that she was going to have to kidnap Grete in a moment, she wanted to drive them out of the building anyhow. She swiftly smashed her daggers' handles into their cheeks before ascending the stairs.

Green Butterfly must not have wanted to run into Amelie, as she took a different staircase up to the second floor. After she and Monika both got there, they headed for the workspace in the back.

Inside the room full of tools and lathes, the girl Monika was looking for was sitting on the table in its center. As Erna trembled behind her back, the girl smiled and dangled her legs off the table. "Yo, Erna told me everything," Annette said with a grin. "Did you hit your head or something, Sis?"

Her smile was as innocent as ever, but there was violence flitting just below its surface. The girl before Monika was barely more than a child, yet there was something terribly evil about her presence.

Monika coldly accepted the realization of who Annette really was.

"I know you know," Monika said.

"Hmm?"

"You assassinated Matilda, didn't you?"

"............"

After the Corpse mission, the girls met a woman who identified herself as Annette's mother—Matilda. Back when they helped Matilda flee the country, there had been something off about Annette's behavior.

Annette's eyes widened a smidge, then she stuck out her tongue a little. "Oh, huh. Tell me, Sis, did I make it seem like that's what I did?"

"I can see who you really are. You secretly leave all the tedious stuff to your teammates, then take the people who annoy you and murder them just 'cause you want to. That's a nice little position you've carved out for yourself."

Unlike the other girls, Monika had uncovered Annette's true nature. She was pure evil—a natural killer. When Klaus put together Lamplight, he'd given them a joker.

As far as Annette went, Monika had one big concern about her. Annette completed her assigned tasks, but her mindset was too reckless and free-spirited. Klaus might be okay with that, but Monika wasn't so sure.

The problem was, *Annette had never truly known failure.* She'd never been humiliated the way Monika had, and because of that, all her potential remained locked away. With talent like Annette's, she could be so much more than she currently was.

Thanks to Monika's current situation, though, she could provide that failure and force Annette to evolve. She could become an obstacle that Annette needed to overcome.

"I'm about to give you some reeducation," she said. "Come at me, you little *runt.*"

The word was the only trigger Annette needed. She moved like a bat out of hell, hopping down from the table and twisting her body. Her skirt twirled up to release a series of unsettling, centipede-looking machines from within it.

"I'm code name Forgetter—and it's time to put it all together, yo!"

"Too slow."

Monika didn't give her a chance to use her contraptions. Annette's specialty was assassinating people from behind a guise of innocence. Hand-to-hand combat, on the other hand, was a shortcoming of hers. There was no way Monika was going to lose to her in a head-on brawl.

She took the hand Annette was using to hold her remote control and struck it with the back of her knife. Then she kicked away the machines swarming at Annette's feet and dashed them against the wall. The centipede robots had been loaded with small bombs, and they exploded on impact, sending fire rushing up the wall. Fragments from the bombs hit Annette and Erna in the head, and the two of them keeled over.

"………"

Annette stared vacantly at Erna, who'd passed out and was lying there motionlessly. Then she wiped off the blood dripping down her own fore-head, rose to her feet, and produced a metal rod from within her skirt. She gave Monika an expressionless glare. Her eyes were like black pits.

Even against Annette's full strength, though, Monika had nothing to fear. She took a look at the flames spreading through the workshop. It was getting to be time to leave. Klaus wasn't there yet, but there was a real danger he would come rushing over, and on top of that, she still needed to collect Grete's unconscious body.

"Do it," Green Butterfly said quietly.

Annette stood motionless as Monika addressed her. "Remember this," Monika said coldly. "Remember this feeling of absolute powerlessness— of being able to do nothing when someone you desperately want to kill is standing right in front of you."

She swung a dagger at Annette's side and shattered her ribs.

The force from the impact sent Annette smashing into the wall. She vomited up blood, then passed out.

*When she wakes up, she'll have friends by her side.*

Monika was confident that they would console her. It would be Annette's first time tasting defeat, and she would have no way of removing the pain from her body, but the others would guide her through it with a gentle hand.

Annette's growth would be a huge boon for Lamplight. All Monika had to do was believe that and keep playing the villain.

The flames began spreading and growing out of control. Green Butterfly cracked a joke. As Monika was ignoring her, she sensed someone behind her.

""_____""

Over at the workspace's entrance, Lily and Sybilla were staring at her in shock. They must have come in right as she was attacking Annette. Unable to look them in the eye, Monika turned to stand beside Green Butterfly and tossed a vial of kerosene on the floor to cut herself off from them with fire.

"—I'm sorry."

As the flames raged, Monika finished her raid, leaving nothing behind but that one quiet whisper.

Green Butterfly gave Monika's attack a grade of "Perfection."

With that, Monika succeeded in winning a bit of her trust. However, that did nothing to change the fact that Lily was being held hostage. That, combined with the fact that Klaus was hunting her in earnest now, was a problem. If Monika got caught, Lily would be in danger.

Monika's plan needed to move to its next phase.

Green Butterfly didn't stay by Monika's side around the clock. At one point, she left to carry out a Serpent op that she wasn't ready to divulge to Monika just yet. Later, Monika would learn that she'd been off killing a woman named Mia Godolphin, but sadly, Monika had too much on her plate already to try stopping her.

Instead of being there in person, Green Butterfly had her surveilled. Wherever Monika went in the city, she could always feel herself being watched. However, the fact that she could sense the lookout's presence so trivially meant that they couldn't have been all that talented.

The evening after her attack, Monika hid her face under a hood and visited a small coffee shop in a Hurough alleyway. She sipped her bitter coffee and waited for her counterpart to show up. The chaos that had engulfed the city in the wake of Prince Darryn's assassination made it nice and easy for Monika to go unseen.

Right as the shop started to get crowded, Thea came in—in disguise—and sat down two seats over from her. The disguise was by no means as elaborate as one of Grete's, the kind that allowed her to completely take another person's place, but with her hair tied back and her makeup on thick, Thea successfully avoided looking like herself.

*"Answer me, Monika."*

They conversed exclusively through the rhythm at which they tapped the counter. That was one of the many communication methods Lamplight had at their disposal, and it was enough to fool a shoddy lookout like the one Monika had.

*"Why did you attack Annette like that? Did you really have to go that far?"*

Despite the method of communication, Thea's words were heavy with emotion. *"She needed direction,"* Monika replied. *"Plus, there was your situation."*

*"What do you mean?"*

*"You needed to be able to volunteer to look for me without Klaus getting*

*suspicious. Because of what I did, you actually meant it when you told him you wanted to track me down."*

Thea grimaced in disapproval.

The issue Monika had been worried about was whether Thea would be able to fool Klaus immediately after the attack. That was why she needed to attack Annette the way she did—so Thea would get angry at her for real without needing to fake it.

Monika could tell that an argument was brewing, so she moved on before it had time to find its footing. *"I left a to-do list for you in the shrubbery at Montegnée Park. Get it done."* Then she called over the proprietor and asked for her check.

Thea frowned. There was still so much she wanted to discuss. *"And I can't let Teach find out?"*

*"Yeah. I've got…a reason why I can't let Klaus know what's going on."*

*"What's that?"*

*"I can't tell you what it is, either."*

The longer the conversation went on, the greater the danger of the lookout catching on to them. Monika ended things with one final message. *"I'm counting on you. You're the only one I can ask for this."*

Without turning to see Thea's expression, she left the coffee shop.

Monika headed back to the hideout Green Butterfly had prepared for her. The hideout was in a building in an alley just one road off Hurough's main street in the heart of the city. The building's first floor was a restaurant, its second floor was a law office, and its fourth floor was a theatrical troupe's training room. The third floor was Monika's. The building's owner was likely a Neo-Imperialist of some sort and was close with Green Butterfly. Green Butterfly didn't tell Monika any specifics, just that she was free to use the floor as she pleased.

The floor had once been a real estate agent's office, but now it was completely empty. There were marks on the wooden floor from where the desks had been. The sound of actors doing vocal exercises was just barely audible from the fourth floor.

All the way in the back of the hideout, there was a girl lying on the floor with both her hands bound. She'd just woken up, and she cast a vacant look Monika's way. "Monika…"

"Sorry, Grete." Monika took the bottle of mineral water she'd bought and held its mouth up to Grete's. "You've probably figured it out by now, but your wounds aren't that bad. That blood on your clothes isn't yours. I had to kidnap you."

The blood stuck to Grete's outfit was smudged on the floor.

Instead of accepting the water, Grete chose to pile Monika with questions. "Why did you attack us?" she asked, calmly and methodically laying her questions out one after another. "Did you betray Lamplight?" However, the vast majority of them were things Monika was unable to answer.

Even so, their exchange allowed Grete to pick up on most of what was going on. "Would you tell me this, at least?" she said. Despite the situation, her voice remained mild the whole way through. "What did you kidnap me for?"

"You're probably gonna have to make some kind of mask. I'll get my orders at some point." Again, Monika didn't give her the real details. She had no way of knowing if Green Butterfly was listening in somehow. She would find an opportunity to fill Grete in. "That said, the biggest reason is as a countermeasure against Klaus." She shrugged and drank the water Grete had turned down. "I'm going to fight him soon, and there's no way I'm going to be able to beat him. I needed a plan that'd let me escape. Sorry, Grete, but I'm gonna have to keep you locked up here until you're nice and weak. That way, when the chips are down, Klaus'll prioritize saving you over capturing me."

Grete gave her a quizzical look. "If all you wanted was to give the boss a scare, I feel as though you could have picked anyone."

"Wait, seriously? You never realized?"

A thin smile stole its way across Monika's face.

"Out of everyone on the team, you're the one Klaus loves the most."

Grete's eyes went wide.

A wave of astonishment rose up within Monika. Based on Grete's reaction, she really hadn't known. "That love of yours might not've been so wasted, after all," she said teasingly.

Klaus took care not to visibly give any of the girls preferential treatment, of course. He probably even tried to interact with them all equally. But even so, Monika knew. There was a slight difference in the way Klaus felt about the rest of the girls and the way he felt about Grete. It wasn't quite romantic love, but there were definite hints of a certain warmth and tenderness there.

Monika averted her gaze. "...I really do envy you."

"Huh?"

"I told you once, remember? I'm the kind of person who can't help but get jealous when I see someone else get all earnest about their love."

Grete always seemed so radiant to her. It would be so much nicer if love could be straightforward for her, too.

"........."

For a moment, it looked like Grete might break into tears. She had always been a clever one, so she might well have intuited Monika's secret. Monika was fine with that. Knowing Grete, she would carry it to the grave.

Grete bit down on her lip and looked Monika straight in the eye. "Monika," she said, her voice burning with conviction. "Could you take off my disguise for me?"

"Your disguise? What do you mean?"

She repeated Grete's own words, but Grete gave her no answer, like there was no explanation she needed to give. As far as Monika could tell, though, Grete wasn't wearing anything of the sort.

A chill ran down Monika's spine.

She reached for Grete's face in disbelief. Merely touching her skin wasn't enough for her to tell, but the moment she dug her nails in, something felt incredibly wrong. Grete was wearing a mask on her face that very moment.

With bated breath, Monika snatched it off. Beneath it, *the left half of her face was completely covered in a hideous birthmark.*

That was Grete's secret—the one she kept even from her allies.

"........."

Looking at it up close like that, Monika couldn't help but let out a gasp. There was no kind way to put it. The birthmark was hideously unflattering. It summoned up instinctive feelings of revulsion.

Seeing Monika's reaction, Grete took a chiding tone. "Would you still say you envy me?"

Monika wouldn't. She couldn't. She saw now how thoughtless she'd been, and that shut her right up.

"You know, the boss saw my real face and accepted me for who I was."

"…Yeah. Makes sense, knowing him."

"It does. And what about your beloved, Monika?" Grete said, her voice firm and unfaltering. "I don't know who exactly it is, but…do you really believe they would be so narrow-minded and repulsed by your feelings? If you decide all on your own that your feelings would never be understood, aren't you just giving up?"

Each and every one of Grete's words pierced Monika right where it hurt. She didn't want to, but she envisioned it all the same—a future where she revealed her feelings to Lily, and Lily accepted them just the way Klaus had accepted Grete's birthmark. She shook her head to drive off the fickle fantasies. "Even if I told her, what good would that do?"

"If nothing else, it might have let us avoid our current situation."

Despite herself, Monika let out a laugh. "Pretty hard to argue with that one."

"Please, Monika, I'm begging you. Don't try to shoulder everything all on your own…"

"That ship's already sailed." Monika gave her a self-deprecating nod. "But thanks, Grete."

Grete gave her another, even more pleading look.

Monika took the mask and delicately tried to replace it, pressing it cleanly into place so the birthmark wouldn't catch anyone else's attention. Once removed, though, the mask refused to go back on right. "I'll get you something else to use later," she said, then gently laid the mask down on the floor.

"It's scary, telling someone how you really feel," Monika murmured as she looked at Grete's birthmark. "But can you blame me? In this world running rampant with fear, love like mine is taboo. It's a crime, a mental illness. All my feelings are gonna do is cause problems for people."

Grete's expression contorted like she wanted to say something, but Monika forged ahead.

"And see, that right there is why I decided to destroy the world."

Monika needed to get started on her next set of preparations.

Soon, she would do as Green Butterfly ordered and fight Klaus. She would lose that fight, no doubt. She knew that going in.

Her *real* fight was going to take place after that.

At that point, nobody else had realized just what a cruel future she was headed toward. Not Green Butterfly, not Thea, not Klaus.

"I really do hope," Monika said as she left, "that you and Klaus find your happily ever after."

# Chapter 9

# Glint and Scarlet Leviathan

The unrest in Hurough continued unabated.

When the CIM team that had barged into the *Conmerid Times* office marched back out the front door, the people swarming by the entrance immediately realized that something was off. Upon hearing the agents shouting angrily into their radios, they discovered that Editor in Chief Raymond had vanished.

Between the strange newspaper company reporting on the assassin and the disappearance of the editor in chief who leveraged his authority to get the article printed, there were mysteries aplenty, and that was before news came in about the bombing a few buildings over. According to eyewitnesses, the person responsible was none other than the cerulean-haired killer depicted in the article.

It was clear to everyone that a storm was coming. However, they had no idea what form it would take, so there was nothing they could do but panic.

For several days running, activists had been making speeches in front of the train station lambasting the CIM for its failures. There were people handing out flyers saying that the whole thing was a conspiracy by the United States, and there were other people accusing the first group of being Galgad spies and beating them up. The city was in complete turmoil.

Over by the large clock tower that held the Houses of Parliament, there was a massive protest. The protestors had decided that all the chaos had been the work of spies, and they were demanding that any foreigners be rounded up. "Lock 'em all up and press 'em till they talk," they shouted as they held portraits of the late Prince Darryn. There were over three thousand of them marching, and the police ultimately had to step in to break up the demonstration.

As unrest overtook the city, one girl watched it all play out with visible glee.

From her hiding spot up in a building just off of Queen Clette Station, the girl chuckled to herself at the chaos spreading below. She was Green Butterfly—the person who'd orchestrated the madness. She was holding a radio, and information poured in through it from the many Worker Ants and other underlings who answered to her. At the moment, she'd just been informed of the result of Monika and Klaus's battle.

"Perfection."

By the time she finished listening to the report, a broad smile had spread across her face.

"Beautifully done. Gee, to think that she didn't just wound Bonfire, she even lived to tell the tale."

The wound she'd dealt to Klaus's left leg was more than Green Butterfly had dared to hope. If she'd cracked a bone, it would take him two or three whole months to be back at peak form. Until that happened, he wouldn't be able to bring the full extent of his strength to bear.

They'd just taken a definite step toward putting the man down for good. And what's more, Green Butterfly still had Monika as a pawn in her arsenal.

*Bonfire will have his hands full with her for the next little while. How much will she be able to wear him down, I wonder?*

Monika had put in more work than Green Butterfly had ever imagined she would. She still didn't fully trust Monika, but for now she was going to continue expecting great things from her.

*Honestly, considering how bad she messed up Bonfire's leg, can I just go ahead and count her as a genuine ally? Or is that just me being a sucker?*

Was it safe to dismiss the possibility of Monika being a double agent? Bonfire was the Din Republic's strongest spy. There was no way it was worth taking out his leg just to win Serpent's trust.

*I guess I shouldn't let my guard down yet, but it's probably safe to assume she has no plans of returning to Lamplight. Gee, depending on how things play out, maybe I could tell her what Serpent's goal is.*

Green Butterfly let out a long exhale and stepped away from the radio. *After all, it's not like anyone could disapprove of Serpent. Not after finding out* why we exist.

That was how it went for Green Butterfly, at least. She'd once been a Fend spy who wished for nothing more than her nation's prosperity. However, the global intelligence community had yet to grasp just how deep the world's despair ran, and when Green Butterfly learned the truth, it felt as though the ground had just crumbled beneath her feet. That was when Serpent recruited her.

She looked at the clock and discovered that it was already evening. She needed to report in as part of her Serpent duties.

They never used radios for sharing critical information. Instead, she learned meeting sites via cryptograms hidden throughout the city. Then she would go to the spot at the designated time and leave a dead drop.

In Green Butterfly's opinion, the whole thing was a pain in the ass.

*"It's 'cause you're still so naive, Green Butterfly. Don't forget that."*

As if she could forget a message delivered so condescendingly.

"Kill me now," she said, clicking her tongue as she reached for her coat.

As she extended her right shoulder to slide it through the sleeve, a sudden jolt of pain ran through it. She clamped her left hand down on it and fought to keep her footing.

"_____"

It had been over ten months, but the wounds still stung. By all rights, they should have healed by now, yet they tormented Green Butterfly on the regular like she'd been cursed.

The wounds in question were scars—two of them, etched down her shoulders like lightning bolts.

Green Butterfly loved to dance, so having scars on her arms like that was a massive burden. Ever since she got them, she'd been forced to wear outfits that covered her shoulders and upper arms every time she set foot in a dance hall.

*Oh, go to hell.*

She clicked her tongue again as the memories resurfaced.

*You wretched hag... You keep finding ways to make me hate you, even from six feet under.*

How many times was it, she wondered, that she'd bit her lip to choke back that same feeling of revulsion?

Ten months ago, Green Butterfly met an Inferno member in their final moments.

That member's name was "Firewalker" Gerde.

The briefing said she was old and decrepit.

That was what "Torchlight"—or rather "Blue Fly" Guido had told her after switching to Serpent's side. A faint glimmer of sadness passed through his eyes, after which he went back to talking and polishing his trusty sword.

"But hey, that's what happens when you're seventy-two. She's a regular old granny now. Her golden days came and went a looong time ago. She's been withering away, especially this past decade."

Upon hearing that, Green Butterfly volunteered to be the one to kill her.

On Guido's recommendation, that was what they were doing—assassinating every last member of Inferno. Just as Purple Ant had beaten Hearth over in the United States of Mouzaia, Green Butterfly had been tasked with killing Firewalker. The Fend Commonwealth was Green Butterfly's home turf, so she was the logical choice.

Thanks to Guido's intel, luring Firewalker to the designated site was a piece of cake. There was a dance hall under Green Butterfly's patronage out in the Hurough suburbs. It was normally a place for high society types to hobnob, but Green Butterfly picked a night when it would be empty to summon her target there.

Right as midnight rolled around, an old woman marched in.

"Hmm? And what's this, then?" The woman took a look at Green Butterfly, who was sitting on a chair in the middle of the hall. "Here I was thinking Guido called me out here, not some young whippersnapper. Did that numbskull leak our code or something?"

Despite being an old woman, Gerde certainly didn't look the part. She was wearing military cargo pants and a tank top that left much of her upper body exposed. Her arms were far more packed with muscle than should have been possible for a woman her age, and they gleamed as they reflected the hall's lights. If she went out in public looking like that, she would draw all sorts of attention.

That was her. The invincible sniper who'd spent over half a century roaming the battlefield. Green Butterfly had heard the legends, and she couldn't help but get nervous. "...Care to negotiate, ma'am?"

"Hmm?"

"Your teammate 'Torchlight' Guido betrayed you and switched sides to the Empire."

Gerde's expression didn't so much as twitch.

Green Butterfly assumed that her composure was feigned. She went on to prove her claim. "He told me about the Heat Haze Palace rules. Rule fourteen is, no forcing the other residents to drink. Rule fifteen is, no using gunpowder in place of an alarm clock. Those two were written for you."

"Yeah, that they were." Gerde's stony expression broke, and she let out a cheerful laugh. "In my defense, the gunpowder thing was to teach Little Klaus some manners. Ah, the boss *really* had my hide for that one."

For some reason, Gerde seemed amused. As Green Butterfly stared at her in confusion, Gerde sauntered over to the chair across from hers and sat down with a little grunt.

"So Guido betrayed us, did he? Well, I can't say I'm surprised," she said nonchalantly. "Ah, so that's why he sent Little Klaus off on his own when he did. Even Guido is scared of the kiddo, huh?"

"You don't seem upset."

"Sorry, missy, but situations like these are old hat." Gerde began bending her fingers down and counting. "At this rate, the boss is a goner. That idiot Lukas is liable to get *himself* killed even if you don't lift a finger, and Wille will probably follow his brother to the grave. As for Heide, dying once might do her some good. And Little Klaus... Well, he should be fine, so long as he handles himself well."

After folding her fingers down one after another, only one remained. "Well, at least there'll be one survivor. That'll do," she said with a satisfied nod.

Green Butterfly couldn't help but notice that Gerde hadn't factored her own survival into her calculations. She leaned forward in her seat a little. "I could kill you whenever I wanted, you know."

".........."

"I'd love some intel, if you don't mind. I mean, gee, you know things, right? About the Nostalgia Project? If you give me the lowdown, I'm prepared to spare your—"

Before she could finish her sentence, her whole world shook.

It took her a moment to realize she'd just been punched in the head. It had happened so suddenly she wasn't able to comprehend it, and she toppled over backward without so much as getting a chance to break her fall.

In Gerde's hand, she was clutching what looked like a black rod. When Green Butterfly fixed her prone gaze on it, she saw that it was the barrel of a rifle. Gerde must have been keeping it hidden beneath her clothes. The old woman quickly took her concealed rifle parts and began reassembling it.

By the time Green Butterfly was able to regain her footing, Gerde had already finished putting the gun together and pulling the trigger.

Two shots roared out, and blood exploded from Green Butterfly's shoulders. The bullets had carved deep into her flesh. The pain was so intense it was maddening, and Green Butterfly could feel her mind going numb.

"You really ought to give me more credit, missy. You think you can force *me* to negotiate?" Gerde had spared her on purpose. If she wanted to, she could have just as easily sunk those bullets into Green Butterfly's skull. "You know, I think my hearing's been going as of late. Would you mind running that by me again? What did you say you could do to me whenever you wanted, again?"

Without a shred of mercy, she stomped down on Green Butterfly's head as the younger spy crawled ignobly on the ground. However, the pain in Green Butterfly's shoulders meant she was in no state to fight back.

*That bearded bastard! You call that "decrepit"?!*

Guido was the one who'd given her that intel, and she cursed him for it.

*Anyone with eyes could tell that the old bag is still one of the strongest spies in the world!!*

Guido hadn't been lying to her, not intentionally. The part about Gerde having withered away had been true. However, the simple truth was that even with her golden days long behind her, Gerde was still monstrously strong. Inferno's standards were just so deranged that her current strength was decrepit by comparison.

Green Butterfly felt a hard sensation of a gun barrel pressing against her head. Above her, she heard Gerde's voice bristling with hostility.

"Best get talking, missy. Where did you hear the term *Nostalgia Project*?"

Green Butterfly realized she'd been squeezing her fists tight without meaning to, and she relaxed her hands and steadied her breathing.

*Ugh! Every time I remember it, it creeps me out all over again!*

For Green Butterfly, her current mission was one of revenge. Gerde had humiliated her, brought her within inches of literally having to beg for her life, and that made the elder spy her mortal enemy. Much as Green Butterfly wanted to kill her, though, the crone was already gone. Instead, Green Butterfly was going to have to settle for going after the man who Firewalker had been so sure would survive—"Bonfire" Klaus—and proving the old woman wrong.

All that time, Green Butterfly had been laying the groundwork.

Klaus had been worn thin in both body and mind, and even now he was still rushing about in pursuit of Monika. Rather than giving his wounded leg time to heal, he was undoubtably still doing intelligence work.

It wasn't Green Butterfly's job to finish him off. She still had plenty of schemes in the tank to push Klaus to his limit with. Then, once he was well and truly exhausted, she was going to meet up with her Serpent teammates who were currently on another op, and they were all going to rush him down at once.

Green Butterfly was just one step away from completing her mission.

*But gee, if there's one thing that gives me a bit of pause...*

She finished putting on her coat as she sorted through her thoughts.

*...it's that* Conmerid Times *article. I can't for the life of me figure out what they're up to.*

The article that morning had come completely out of nowhere.

THE BLUE-HAIRED GIRL WHO KILLED PRINCE DARRYN

Even now she still couldn't make heads or tails of the article. How did that newspaper company get their hands on photos of Monika? Who fed them the article? And to what end?

She tried asking Monika about it, but the only answer she got was "Hey, beats me," and Green Butterfly had no way of verifying whether she was telling the truth. The whole thing seemed fishy, but that alone wasn't reason enough to cut Monika loose. There was a chance it was some scheme of Lamplight's. For the time being, she'd ordered her people to keep digging.

*They should be getting their results in any minute now...*

Right as the thought crossed her mind, she heard footsteps by the entrance. Their owner announced himself with the prearranged code, then came into the room Green Butterfly was in.

"Ma'am..."

It was one of her Worker Ants, a timid-looking CIM agent in his twenties. He'd clearly come in a hurry, as he was out of breath.

Impressed by his excellent timing, Green Butterfly ordered him to give his report.

"Raymond Appleton is still missing, but the CIM was able to track down some information on the man. Apparently, he's spent the last few days staying in close contact with an underworld group called the Fires of War."

"The Fires of War? I've never heard of them."

"They're a newly formed organized crime group. They've grown in influence rapidly, and they claim they're going to save the nation."

"Oh?" Green Butterfly replied. There was no small number of sketchy activist groups operating out of Hurough, and it sounded like the Fires of War was one of them. However, that still didn't explain how they'd gotten those photos of Monika.

At that point, the man frowned in hesitation. "I'm afraid there's more…"

"Out with it," she urged him.

"Twenty minutes ago, a different newspaper put out a special edition. We suspect the Fires of War was involved."

As he spoke, he handed her a copy.

A chill ran down Green Butterfly's spine. She knew this was going to be bad, but she fought the sense of foreboding and read the report. Long story short, it was a follow-up to the *Conmerid Times*' article.

> As warriors fighting to bring salvation to our nation, we bring you information on Prince Darryn's killer.
> - Her code name is Scarlet Leviathan.
> - She's sixteen years old.
> - She's a member of the Galgad spy team Serpent.
> - She has blue hair and is 4'11".
> - She's hiding somewhere near Hurough.
>
> If you've seen her, please contact us.

"What……?" Green Butterfly gasped.

The article had been published alongside a photo of Monika's face, and it listed her both as Prince Darryn's killer and *as an Imperial spy*.

"Noooooooooo, no, no, no, no, no, no, no, no, no, no, no, no, no, no, no, no, no, no, no, no, no, no, no, no, no, no, no, no, no, no, no!"

Unable to hid her panic, Green Butterfly began yelling. She scanned back through the article, hoping in vain that she'd misread it.

"This is deranged!!" she shouted. "How did this ever make it to print?! Have they lost their minds?!"

She couldn't even begin to fathom what their goals or motives were.

The company that put out their special edition was a newspaper with the fifth-largest circulation in the country. It wasn't like they were some fly-by-night hack shop. It was unthinkable for a company their size to be blasting out misinformation on such a large scale. Going ahead and publishing a report on the suspect without waiting for the government to make an official statement was an act of utter lunacy.

"The CIM believes that the people's distrust of the government, especially in the wake of the crown prince's assassination, has given people from the underworld outsize influence."

"Sure, but even so!!"

"It all goes back to the the Fires of War's leader," the man declared. "She was the one who took all the battling organized crime groups and brought them together by brokering negotiations. By stirring up their mistrust of the government, appealing to their senses of chivalry, and giving all those frustrated people structure, she was able to take complete control. We believe that she was the one responsible for winning over the newspaper's decision-makers and getting them to put out that special edition."

Green Butterfly started crushing the newspaper in her hand. Under normal circumstances, there was no way a journalism company would stick their neck out like that.

*I underestimated what an impact losing a member of the royal family would have. We've got chaos begetting chaos out here. At this point, just about anything could happen.*

Serpent had known that shooting Prince Darryn was a risky move to make, of course. They were well aware that doing so could very plausibly end up starting a war. Extenuating circumstances had forced their hand, but at least they'd done so with eyes wide open.

Now no one could predict which way the winds would shift, and amid all that turmoil, someone out there was starting to pick up momentum.

"Just who is this leader? And where did she get her intel on Serpent?"

"We don't have any details. The closer people are to her, the harder it is to get anything out of them," the man said in frustration. "All we've heard is that hero of salvation…is supposedly a beautiful girl."

"A girl?" Green Butterfly asked. Now, that was an unexpected morsel of information.

Right as the words left her mouth, she heard a voice rich in elegance and charm.

"Goodness. You wouldn't happen to be talking about little old me, would you?"

Over by the doorway, there was a dark-haired girl wearing a gentle smile.

Green Butterfly knew that girl. She'd spotted her a handful of times while Lamplight was conducting their mission in Fend. It was "Dreamspeaker" Thea—a spy blessed with an alluringly curvaceous body and a voice that was pleasant to the ear.

The moment Green Butterfly saw her, it all clicked into place. So this was the leader. Green Butterfly had known that Lamplight had a girl who specialized in forging relationships, but the level of talent on display was beyond anything she'd anticipated.

"I take it you're Green Butterfly? It's so nice to meet you." Thea's heels clicked as she sauntered on in.

How did she find this place? Did the Fires of War track it down, or could it be...?

Green Butterfly cast aside the coat she had just put on, leaving her arms bare and exposed. "What do you want? You've caught me in a *very* bad mood."

She had a million questions she wanted to ask Thea. It was nice of her to save Green Butterfly the trouble of having to track her down.

Green Butterfly shot a glare at her subordinate. "What are you just standing there for? Catch her. You don't want Purple Ant to torture you again, do you?" she threatened him. The man went pale and drew his knife as fast as he could.

Thea narrowed her eyes in displeasure.

Purple Ant had lent Green Butterfly a dozen Worker Ants, and while she only had one of them there with her, his assassination skills were a force to be reckoned with. The man was a first-rate CIM agent, and he already had fourteen kills to his name.

"Ha-ha," Green Butterfly laughed. "Go beat that girl within an inch of her life."

The Worker Ant charged. Despite his timid expression, his movements were ferociously swift. He bore down on Thea in an instant and, with a battle cry, thrust his knife at her. There was no way Thea could possibly defend herself. She made no effort to ready a weapon, and she wasn't even looking at the knife.

**"Protect me."**

The moment the words left Thea's mouth, a swarm of arms reached out from behind her, twelve of them in all. The Worker Ant was horribly outnumbered. The arms grabbed his hand holding the knife, his head, his neck, and his legs one after the other, pinning him in place in the blink of an eye.

Before Green Butterfly knew what was happening, six unsavory men and women had appeared in front of Thea. After containing the Worker Ant and knocking him out, they turned their glares on Green Butterfly as though locking in their next target.

Those were the Fires of War mafia members. Thea had brought muscle with her. "Much appreciated," Thea thanked them, then elegantly strode her way over to Green Butterfly.

"Gee, you look like a cult leader." Green Butterfly chuckled. "You think *this* makes you a hero?"

"I mean, you've certainly made proper villains of yourselves." Thea extended her arm and thrust her index finger at Green Butterfly. "Listen up! That girl is with the group that assassinated Prince Darryn! She's one of the Serpent members who's been working with Scarlet Leviathan to plunge the world into chaos!"

The six pairs of eyes darkened.

Thea barked out her order. **"Capture her."**

On her signal, the mafia members charged.

Green Butterfly whirled around and made a beeline for the window behind her. *Dammit, I need to get out of here!* Her gun only had fourteen bullets in it. If she tried picking a fight, she would run out of ammo before she knew it.

As the sun set on Hurough, Green Butterfly smashed in the window, dove out into the city, and landed on the adjacent building's roof. The jump had taken her from a fourteenth-floor window to an eighth-floor rooftop, but she ignored the shock to her legs and landed with ease.

"Uuugh, this sucks."

She aimed her gun upward and fired two shots into the air. That was her signal to the nearby Worker Ants that there was an emergency. There was a march happening on the street directly below, and the protestors screamed when they heard the gunshots. As they began scattering every which way, the situation at ground level descended into absolute bedlam.

The police who'd been clashing with the protestors were at their limits just trying to keep things contained.

Thea and her followers showed no signs of giving chase.

*At the end of the day, they're just glorified gangsters.* Green Butterfly looked up at the building she'd just jumped out of. *It's not like they've trained to leap from rooftop to rooftop or anything. Maybe escaping will be easier than I thought.*

It was a talent that any spy around could pull off, but these were no spies. There was nothing Thea's mafia goons could do but stand by the window and look down powerlessly at Green Butterfly.

*Time to get out while the getting is good,* Green Butterfly mused. She was optimistic about her chances—right up until the bullet grazed her cheek.

"___!"

She whirled around to discover she was surrounded by mafia members with their guns trained on her. The roof of the building she was on, the roofs of the surrounding buildings, and the upper-floor windows of the taller buildings were bursting at the seams with gunmen. All told, there looked to be about a hundred of them. Were they all members of the Fires of War?

*How did she get so many people so quickly?!*

Green Butterfly was forced to admit that she'd underestimated Thea. If she hadn't been certain she needed to get away earlier, she sure as hell was now.

The mafia members opened fire without a moment's hesitation. Fortunately for Green Butterfly, though, these were mere street thugs, not soldiers with proper marksmanship training. Their aim was mediocre at best, and she managed to dodge their entire initial salvo. However, the problem was their raw numbers. In order to escape their siege, she had no choice but to use every smoke bomb she had on her.

As she hid herself in the fumes, she took two hand grenades and tossed them out in random directions in an act of indiscriminate terrorism. She had no compunctions about dragging civilians into the fight.

Screams rose up from the ground and threw off the Fires of War's chain of command. Green Butterfly charged out of the smoke screen, wove her way through the panicking gunmen's ranks, and descended to the street. A random man walked beside her, and she knocked him out with a punch and stole his coat.

*I used up most of my getaway gear back there. All I can do now is go to ground.*

She put on the coat and scanned the surrounding area to see if there was anywhere she could hide. Luckily, it didn't take her long to track down an abandoned building. She used the fire escape to get up to the second floor, then smashed the lock with her gun. From there, she tied the coat in a special knot around the railing in front of the door. It was a signal to her Worker Ants so they knew where to find her.

*With a little prep, I should be able to get to safety. All I need to do is buy some time, and—*

She froze midway through her thought. She'd assumed the building was empty, but as soon as she went in, she sensed someone's presence.

"Well, well, well. You certainly got here quick." That someone was Thea. She'd been waiting for Green Butterfly with a smile just as triumphant as before. "With how many locals I have on my side, circling ahead of you was child's play."

Everything had played out just the way Thea planned.

Green Butterfly's face grew hot when she realized she'd been manipulated, but she quickly collected herself. There was no denying it—Thea was good, and she'd devoted a whole lot of effort and resources toward choking out Butterfly's life.

"It's so wild that it almost makes me wanna laugh," Green Butterfly said, sticking out her tongue to taunt Thea. "I mean, what's up with all your fanboys? Dunno if you forgot, but you're one of the spies ravaging Fend, too. You must've fed 'em a whole load of lies to get them to follow you, huh? Gee, that was a pretty messed up thing to do."

Considering how loyal the mafia was to her, they must have actually believed the yarn about Thea being a hero who was going to save the country. That was one hell of a con Thea had played on them.

Thea cast her gaze downward. Green Butterfly hadn't expected Thea to take the verbal jab quite so hard. After letting out an anguished exhalation, Thea shook her head to the side. "You're right. I did lie to them. I never once told them that I was a spy, too." She raised her head. "But when I said I was going to save this nation, I meant every word of it. We all want to rescue Fend from Serpent's noxious clutches. That objective we share is the truth."

"You've gotta be joking. The Commonwealth isn't even your country."

"No, it isn't."

"I don't get it. What does a Din Republic spy get out of saving some foreign country?"

"That's not what it's about," Thea replied with a proud laugh. "My goal is to become a hero who saves everyone, even my enemies."

Green Butterfly couldn't begin to make heads or tails of that, but there was something unsettling about the confidence in Thea's expression. "Well, that's the dumbest thing I've ever heard," Green Butterfly spat.

After all, Green Butterfly had no way of knowing. She had no way of knowing about the heroic aspirations Thea had nurtured ever since she was saved by "Hearth" Veronika, and she had no way of knowing that Thea had sublimated that intense motivation into a new power.

There was a fighting style for spies the Lamplight girls had learned from Avian—liecraft. It was a way to beat powerful foes by taking their innate talents and combining them with a synergistic form of deception. Thanks to the training she'd gotten from "Feather" Pharma, Thea had been able to master the technique. Her ability to peer into people's hearts made her a master at forging connections, and she'd used that talent to fool an entire organization into worshipping her as a hero.

Negotiation × Idolatry = In Praise of Folly.

There in the Fend Commonwealth, Thea's ludicrously powerful liecraft had come into full bloom.

Green Butterfly might not have known what Thea's power was, but she recognized that the girl standing before her was her enemy, and she began carefully observing the situation. Thea may have circled around and gotten the drop on her, but she wasn't carrying any weapons to speak of. What's more, her right arm was badly injured. Even further, the building was deserted. All it had were big, empty rooms.

*Why did she rally all those underlings, then come here alone?*

Thea was practically radiating confidence. She was carrying herself like she'd already won, and that rubbed Green Butterfly the wrong way.

*...Is she underestimating me? Is that it?*

If so, that was awfully conceited of her.

Green Butterfly pulled out an ice pick. Conventional bladed weapons had a habit of getting caught on bone, so if you knew how to aim directly for the heart or the carotid, ice picks were far more reliable. She aimed its point directly at Thea. "Just so you know, I can hold my own in a fight just fine."

"Oh, I can see that."

"And plus, my pawns have arrived."

The sound of footsteps came from the door Green Butterfly entered through as Worker Ants began filing into the room. Purple Ant had brainwashed them into training, day in and day out, and their skills put mafia members to shame. It had taken them barely any time at all to come to Green Butterfly's aid, and now a full half of the Worker Ants she had undercover in Hurough were there with her. Oddly enough, there were six—the exact same number as the mafia members who had been surrounding Green Butterfly earlier.

Now the tables were turned.

Green Butterfly brandished her ice pick and cackled. "Gee, you'd better hurry up and call in whatever little mafia friends you've got waiting outside. Wouldn't want you dying alone, now, would we? Ah-ha-ha-ha! I'll tell my Worker Ants to blow themselves up and have them run your goons down!"

The Worker Ants gulped, but if she gave the order, they would carry it out without question. They'd long since been stripped of the willpower to fight back.

Thea's fists trembled with rage. "I'm not going to let that happen."

"Hmm?"

"My plan was never to have the mafia actually fight for me, you know. I just asked them to lend me a hand luring you here."

"It's pathetic, how much of a soft touch you are."

"It's fine. The Fires of War was always meant for one purpose—controlling the media."

Green Butterfly felt a chill, and she let out a confused grunt. An overwhelming desire for bloodshed had just filled the room. It was so intense she could practically envision a starving beast snapping at her throat. All of a sudden, the situation was becoming clear to her. Now she understood the goal behind those articles.

"I hear you threatened to pin the blame for Prince Darryn's assassination on Lily," Thea explained. "Now, though, I'm afraid that won't play. The whole world believes Monika did it, and Monika went so far as to show herself in public and bomb a building. With all that stacked against you, do you really think anyone's going to give you the time of day if you tell them Lily did it? The truth has already been decided."

However, that "truth" was wildly different from the one Green Butterfly had been expecting. And what's more, the new culprit had been falsely painted as a Galgad spy.

"There's no way you'll be able to paint Lily as the killer anymore. She's completely safe."

As Thea smiled, another girl strode out from the pillar behind her.

"I've freed Monika from your control."

There Monika was, with revolver in hand.

So that was where that foreboding bloodlust had been coming from. Green Butterfly retreated and kicked one of her Worker Ants in the back.

With that as their signal, the six Worker Ants sprang into action. As four of them opened fire with their guns, the other two got in position to intercept Monika's assault. It was a beautiful bit of coordination and more than enough to kill a single spy.

The four bullets flew straight at Monika, and they all should have landed direct hits. Right before they did, though, Monika's body blinked to the side. All the bullets zipped past her left flank.

Monika closed in on the Worker Ants before they had time to fire a second round of shots, and from there, her movements flowed into each other without so much as a single wasted turn.

She started by shooting one of the Worker Ants in the shoulder. One down.

One of the women came at her with a knife, but Monika crouched down and dodged it. Then she scooped up the gun the first Worker Ant had dropped and shot the man and woman to her left and right simultaneously. Two and three down.

That left the enemy formation in shambles, and Monika had no intention of giving them a chance to regroup. She shot a fierce, high kick at one of the remaining men, right in his jaw, to knock him out. Four down.

That left two men standing, and they charged at her from both sides with their knives. Just like when she dodged the bullets earlier, though, she evaded with footwork so swift it was like she'd vanished entirely. Then she took her dual pistols and smashed them into the men's shoulders to take them out of commission. Five and six down.

Once she was finished, Monika tossed aside her stolen gun. She looked almost bored.

Green Butterfly shuddered as she watched it play out from the side.

*How did she take them out so fast?!*

Her breath caught in her throat. She couldn't believe what she'd just witnessed. She'd always known that Monika's skills were the real deal, of course. She herself had placed a fair bit of stock in that fact. What Monika had just done, though... That blew Green Butterfly's wildest expectations out of the water. But as for what surprised Green Butterfly most of all...

*...That was the same footwork as Firewalker's!!*

That movement was so blisteringly fast it was easy to mistake it for teleportation, and Green Butterfly had experienced it firsthand. Its user could be stationary one moment, then zooming at top speed the next, allowing them to dodge bullets with ease and obliterate all comers. It was a huge part of why Firewalker had been hailed as invincible, and no matter how Green Butterfly sliced it, what Monika had just used was undeniably Firewalker's technique.

Thea laughed, clearly impressed. "Those were certainly some fancy moves. Did Vindo teach you those?"

"More like he *beat* them into me. I still haven't quite mastered them yet. He and Klaus could still run circles around me."

"At this point, I've just about given up trying to tell who's faster than who."

Upon seeing the two of them chat like that, Green Butterfly broke out in a cold sweat. The conversation she was witnessing was giving her chills like she couldn't believe.

*This feeling... It isn't possible!*

There was a girl who wound the masses around her little finger and reshaped the world as she saw fit. And beside her, there was a girl who accompanied her and mowed down those who opposed them with peerless might.

Green Butterfly's logical side was screaming at her that she was wrong. The girls standing before her had shown some glimpses of talent, but they certainly weren't on par with the best in the world. The notion was unthinkable. Yet even so, Green Butterfly's brain couldn't help but draw the comparison. It saw something behind Thea and Monika, something vast and terrifying.

In Green Butterfly's mind's eye, she saw their faces overlap with those of "Hearth" Veronika and "Firewalker" Gerde—the duo who once ruled the world through the shadow war!

*Who are these people?!*

First off, the girls' plan was deranged. Not only had Monika intentionally painted herself as the criminal who'd offed a royal, she'd even gotten her ally Thea to pressure the papers into reporting it. No one in their right mind would go to such lengths.

All that time, the two of them must have been communicating through some method that had escaped Green Butterfly's notice.

That photo in the paper—the one of Monika killing Mia Godolphin—was a forgery. The corpse was probably a fake. It would appear that someone on Lamplight—Grete, if Green Butterfly had to hazard a guess—was a master of disguise. The girls had asked her to make a mask so they could dress up some other corpse as Mia.

Right as Green Butterfly finished deducing that, Thea took a step forward. "A little bird told me you wanted to become Monika's partner. Don't make me laugh," she said forcefully. She glared down at Green Butterfly with a look of utter contempt. "People like you need to know their place. There's only one partner in crime for Monika here, and it's me."

Monika frowned for a moment like she wanted to say something, but she certainly didn't dispute Thea's assertion. She held her gun tight and kept watch in case Green Butterfly tried anything.

Green Butterfly took another look back over at her Worker Ants. Monika had shot out their joints, leaving them unable to stand. Their wounds weren't fatal, but there was no way they were going to be able to fight Monika in their current state.

Green Butterfly let out a big sigh. "Hey, Monika."

"What, not calling me Scarlet Leviathan anymore?"

"Yep, and it's a shame. Gee, I really was looking forward to working with you. We would've got to split our despair. But I can see you've made your choice."

"You say that like I give a damn about what you wanted."

"Eh, it's fine. I won round one, and I guess round two goes to you. I get it, I get it, I really, totally do."

Green Butterfly squeezed her ice pick and gave her two foes a grin.

"Let's start up round three, shall we? I'll show you just what Green Butterfly is capable of."

The moment she flashed her jagged teeth, the room's windows shattered. Bullets went flying as a group of armed assailants stormed inside.

Monika and Thea immediately put some distance between themselves and the windows.

"The CIM?! What are they doing here?!"

Sure enough, the newcomers were a Fend Commonwealth intelligence unit.

Green Butterfly stepped back as well, then locked eyes with one of the agents to indicate that it was Thea and Monika they wanted to attack, not her.

"Monika, we need to get out of here!" Thea cried. "You don't want anything to do with the CIM right now!"

Monika followed her lead and began retreating. She fired one frustrated parting shot at Green Butterfly, but all Green Butterfly had to do was tilt her head a little to dodge it.

"Stubbornness! Killed! The cat!" Green Butterfly shouted, pointing at Monika as the latter fled. "You made the wrong choice, you incompetents. Tremble in fear at the ruin that awaits you—and perish in agony as the jet-black nightmare takes you!!"

The point she was making was clear—this was where the real battle began.

◇◇◇

After bandaging up his wound and taking Grete to the hospital, Klaus returned to Queen Clette Station with Erna, Sybilla, and Lily in tow. He was pretty sure Thea was at the same location, and immediately after they began their search, they heard shots being fired over by the west side of the station.

By the time they got there, the entire area had already descended into panic. There were mafia members firing shots from the rooftops, and while Klaus caught a brief glimpse of a girl with scars on her shoulders matching Green Butterfly's description, she quickly vanished behind a smoke screen. He thought about pursuing her, but he hesitated. The girl had just thrown grenades down at the masses walking in the streets.

Foreign citizens or not, Klaus wasn't about to stand by and let a bunch of civilians die. "Sybilla," he said to get the attention of the one girl capable of handling a coordinated maneuver with him.

Sybilla gave him a confident "Way ahead of ya!" and the two of them took off in unison. After snatching the grenades out of the air, Sybilla tossed them over to Klaus, who popped open a manhole cover and hurled them into the sewer. Flames gushed up from the opening, and the thunderous boom caused the people around them to scream even more. The situation was getting out of hand, fast. A couple of civilians still got hit by stray bullets and collapsed. Now that Green Butterfly was gone, Klaus and the girls had little choice but to prioritize treating the wounded.

After they'd been waylaid for a good long while, they spotted an unexpected face.

"Teach?!"

It was Thea. Based on her reaction, she hadn't expected them to be so close by.

"Hello, Thea," Klaus growled. "You've had a busy few days. Did you have fun, putting together the Fires of War?"

"No, I promise, it's not what you..." For a moment, it sounded like she was going to try to deny it, but she soon shook her head in resignation and offered Klaus an apologetic bow. "...I'm sorry. Once we're through here, I'll take whatever punishment you want to give me. I was acting on Monika's orders, though. She said I absolutely couldn't tell you what was going on."

There were a million things Klaus wanted to scold her for, but there would be time enough for that later. Thea had once tried to help Annette's mother, a foreign spy, escape. Monika had helped her with that, so much of what Thea had done those past few days had probably been her way of returning that favor.

Right now, though, there was something Klaus needed to confirm. "And? Where's Monika now?"

"Huh.........?" Thea gave him a blank look and looked over her shoulder. However, Monika was nowhere to be seen. "What? But why?" The blood slowly drained from Thea's face. "It doesn't make sense. She was just with me. Where could she have gone?"

Monika and Thea had been separated.

As Thea tried to make sense of it, the other girls started gravitating their way. Mournful tears were streaming down their faces.

Klaus dispassionately continued his line of questioning. "And what did she say the plan was?"

"She told me we were going to join back up with Lamplight... That the way things were going, she was liable to get blamed for the assassination, so we would need you to help her hide..." The further Thea got into the second sentence, the frailer her voice became. Her fingers trembled, as though she could sense that something was terribly amiss. "Then we were all going to fight the CIM together so we could prove her innocence…"

"So she tricked you, too." Klaus couldn't bring himself to scold Thea. Monika had been putting everything she had into conning Thea, and seeing through something like that was a tall order. As a matter of fact, Klaus himself had been deceived in much the same way. He hadn't figured out the full truth until just recently. "I was operating under the same assumption—that Monika joined Serpent as a double agent and was always planning on returning to Lamplight. I was fully prepared to stand against the CIM to protect her from the false allegations."

Monika's defeated smile flashed back through Klaus's head.

He let out an exhale. "However, I underestimated her resolve."

Klaus and Monika had never been on quite the same page, and because of that, he hadn't been able to stop her.

Klaus had already told his theory to the other girls. They all had stared at him in horror, and some of them had even broken down in tears. None of them wanted to believe it was true.

"Monika never had any intention of clearing her name or of returning to Lamplight. Her plan is to continue presenting herself as the Galgad spy who assassinated Prince Darryn, to lure the CIM after her…"

Klaus's voice was solemn.

"…and to die."

# Chapter 10

# Traitor

Over on the east side of Hurough, there was a set of wharfs collectively referred to as the Dock Road. The wharfs extended out from the Turko River as it ran through the heart of the city. A century prior, they'd been the largest port in the world, and huge amounts of imported goods had flowed in from countless different nations. The area was crammed full of gigantic brick warehouses and spherical tanks for holding crude oil.

Sunset had already come, but the darkness found no purchase on the Dock Road. Cargo was loaded and unloaded there around the clock, and the entire area was kept well illuminated. Over on the wharfs, in fact, it was just as bright as it had been in the middle of the day.

Monika stood perched atop a Dock Road warehouse, surveying the wharfs from a distance as she caught her breath. In her hand, she was holding a radio she'd stolen off Thea. However, she wasn't getting any response.

*I thought I could at least pass along a message, but it looks like that's a no-go.*

The only thing coming from the speakers was a fuzzy noise that sounded like rainfall. The signal was getting jammed.

*Makes sense, what with how many CIM members they're mobilizing. They're putting a whole lot of manpower into this.*

As the fact sank in, she turned her gaze over to the setting sun. It felt like she saw her own fast-approaching fate reflected in its descent below the horizon.

What other option could she have taken?

She'd asked herself that question time and time again, but she'd never found a good answer.

*Serpent's got their hooks into the CIM deep. Talking things out with them was never going to work. I don't know why, but they've got it fixed in their heads that it was a Din spy who assassinated the crown prince.*

The CIM was desperate to find the prince's killer. After all, it was their reputation on the line. If they failed so thoroughly as to let the assassin escape, it would make a laughingstock of their entire nation.

That left Lamplight with two options: sacrifice a single Din spy or push back against the CIM with everything they had and prove that a Galgad spy was the one pulling the strings.

Obviously, the latter was the preferable of the two.

*The problem is, everyone knows that Klaus works for Din, so him fighting back too publicly would cause a diplomatic incident. It could put the entire team's safety in jeopardy.*

The thing was, the CIM was under Serpent's control. There was a good chance that their claims of innocence would simply be ignored, and if things turned into an unproductive war of attrition, then eventually someone on Lamplight might end up losing their life. Who would be the next victim to fall after Avian? Grete? Sybilla? Thea? Sara? Annette? Erna? Lily, perhaps? Or maybe even everyone? Every time Monika envisioned that tragedy, her whole body broke out in a cold sweat.

*I don't know if I actually believe it'd play out like that,* she thought quietly to herself, *but I want to protect them both. I want to protect Lily...and I also want to protect Lamplight.*

No matter how many times she mulled it over, it never changed her decision. All she had to do was sacrifice herself, and everything would be settled. The killer's death would put the Fend populace at ease. The CIM would get to protect their honor. The news would report the killer as a Galgad spy, so the Din Republic would get to avoid having an international incident with the Fend Commonwealth. And Lamplight would have suffered only minimal casualties before their next battle. It would be happy endings all around.

The one regret she had was that promise she made with Lily.

*"We need to make an oath. I don't want anyone else to die here. We're all*

*gonna make it back to Heat Haze Palace, and we're all gonna make it back alive. I need everyone to promise me that.*"

Every time Monika thought back to that pledge Lily had made in front of the group, she felt her expression soften a little.

"Sorry, but I might not be able to keep that promise." She let out a self-deprecating chuckle and quietly cast her gaze forward. "After all...I'm just a stupid, no-good traitor."

Monika had failed to become a double agent. She'd taken Lamplight and Serpent and abandoned them both. She'd even rejected Klaus's assistance, and now as she stood there, she was truly alone.

The bill was fast coming due.

One final battle awaited her—and she had no chance of winning against the full might of the CIM.

As the chaos raged, Amelie returned to the CIM headquarters.

The traps Klaus laid were ingenious, and Amelie had failed to spot them all during her escape from Lamplight's base. She was pretty sure she'd pushed some sort of switch. That had sent a wireless signal over to Klaus, no doubt, so he probably knew that she'd fled. If he was so inclined, he could have all her Belias agents slaughtered.

Even knowing that, though, Amelie had no choice but to act.

*You're out of time, Bonfire. The unrest has spread too far. Even if it means sacrificing my team's lives, I need to report in to my superiors.*

Doing so pained her, but as a spy, it was the right call to make.

As soon as she arrived at the headquarters, she immediately headed for the room that housed their governing body, Hide, and relayed the truth to its five members behind their partition. She told them about how she'd been working with Lamplight to track down "Cloud Drift" Lan, but how they set her up and captured her. She told them about how, once Lamplight took her agents hostage, she had no choice but to obey them.

Hide listened to her report in silence.

Amelie could feel her skin prickling from how much raw tension was in the air.

"We'll handle the matter of Belias's failure later. There will be consequences, but now is not the time for that," one pompous voice declared. The other four voiced their agreement.

, A deep male voice boomed out. "Amelie, tell us *exactly* what you've witnessed."

"...As you wish."

"Was it 'Cloud Drift' Lan who shot Prince Darryn?"

"No, I don't believe it was. The night His Highness was slain, I saw Cloud Drift's injuries with my own eyes. She was in no state to carry out an assassination. If nothing else, she wasn't the one who pulled the trigger."

"The papers are saying it was a spy called Scarlet Leviathan. Is there any truth to that?"

"I'm afraid I can't rightly say," Amelie replied candidly. Aside from the killer, there probably wasn't a single person who truly knew the answer to that question.

A gloomy male voice came from behind the partition. "Hmm, how odd... It certainly lacks *elegance*...," he said, putting a peculiar stress on the final word. "The intelligence that a Din Republic spy was plotting to kill Prince Darryn came directly from Magician. **Are you suggesting that we made an absolutely unthinkable error?**"

The air in the room dropped a few degrees. There was discord brewing within Hide's ranks. The gloomy man was calling Magician out.

The next voice Amelie heard was husky and female. It belonged to Magician, no doubt. "It wasn't an error."

"Really, now?"

"All this means is that the newspapers had it right—that the killer was a Galgad spy disguising themselves as a Din spy. It was a tiny misunderstanding, nothing more."

After Magician gave her excuse, a long silence descended on the room. Then the deep-voiced man spoke again. "Amelie, we ask of you this," he said menacingly. "What side does Scarlet Leviathan work for? The Din Republic or the Galgad Empire?"

Amelie hesitated for a moment. This time, though, she had an answer. All she had to do was state the facts. "I personally witnessed 'Scarlet Leviathan' Monika *attack her Lamplight teammates*." Monika hadn't so much as hesitated before turning her blade on her own allies. "I believe her to be a mole working for the Galgad Empire."

She could hear breaths being released from behind the partition. There was another long silence, after which the five Hide members came to a consensus. "Relay the news to every active CIM unit. Our opponent is from the Galgad Empire."

Then came the order.

"Scarlet Leviathan is to be killed at once. The CIM's dignity rests on ensuring that she not be allowed to escape."

Amelie curtsied. "I will see that it is done."

That was about how Amelie had expected things to go. If the Anti-Imperialists and Neo-Imperialists could agree on one thing, it was that Monika needed to be eliminated. Hide's verdict had been inevitable.

*Though, I suspect this is all playing out exactly as she planned.*

Amelie had seen the sadness lurking in Monika's eyes. That was the one piece of information she hadn't passed along to Klaus.

In any case, Amelie was under no obligation to protect her. There was no hesitation in her mind. Right now the entire populace of the Fend Commonwealth wanted Scarlet Leviathan dead.

Upon learning the full truth, Thea was aghast. The fact that she'd been betrayed must have come as a great shock, and her shoulders trembled as tears welled up in her eyes. "That can't be," she choked out, but not a single one of her teammates spoke up to refute Klaus's claims. Back when he first told them, they'd reacted the exact same way. They didn't want to accept the facts even as the fear welling up in their hearts threatened to overwhelm them.

"That *traitor*!!" Thea cried, clenching her fists in anguish. "We have to stop her! Letting Monika sacrifice herself like this isn't the way we—"

The rumbling of footsteps cut her off.

A group of people in dark coats had just moved in to surround them. They'd used the panicked crowd to mask their approach. All in all, there were about twenty of them.

"You're with the CIM?" Klaus calmly asked. If they tried to attack, he was more than ready to send them flying.

A man strode forth from the group. He had dark skin, blond hair, and that unique sort of composure about him exclusive to the strong. Klaus had spotted him in front of the *Conmerid Times*, too. An anachronistic saber hung from the waist of his jet-black coat. "Are you Bonfire?" the man asked. His eyes gleamed with contempt, like he was looking at something beneath him. "I'm 'Armorer' Meredith, the man in charge of the CIM's Vanajin team. Think of us as coworkers to the Belias team you fought."

"I see. And what brings you here?"

"I'd rethink my attitude if I were you. We have hostages." Meredith shot a look over to where another group of men were holding a pair of dark-red- and brown-haired girls captive at gunpoint.

"Sara?! Lan?!" Sybilla cried.

The two girls bit their lips in chagrin when she called their names. "I-I'm sorry. They were on top of us before we knew what was happening..."

"Prithee, forgive me. There was naught we could do against their numbers."

Klaus remained unshaken. "Amelie led you right to them, I take it."

He was aware that she'd escaped, but he'd never gotten a chance to give Sara and Lan new orders. It had happened right in the middle of his fight against Monika.

Meredith let out a snort before going on. "The CIM is moving in to eliminate Scarlet Leviathan. Give us all the intel you have on her. The way I see it, she's just as much a traitor to the Din Republic as she is to anyone."

".........."

"If you try to protect her, we'll have no choice but to view you as enemies of the Crown as well."

Klaus's thoughts turned. Considering his injured leg, would it be possible for him to kill all twenty Vanajin members to keep them quiet while simultaneously protecting the girls, including the hostages? It was possible, certainly, but it would carry substantial risks, and even if he succeeded, he didn't see any way for it to go well in the long term.

"Just obey us like good little boys and girls," Meredith said confidently. "We don't want to cause any diplomatic issues with the Republic if we don't have to. Surely, this is better than having us make it public that Scarlet Leviathan came from the Din Republic, right? You want a war, that's how you get a war."

Klaus needed to make his decision.

He pulled out his gun, then tossed it on the ground. The girls sucked in frustrated breaths.

"It's fucked, y'know," Sybilla spat. "Your whole damn country is fucked."

The expressions on the Vanajin members surrounding them went harsh, and they stared daggers at Sybilla. "I see your girl has a mouth on her," Meredith spat back, unimpressed.

Klaus took advantage of that tiny opening to move his fingers.

Eventually, Vanajin dragged Klaus and the girls away to handcuff them, stick them in cars, and blindfold them to completely restrict their movement. While that was going on, the girl farthest from Klaus followed his hand signal. By taking full advantage of the moment Vanajin's attention was gathered on Sybilla, she was able to nonchalantly sidle backward and disappear into the Hurough crowd.

◇◇◇

As the sun finished its descent, it painted the sky orange with its afterglow.

Monika continued waiting atop the warehouse as more and more people gathered on the Dock Road, all radiating hostility. She could feel their gazes piercing her like needles.

Monika wasn't surprised that the CIM already had her surrounded. She was making no attempt to flee or hide, and that must have been setting off alarm bells for them. For the moment, the CIM was spending the entirety of their efforts clearing the area of civilians. They weren't going to go in for the kill until they had that finished. It wasn't like Monika had anywhere to run, after all.

Monika got where they were coming from, but still. "Would it kill you to hurry it up a bit?" she grumbled.

Then she heard a lazy drawl from the next warehouse over. "Fouuund youuu."

It was Green Butterfly.

"Hee-hee-hee-hee-hee-hee-hee-hee!" She let out a vulgar laugh and flashed her jagged pearly whites. "Gee, Mooonika, how's it goin'? Check out aaall those CIM heavy hitters showing up. They're here to kill you, you know."

"You sure you want to be standing there? They're gonna see you."

"Oh, that's fiiine. The CIM would never attack me," Green Butterfly boasted. "No way, no how."

Green Butterfly had the power to deploy the CIM as she pleased, and Monika had figured out the trick she used to do it. Monika had a question she needed to ask her, and it had nothing to do with any of that. "I just want to know one thing."

"Oh yeah? Gee, what's that?"

"What would've happened if those papers had reported that you were the killer instead of me?"

"Ha-ha, what? I would've just had the CIM bury the article, that's what. Then we would've announced someone on Lamplight as the killer, and no one would've paid that nonsense a second thought."

"Cool. Glad to hear it." Monika's expression softened a little, and she nodded. "I knew I made the right choice."

"Look, I dunno what you're so satisfied about... But it looks like your time's up."

The air of hostility permeating the area grew stronger. The CIM was finished with their prep work.

"So long, Scarlet Leviathan. I'll make sure I bear witness to your death," Green Butterfly whispered. She leaped off the warehouse, then vanished.

The moment she did, a group dressed in suits appeared as though to take her place. It was a CIM unit. All its members had their guns at the ready and were staring at Monika with murder in their eyes. There were fourteen in all.

The man standing at their center had a keen gleam in his eye. That was probably the team's boss. He was wearing a dark mask over his mouth with an image of a carnivore on it. The raw bloodlust he was giving off told Monika that the man was the real deal.

The CIM members didn't introduce themselves, nor did they say a single word that didn't need to be said. They revealed nothing—not that they were Carval, a team made up of the CIM's finest operatives; nor that they'd been operating abroad and had been ordered to return as soon as possible once Prince Darryn died; nor that they were a combat unit with unmatched skill that was supposed to be carrying out an assassination in the Galgad Empire.

Aside from Hearth, there was no target they'd ever failed to put down. That was the level those people operated on.

Behind them, there was a member of the CIM's Hide leadership, "Cursemaster" Nathan, as well as seventy-five members of Vanajin, the CIM's largest counterintelligence unit, and sixteen members of Belias, the counterintelligence unit that answered directly to Hide. All in all, the CIM had deployed over a hundred operatives, each and every one of them specialized in fighting spies.

"*Our righteousness is absolute,*" declared "Silhouette" Luke, Carval's boss. His voice came out muffled through his mask. "*We are always just, and we do not err.*"

Monika shrugged. "If you say so."

"You are an enemy of the Crown, and we offer you a dignified death."

With that, they began their mission.

They'd brought far, far more forces there than they needed to kill a single girl. It was going to be a massacre.

After marching Klaus and the girl into a room, the CIM finally removed their blindfolds.

The building was one of the CIM's many bases. Considering the time it had taken them to get there, Klaus assumed they couldn't be far from Hurough. With no windows in the room, though, it was hard to be any more specific than that. They were in a cell. There wasn't so much as a single chair, and the only way in or out was through a heavy metal door.

"Wait here and don't cause any trouble," one of the Vanajin members ordered them, then left the cell. Vanajin had probably been called in to participate in the anti-Monika strike force.

Vanajin had confiscated their guns, so breaking the door would be tricky. There were six of them in the cell: Klaus, Lily, Sybilla, Thea, Sara, and Lan. Considering how thorough the CIM was being, they had to imagine that Annette and Grete were being detained over at the hospital, too.

Klaus leaned against the wall and let out a long exhale. There was nothing they could do but surrender themselves to the passage of time. Klaus had given Vanajin some intel on Monika during the ride over, but only superficial details of little import. They wouldn't be called again until the whole thing was over.

"C'mon, Boss!" Sybilla shouted, unable to contain herself. "What're you just sittin' there for?! You gotta have some trick up your sleeve. You gotta!"

Klaus closed his eyes. "All we can do now is wait," he said plainly. There was, in fact, nothing he could do.

He heard the sound of teeth grinding. "What the *fuck* have you even been doing?!"

Klaus opened his eyes and found Sybilla standing before him, tears streaming down her face. Her hands were balled up tight into fists, and she was glaring at him like she was about to strike him at any moment. Her face was flush red. "You've been useless this whole goddamn time! You let Monika betray us, it took you forever to find her, and when you did, you let her get away! That shit ain't you, man! The fuck's wrong with you?!"

"Sybilla, come on...!" Lily said, grabbing her arm in an attempt to calm her down.

However, Sybilla shook her off and buried her face in her hands in anguish. "I know I'm just takin' my anger out on you, but still... STILL!" Her shoulders heaved, and when she spoke next, her voice came out thin and sorrowful. "There was this part of me that believed... I figured you'd find some way to fix it, in spite of everything..."

She feebly hung her head.

Klaus quietly watched his dejected subordinate. The others cast sympathetic gazes Sybilla's way. They probably all shared the exact same complaints she'd just voiced, and they were right to. Klaus had suffered a long string of embarrassing failures lately. He could hardly blame them for being disappointed in him.

"Teach had his hands full, too," Lily said, trying to defend him. "And besides, he's not the only one to blame here. If we'd just worked harder—"

"No, that's not it," Klaus replied. "There was a different reason she was able to give me the runaround, one that I only recently realized."

The girls all gave him a quizzical look.

Now that he thought about it, things had felt off for a while, chief among them the fact that he'd failed to notice how Monika changed right before their attack on Belias. It wasn't until he fought her in person that he understood what that feeling was. The answer was mind-bogglingly simple. "It's because of how rapidly Monika's improved."

""Huh?""

"She grew faster than I anticipated and successfully concealed her plan. She beat me, plain and simple."

He felt a hint of chagrin in that realization, but perhaps he ought to have been celebrating how far his student had come.

Lily stared at him in shock. "...What? No, no, no. I know it was just once, but still, there's no way she actually beat you—"

"She's still sixteen, right?"

She was coming up on seventeen, but either way, that was still pretty darn young. Ominously so. Klaus thought back to his own sixteen-year-old self and gave the girls his candid thoughts.

"I think she's stronger now than I was at that age."

""""""Huh?"""""""

The girls' eyes all went wide in unison. However, that was Klaus's honest opinion. Klaus himself had grown a lot since he was sixteen, of course, but while he had no intention of relinquishing the title of the World's Greatest, he realized now that he was going to have to work to keep it.

"Th-there's no way...," Lily stammered, still frozen in shock.

Her disbelief was understandable, but after fighting Monika, Klaus knew. He'd seen the raw talent her predicament had awakened in her.

Every so often, the world gave birth to a monster. And just as it had created the peerless spy that was Klaus, it had created another one in that very nation...

"She intends to die taking on the CIM. I would love nothing more than to stop her, but she's made her wishes clear. It's up to us to respect them. And besides, I doubt she's planning on going down without a fight," Klaus told the girls. "So I'm choosing to believe. I believe that that genius will find a way to survive and make her way back to Lamplight."

After going through all that growth, Monika had decided to fight to the end. Klaus knew better than to stand in her way. All he could do was close his eyes and pray for her safe return.

Something very strange was happening on the Dock Road. So strange, in fact, that the CIM spies gathered there couldn't process what they were seeing.

Nathan, the man feared as Cursemaster the world over, witnessed it from his position down on the bank of the River Turko. Nathan had lived through more than his share of battles. He'd joined forces with Inferno during the Great War to throw the Galgad Empire's intelligence network into disarray, and of the five members of Hide, he was the only one who was still operating on the front lines.

He smirked a little. He hadn't felt fear like that in a good long while. "Such elegance..."

Vanajin's boss, "Armorer" Meredith, was on standby behind Carval. His job was to provide backup on the off chance Monika managed to give Carval the slip, and he'd come in assuming that was the same as having no job at all. He wondered why they needed so many forces there. Surely, it was overkill.

Now he admitted how wrong he'd been as he reached for the saber hanging from his waist.

Belias's boss, "Puppeteer" Amelie, brandished her baton beside Meredith and got ready to give her agents their orders on a moment's notice. Their protracted imprisonment had left them drained, but Amelie had trusted the worry growing in her gut and given a rousing speech to all her agents still capable of fighting, then brought them to the battle.

The thought had once crossed Amelie's mind that the Lamplight girls could end up posing a threat to her nation, and now she was more certain of that than ever.

And Green Butterfly, who'd turned back to look, after putting some distance between herself and the fight, let out a shocked gasp. "No way........."

Carval was made up of the CIM's cream of the crop, *and all fourteen of them had just gotten annihilated*. Despite being one of the top-two assassination teams in the entire Fend Commonwealth, all it had taken was a single girl to mop the floor with them. The fourteen spies lay collapsed atop the warehouse roof. Some of them had gotten their knees shot out and others had simply lost consciousness, but there wasn't a single Carval member capable of standing on their own two feet anymore.

Monika had done it all on her own. As soon as Carval came after her, she dodged every bullet they fired her way, then closed in and brought the fight to them. And when she did, she *ran them over*. After switching from her knife to her gun, she began firing practically from all but point-blank and got to work obliterating the Carval members' knees and shoulders. There were moments when she used her enemies as shields to repel bullets, and there were others when she stole her foes' knives and hurled them with unparalleled accuracy.

Monika's marksmanship was on point, too. Each time she downed an opponent, she used their body to hide where she was aiming from so the next one wouldn't see her coming. Whenever one of her foes stopped moving for the slightest of moments, Monika's speed meant they were sure to fall victim to her gun.

It took her less than two minutes to completely incapacitate Carval.

Monika weighed the automatic pistol she'd stolen from one of them in her hand.

*I dunno why, but there's this* heat *in me.*

She let out a long exhale as she detachedly surveyed the situation.

*What is this feeling? It's like none of what I'm seeing is real.*

She'd been fighting her battles back-to-back-to-back, and by all rights, her fatigue should have been peaking. Yet in spite of that, she felt absurdly light, like her brain was secreting something that maybe it shouldn't be.

*Are my opponents moving slow? No, I guess I'm just that fast.*

Not even she knew how to describe the state she found herself in.

*It's like there's this fire burning inside my body.*

That was the closest thing she could come up with. It was hot, so hot she could hardly stand it. The fire burning inside her—inside her heart— had set her ablaze.

On that day, Monika earned herself a new code name. Nathan gave it to her after seeing what happened there on the Dock Road.

When intelligence agencies gave monikers to foreign spies, those names carried a different connotation than the ones used domestically. They were given exclusively to spies who held great significance for a particular mission, spies that agencies needed to be wary of, and in some cases, spies that absolutely needed to be eliminated.

For the Fend Commonwealth, that was exactly what Flash Fire was—a threat that needed to be killed at any cost.

"Why…?"

The words spilled from Meredith's mouth as he looked at Monika. He gave no orders to his men. He simply stared at the scene that had played out before him. He could send in all seventy-four of his agents, but he knew he would be sending them in to die for nothing. The raw drive Monika was working with right now made him sure of that. "Why can't they kill her? Carval is one of the CIM's best teams…" All he could do was lament their fate. "They've taken out countless first-rate spies in their—"

Monika turned toward Meredith. As he looked up at her from the foot of the warehouse, he could see the contempt in her eyes.

"___!!"

He gasped. He commanded the majority of the agents present, and she'd spotted him in an instant.

"Can you hear me, you CIM shit stains?" Monika's voice echoed loud and true. "You get one warning. If you come at me, I can't promise you'll live to regret it. I don't care if you're puppets or slaves or what. Anyone who fights me dies."

It was an odd thing for the person who shot Prince Darryn to say. As far as Meredith could tell, though, every single member of Carval was still breathing. As long as they got some emergency first aid, they would be able to make it out of there alive.

Monika had been pulling her punches—and that fact made Meredith shudder all over again.

"I never cared, you know."

Each and every one of her words echoed loudly across the Dock Road.

"I was never interested in the fate of the world or the spy business or any of that. All I wanted was to get to be myself—and to spend my time with people I liked being with. That would've been enough for me!"

Her voice gradually grew more heated.

"But you brain-dead imbeciles let yourselves get tricked by a bunch of assholes, and you killed the wrong people, and now you're trying to destroy everything I care about. It makes me sick. It makes me *fucking sick*!"

Meredith went silent, unable to comprehend Monika's sudden accusations. The wrong people? What in the world was she talking about? She was a villain who'd wronged the Commonwealth. What right did she have to lecture them?

Monika shook her head in exasperation.

"If none of that made sense to you, that's fine. Doesn't change what I need to do."

She readied a pair of pistols she'd taken off of Carval members.

"I'm gonna raze this godforsaken country to the ground."

With that, she took off.

Monika dashed across the warehouse roof, then leaped off at full speed and opened fire in midair. Her bullets flew unerringly, causing the spies around Meredith to scatter as she landed in front of him.

"Fascinating!!" The first person to react to her nimble moves was Meredith himself. Close-quarters combat was his specialty, and his dauntless nature and magnanimity of spirit were the exact things that gave him the charisma to lead seventy-four agents. "You talk a big game for a petty villain snapping at the Crown! I, Armorer, shall bring you to the gallows myself!"

Meredith drew his trusty saber and steeled his nerve. He was going to kill that girl, even if it cost him his life.

The moment before the two of them clashed, Monika took an evasive maneuver and rolled to the side. They passed each other by without either of their attacks landing. Amelie had been waiting in the wings just nearby, and that was the moment she'd chosen to step in. Monika had been forced to give up on attacking Meredith if she wanted to avoid the Belias bullets.

Amelie gave Monika a taunting look and brandished her baton at her. "This nation isn't yours to do with as you wish, you know."

"Rgh! Amelie…"

"It has been some time, hasn't it?" Amelie smiled when she heard Monika click her tongue. **"Programme 187."**

With impeccable coordination, a group of four Belias agents launched an attack on Monika. The four of them were all holding powerful submachine guns. It was an uncommon choice for spies, who generally preferred more covert tools, but when faced with the simultaneous fire of four SMGs, even Monika had no choice but to fall back.

Her whole body *slid* to the side.

In the blink of an eye, she was ten feet to the side of where she'd been just a moment before. After escaping the SMGs' line of fire, she sank a few bullets into the shooters' shoulders. That was Firewalker's technique, the one she'd inherited from Vindo. It was the perfect way to pull off a high-speed hit-and-run.

The problem was, she hadn't perfected it enough to be able to use it more than once in rapid succession. She turned and fled into the gap between two warehouses.

*This isn't some random skirmish breaking out in the middle of the city. It makes perfect sense they'd bring in machine guns.*

This was no battle between spies anymore. This was war. Fighting them head-on would leave Monika at a keen disadvantage.

*I need to get away so I can catch them by surprise and set* the plan *into motion!*

Right when Monika made up her mind, a peculiar man descended on her from overhead as she raced between the warehouses.

The man's hair was over three feet long, and it fluttered behind him as he landed in front of her. An odd jingling noise rang out. The sound came from the massive amount of jewelry he was wearing. His wrists were laden with bangles, and they clinked loudly against each other and his necklaces.

"Those moves were Firewalker's moves. How elegant."

It was "Cursemaster" Nathan, one of the members of the CIM's Hide leadership. He used his gun to comb back his long hair.

"How delightful," Nathan said gloomily. "Having a spy claiming to be from Galgad go on a rampage like yours will do a lovely job sobering up those unseemly Neo-Imperialists of ours. What a wonderfully elegant development..."

"What a coincidence," Monika replied with a grin. "I was thinking the exact same thing."

"What an interesting girl you are... Was that your objective all along, I wonder...?"

"And if it was?"

"You should have come in at full form." Nathan's bangles jingled as he lowered his voice. "This is what happens when you underestimate the CIM."

All of a sudden, he unleashed a brutal flying kick. It took Monika both hands and every ounce of strength she had just to block it.

The blow itself was light, yet for some reason, it threw her completely off-balance. Unable to keep her footing, she keeled over backward. Monika had never seen that technique before.

She turned her back on Nathan and devoted her full efforts toward fleeing. That one exchange had been enough to tell her that fighting him was a bad idea.

Rather than wasting his energy giving chase, Nathan simply let her go. He knew there was no sense rushing things. Instead, he could just let her continue her rampage, then kill her when the time was right.

Monika knew that the math checked out. She could feel death approaching as exhaustion slowly but surely crept its way through her.

*I don't think my body's gonna hold out...*

By the time she beat Carval, she'd already burned through the majority of her stamina.

When Monika rounded the corner, she ran right back into "Armorer" Meredith. The man's greatest strength was his tenacity, and he was prepared to hunt down his target to the ends of the earth. His body simply didn't tire. In Monika's current state, it was about the worst matchup imaginable for her. "What's wrong, villain? Worn out already?!" he jeered as he bore down on her.

Monika bounced her rubber balls off the warehouse walls to attack Meredith from his blind spot. That was her specialty, and thanks to her surprise attack, she was able to distance herself from him and escape his sight.

Her supply of weapons was dwindling, but she'd successfully fled again.

For all her localized victories and escapes, though, it was clear that their sheer numbers would eventually be enough to overrun her. Monika knew that better than anyone. She knew that she had no shot of winning the battle. She knew that there was no hope for her.

Monika had gone into the fight prepared to die.

*But I'm not done yet... Just a little more... A little more's all I need...*

She ran across the Dock Road as far as her body would take her, planting her devices at the base of every oil tank she passed and hurling mirrors into specific spots while keeping an eye on her surroundings. She badly needed to rest, but there were enemies on all sides. Whenever she took them out with her guns, the gunshots drew new foes to her location, and if she stopped to catch her breath for a moment, Meredith would catch up to her like the hunting dog he was.

"Shit," she grumbled feebly.

"Big Sis Monika!!"

Right then, the last person Monika expected rushed over to her from behind cover.

"Erna?!" she cried.

What was Erna doing there on the battlefield? Had she slipped past the CIM's siege?

Unfortunately, Erna's timing couldn't have been worse. There was a Vanajin member who'd been following Monika from atop a warehouse, and when he heard Erna's shout, he turned toward her and fired. As far as he was concerned, she was there to provide Scarlet Leviathan with reinforcements.

The bullet sank directly into Erna's side.

"——!!"

Blood went flying.

Monika immediately shot the man and rushed over to Erna. Erna pressed down on her abdominal wound in pain as blood spilled through her fingers. She was still conscious, but it was obvious at a glance how badly she was wounded.

"Teach told me...," she said through ragged breaths, "to back you up..."

Monika couldn't make sense of it. How was *this* supposed help her?

As she stared at Erna in confusion, Erna's trembling lips curled into a smile. "This should buy you...a little time. Getting unlucky in a way that doesn't quite kill me...and playing the part of an innocent little girl...are my specialties."

"Wait, you *let* yourself get shot...?!"

Erna was wearing an adorable dress, making her indistinguishable from an ordinary civilian. She certainly didn't look the part of a Din Republic spy. However, there was no way Klaus would have ordered her to go and do *that*.

Erna looked Monika right in the eye. "I have faith that you'll survive and make it back to us, Big Sis Monika."

Then her body went limp. She was out like a light. The hand pressing on her abdomen flopped to the ground, and blood began pooling around her.

"...!"

Monika fired a shot in the air, then fled. Eventually, she heard the sound of Meredith bellowing angrily from behind her. "Halt! There's a noncombatant we didn't evacuate!" His voice was bloodcurdlingly intense. "She's been shot! Get her to a hospital, stat! We're not letting a subject of the Crown die on our watch!"

The CIM desperately wanted to avoid civilian casualties, and their formation loosened. That slight letup in their offensive gave Monika the opening she needed to catch her haggard breath.

"————"

Erna had only bought her a tiny bit of time. However, that was more than enough for Monika's will to fight to resurge. She steeled herself and headed for her destination: a wharf, lit up bright by the dock's lights.

Right before she got there, though, she found one final obstacle standing in her way—her hated nemesis.

"Hey, Mooooooooonika, guess who's done fooooooor?!"

It was Green Butterfly. She let out a toothy laugh, like she'd been waiting for Monika to run herself ragged.

Monika clicked her tongue and stopped in her tracks. "Never thought I'd see *your* ugly mug out here."

The CIM had finished getting Erna to safety, and Monika could sense them gathering. It wouldn't be long before they had her completely surrounded. However, Green Butterfly made no efforts to flee. It was like that was precisely what she was hoping for.

"I figured out who you are, you know," Monika said. "You mentioned that you'd betrayed an organization yourself once. That was the CIM, right? And you weren't just any old agent. You had enough authority to deploy people en masse."

Once Monika deduced that much, it wasn't hard to find the answer.

"There's a traitor hiding in the leadership body, Hide—and that traitor is you."

"Bingo!" Green Butterfly clapped her hands together in glee. "I was trying to drop the hints slowly, but I should've known you'd figure me out quick."

She had a hell of a lot of influence. She would even be able to play off the chummy conversation she was having with Monika, no doubt. She could just tell the others that she'd been hiding who she really was in an attempt to draw a confession out of the killer.

Monika sighed and shook her head. "It's no wonder you're so weak."

"Excuse me?"

"You probably learned something as part of Hide. You said something about seeing how heartless the world was, right? Whatever it was you discovered, you couldn't take it. And you know, I feel for you. But then you went and fled. You sold out your country, killed your own prince, took the masses you should've been protecting and mocked them for their ignorance, sank to Serpent's level, and started spreading your petty nightmares. You're a sad, weak little nobody." A contemptuous smirk toyed at the corners of Monika's mouth. "The two of us have *nothing* in common."

Green Butterfly's face went bright red. Much of what Monika had accused her of was conjecture, but it looked like she'd been right on all counts.

"And so what?" Green Butterfly said, scowling in irritation. "You're still gonna die here. Bonfire abandoned you!!"

Green Butterfly had her there. The CIM had the area fully surrounded. In addition to the SMG-toting Belias members, Nathan was standing beside them with his gaze locked on Monika, and any gaps in their formation she could have used to escape were blocked off by Meredith and his Vanajin agents.

Monika and Green Butterfly made their moves in unison.

Green Butterfly took her gun and fired, aiming straight for Monika's throat. As Monika dodged the shot, she fired off one of her own at Green Butterfly's shoulder. The bullet sank straight into her foe's right arm.

"Just *die* already!" Green Butterfly moaned. Monika kicked her aside and charged at the CIM throng.

Doing so was tantamount to suicide, and unsurprisingly, the CIM opened fire, fully intent on riddling Monika with bullets. In her head, though, she was carefully running the numbers.

*Sure, Klaus didn't save me. But you know what? That's fine.*

She began performing the final steps of her calculations. Thanks to that tiny bit of time Erna bought her, she'd been able to complete her plan.

*He crushed me, just like he always does. And that's enough.*

There was one thing Green Butterfly had completely overlooked. What she should have asked herself was, why had Monika gone and risked her life to have that fight with Klaus? By all accounts, doing so had been wildly unnecessary. If Monika had been expecting to have to battle the CIM anyway, it would have made more sense to preserve her stamina. Her actions made no sense.

Green Butterfly had failed to see the reason behind what Monika did. However, it was hardly her fault. For most people, Monika's motive was something completely unthinkable. For any of the Lamplight girls, though, it would have been dead obvious.

*The one class that always led us to greater heights...was our battles against Teach.*

The thing was, it had been necessary. When Monika had told Klaus to come on and school her back at the church, she'd meant it literally. Monika's goal had been for the Greatest Spy in the World *to show her how to survive being at the center of a storm of bullets.*

Monika recognized that dodging all the CIM's shots was beyond her, so she used her arms to protect her vitals and avoid any lethal hits. As she endured the sensation of lead tearing into her flesh, she lured the CIM her way. The technique Klaus gave her had bought her a few precious seconds.

"Angle... Distance... Focal point... Rebounds... Speed... Timing..."

Monika had gained a new power, and that was precisely what she unleashed. After getting her ass handed to her over and over by Klaus and Vindo, she knew she needed to get stronger. She'd spent days and nights trying to come up with a new way to protect Lily and to protect Lamplight, and it had led her to a new power, one far beyond creepshot.

She thrust her right hand at the CIM crowd and cried out loud and true.

"I'm code name Glint—*and it's time to burn bright!*"

Erna had given her the hint. Erna and the accidents she'd engineered during their fight against Avian in Longchon—the burning lenses.

All at once, the entire Dock Road exploded into flames.

There were powerful lights illuminating every nook and cranny of the port, and Monika had used the mirrors and lenses she'd strewn in her wake to focus them, causing the fibers she'd planted to ignite. The fire had triggered the bombs she'd set at the base of the oil tanks, causing the tanks to burst and the oil to combust. Monika had calculated it out perfectly, and the first wave of flames quickly spread to the port's many warehouses and ships, lighting the entire Dock Road ablaze.

The raging flames quickly engulfed the CIM, leaving them no choice but to flee. One after another, they dove into the Turko River to escape the fire.

The port had been transformed into hell on earth in the blink of an eye, and now Green Butterfly was the only one left out on the wharf. Her hair was singed, and her eyes were wide with horror. "Have you completely lost your mind?! This is... This is just wanton destruction!" she howled. "It won't just be spies. You're turning the whole world against you, everyone in every nation—"

"That was always the plan."

Monika and Green Butterfly were the only ones the conflagration hadn't spread to. Surrounded by the flames, the two of them faced each other.

In Monika's hand was a knife. "You can prey on people's weaknesses and get them to turn traitor all you like, but no matter how many allies

you make, I'll bring enough terror to drown you people out. I'll be a king killer or whatever else I have to be."

There was no mercy in her heart.

"Stay the hell out of my way."

Monika took a big step forward and smashed her knife down as hard as she could on Green Butterfly's collarbone. Green Butterfly screamed, then fell prone.

*Now that that's settled...*

After dealing with Green Butterfly, Monika took a moment to catch her breath. Her situation wasn't much better than it had been before. The fire was fast approaching from her rear, and the river was full of dozens of CIM hostiles.

The fight was still going, and it wouldn't be over until Monika breathed her last.

The world hadn't been kind to Monika.

Every time she thought she finally had something of her own, some power too great for her to oppose always came in to destroy it. Every time she uprooted her life, the universe found new setbacks to throw at her. Her society took the feelings she held most precious and wrote them off as a mental illness. And when she hid those feelings deep within her and quietly nurtured them, a vicious spy exposed them, took advantage of them, and led Monika to ruin.

That was why she fought. That was why she held her head high, knowing that her very existence was one of rebellion.

Lighting Fires × Villain Role = Playing the Heel.

So what if she never got to share with anyone? All of humanity could hate her, and she would be just fine.

*What a perfect liecraft for me*, the contrarian thought as her lips curled into a grin.

# Epilogue

## The Girl and the World

A conversation took place one day in Lily's room in Heat Haze Palace.

"Hey, Monika, I've got a question!"

"I'm right here; you don't have to shout. Also, less talking, more massaging."

"I've been wondering, what's your special talent? You never actually told me."

"Oh yeah, I guess I haven't."

"I think Grete's figured it out, but even though I keep bugging her, she won't tell me."

"I told Sara, y'know."

"You what?!"

"Hey, Lily, look here for a sec."

"Huh? *Ack!* What was that sudden light?!"

"There, done. Thing is, I'm plenty strong without having to rely on fancy tricks. I'd rather avoid having my intel leaked, so I try not to spread it too far."

"Secretive to the end, huh...? So what was that light about?"

"That one I'm definitely not telling anyone. Least of all you."

To that day, Monika had never been able to bring herself to throw away the photo she took during that exchange.

◇◇◇

The Dock Road fire continued well on into the night.

Right around midnight, the administration put out a rare emergency bulletin. Although they announced that the fire had been started by a foreign spy, they chose not to reveal the spy's nationality. "We believe it was the same agent as the one who killed His Highness Prince Darryn," the cabinet secretary declared. "After being cornered by the CIM, the treacherous spy used their gun to take their own life." Then, after advising the public not to blindly believe the rumors that were flying around, he ended the briefing. The press bombarded him with follow-up questions, but he ignored them all.

It was unclear how the public would react to the news, but at least now the matter was settled.

After watching the bulletin from the CIM's headquarters, Nathan let out a long breath. Then he turned to his subordinate Amelie, who was waiting in the wings. "That should help quell the unrest somewhat... I imagine we'll come under fire for letting the suspect kill herself, but at least this way we get to save a little bit of face. You did well, Amelie. I'll be sure to tell the rest of Hide about your team's efforts." "Cursemaster" Nathan was the first member of the CIM's Hide senior leadership whose face Amelie had ever seen. He looked at the television with a satisfied nod. "Now we can finally hold a funeral for His Highness. We'll need to make sure to give him an elegant send-off..."

Normally, praise from someone of his status would have been enough to make Amelie weep tears of joy. At the moment, though, she wasn't in the mood. "Are you sure about this?" she asked.

"Hmm?"

"We never did end up finding Monika's body."

After exchanging some more shots with the CIM, Monika had ultimately disappeared after getting swallowed by the flames. Amelie assumed she was surely dead, but they'd never been able to track down that crucial corpse. "I don't care if she's dead; all enemies of the Crown must hang," Meredith had growled before sending out his units to find her, but their search had ended in vain.

Nathan shrugged. "There are some things the people don't need to know...and the fact that we let the killer escape after causing a fire like that is certainly one of them. There would be riots in the streets."

"...We are always just, and we do not err."

"Exactly. As servants of the Crown, our elegance must be unimpeachable."

From the way he was talking, he didn't seem too concerned about the fact that they'd failed to find Monika. He didn't sound mad, either. Amelie still had no idea what his notion of elegance was. Perhaps on some level, he'd realized that Monika wasn't the real killer.

"By the way, I hear Flash Fire left us a parting gift," Nathan remarked.

"Ah yes. On that wharf..."

Monika had left a girl behind beaten within an inch of her life. There had to be some meaning there. Amelie didn't recognize the spy, but at the same time, there was something oddly familiar about her.

"The girl was 'Magician' Mirena—one of the members of Hide."

"What.........?"

"She's the second daughter of Her Highness Third Princess Hatofe. Her very existence is a secret, so I'm not surprised you haven't heard of her. For a long time now, Hide has had a custom of choosing at least one of its members from the royal family."

Amelie's eyes went wide with disbelief at the revelation. Considering how much authority Fend's monarchy wielded, there were a lot of advantages to having a royal in your ranks. Mirena had even been the go-between for the CIM and the royal family for that very incident. Still, Amelie could hardly believe that a girl that young had been behind the partition that whole time.

"Amelie, I need you to interrogate her," Nathan said with steel in his voice. "I believe Flash Fire was trying to tell us something..."

While Amelie and Nathan were dealing with the aftermath, Lamplight sat in their detention cell and waited for good news.

At the moment, the CIM still hadn't told them anything. Instead, they were relying on the Lamplight wireless radio sitting in the middle of the room. Klaus had smuggled it in. Thanks to how it had been constructed, it could pick up signals from a massive distance.

They knew Monika had stolen Thea's radio, and they knew she would have held on to it tight.

Klaus and the girls stared at the radio, hoping beyond hope that Monika would call. From time to time, they would take turns calling her name into it.

"Monika's alive. I know she is," Klaus said quietly. "All we need to do is wait to hear from her."

Not a single person present could tear their eyes from the radio.

Monika walked through the night.

Her body was giving off a burnt smell. After trading shots with the CIM from within the raging flames, she'd chosen to flee. She'd caused enough damage as a "Galgad spy," and it was time to prioritize surviving. To that end, she made the all-or-nothing call to dive into the firestorm and pray she could make it out the other side.

To the CIM, it should have looked like she died. Hoping they would decide their mission was complete, she fled.

After applying emergency first aid to her bullet wounds, she jumped on board a passing truck while taking care not to let the driver notice her. When it arrived on the southeast side of Hurough, she jumped off and started looking for somewhere she could rest and recuperate.

*This is bad… Feels like I'm about to pass out…*

Her body was reaching its limit.

Monika had used up everything she had back there. She was out of bullets, out of bombs, out of mirrors, and out of lenses. All she had was a single half-broken knife. She barely even had enough blood left in her body to keep moving. If she let her focus slip for even half a second, she was liable to collapse where she stood and pass right out.

Her goal was to reach the spot Lan had shown her—"Firewalker" Gerde's secret hideout.

The old wooden apartment building had barely any tenants, there was food and water there, and the CIM didn't know about it. All she had to do was get there, and she would be able to rest safely.

She knew her body was about to give out, but she dragged herself step by step past the houses dotting the quiet town.

"Excuse me, miss, are you okay?"

Midway through her journey, she heard a young voice come from behind her.

When she turned around, she was greeted by a young girl dressed in pajamas who looked to be all of about six. The girl was holding a pink teddy bear. Based on how she was dressed, she'd clearly just jumped out of bed.

"It's dangerous to be walking around. There's a bad guy hurting people over in Hurough, see. Mommy and Daddy were scared, both of them were. I don't think it's good to be outside right now."

She must have spotted Monika through her window and come rushing out. It was night, so it was too dark for her to see Monika's injuries.

Monika grinned in spite of herself. "It's okay. The bad guy's gone now."

"Really?"

"Yeah, for sure. All the big Fend heroes came together to beat her up. I'm telling you, they really gave it to her good. The bad guy got totally destroyed, and she burned up in the fires of justice. Head on back to bed and rest easy."

An innocent smile of genuine relief spread across the girl's face. "Oh, thank goodness," she said as she went back into her house.

After watching her go, Monika continued her trek toward Gerde's hideout.

People across the country would be celebrating come morning. The CIM had killed Prince Darryn's assassin with aplomb. The news would be met with applause, and peace would return to the land. Then, as the chaos subsided, people would begin smiling again. Children like the girl she just met would go back to showing big, toothy grins.

Now that the world was rid of Monika, people would welcome it wholeheartedly.

Monika sighed. That was fine. If that was what it took to rid the world of one of its fears, then that was fine.

"Screw off, you monster. Like, for real."

A voice came from down the road. It was a vulgar voice, the kind that was rough and filthy and spoke to the small-mindedness of its owner.

"I mean, what's the deal here? The student of a monster's gotta be a monster, too? Makes me not wanna even get out of bed in the morning."

The man before her had hair like a mushroom. He was short of stature, and he smacked his forehead with the melancholy look in his eyes of a man who derided the world and everything in it. He let out a melodramatic sigh as he walked toward her with his sniper rifle resting on his shoulder.

Monika recognized those features. The man was a dead ringer for the portrait Klaus once drew.

It was White Spider.

A contorted grin crept across White Spider's face. "Though, I did have to get pretty dang lucky to find you here, so I guess it cancels out," he said.

A lot of things made sense to Monika now. She had known that Green Butterfly wasn't the only Serpent member in Fend, after all.

"Tell me," she said, glaring at him. "Are you the guy Green Butterfly answers to?"

"Something like that, yeah."

"Ah. And you're the one who shot Prince Darryn, too."

"I'll leave that one to your imagination." White Spider lowered the sniper rifle from his shoulder and readied it. "And on that note... Gonna need you to die."

It took everything Monika had to block his bullet with the back of her knife. The punch it packed was enough to put all those pistols from earlier to shame, and the force of the impact alone was enough to break Monika's wrist. She kept an eye on White Spider as she rolled away, keenly aware that her right hand was out of commission.

"Wait, you found her before I did? Damn you. How dare you leave the Unrivaled in the dust."

A new man's voice came from the opposite direction as White Spider.

The first things that caught Monika's eye were his *three right arms*. Two of them were prosthetics, no doubt, and they gave off an unnatural metallic gleam where the moonlight struck them. As far as the man himself went, he was certainly tall and stocky, but the coat hood covering his head made it hard for Monika to make out his face.

"With this loss, though, I see where things stand. I relinquish the title of Unrivaled. Now I can retire."

"Black Mantis, my guy, c'mon. You gotta stop trying to retire over every tiny thing."

"...My Surmounters are still out of order. My heart isn't in it."

"Seriously, dude, quit grumbling and help me out here. How was I supposed to know things were gonna get this messy?"

"I guess it's no wonder you're calling on my aid. Such is the lot of those overblessed with talent. I can feel the hopes of millions of Imperials resting on my shoulders... Once again, retirement inches away from me."

"I am literally begging you to stop giving narcissistic speeches every time I need you to get your rear in gear."

After bantering for a bit, the two of them turned their attention back to Monika.

"All right, guess we'd better finish you off."

Monika didn't hesitate. Instead, she poured every bit of energy she had left into escaping. She leaped to her feet, then fled away from the street and toward the houses to escape from the duo closing in on her from the front and behind.

"Damn, you can still run?" White Spider called after her in amusement.

Based on their conversation just now, Black Mantis was another member of Serpent. Green Butterfly was just a pawn to them, but that guy was on a different level.

Monika had no bullets or stamina left, and her dominant hand was broken. Plus, it was two against one. There was no way she could beat them. That there was a fact, one that no amount of pluck or determination could overturn.

After escaping their line of sight, Monika plotted yet another course for "Firewalker" Gerde's hideout. As far as she could tell, Serpent had simply anticipated her escape route and moved to cut her off. There was no reason for them to know about the hideout.

If she could make it to that wooden apartment building, she just might survive.

She could feel the strength draining from her legs, but she kept on desperately putting one of them in front of the other.

*"Monika!"*

Then she heard a voice from the radio in her pocket.

*"If you can hear me, please, say something!"*

Monika's eyes went wide, and she stopped in her tracks.
"Lily...?"

She'd turned on the radio just before her fight with the CIM, and that was unmistakably Lily's voice coming through it. It had finally connected.

Previously, the massive number of radios the CIM was using had been hogging all the bandwidth. They must have just halted their search for her.

"*Where are you? Are you okay?!*"

"I'll make this quick." Monika held the radio to her ear and resumed running. She heard Lily gasp on the other end. "Green Butterfly is with Hide. I just ran into White Spider in Immiran. He was the one giving Green Butterfly her orders, and he's the one who shot Prince Darryn. There's a guy with him called Black Mantis who's got a bunch of arms—"

"Whatcha talkin' about?"

When Monika arrived at the apartment building, she ran right back into White Spider and Black Mantis. They'd gotten there first. There were nasty grins dancing on their faces, like a pair of hunters who were delighting in watching their frantic prey.

For a split second, Monika's brain kicked into overdrive. There was a piece of intel she needed to pass on, and she needed to do it now.

"Get code name Insight. We need them. They're the only person who can beat Serpent."

White Spider's and Black Mantis's eyes narrowed a smidge.

Monika knew better than to mention any details around them, but Klaus had put together an unorthodox plan just before Lamplight left for the Commonwealth. Rather than the eight girls, it revolved around the one Din Republic spy he trusted more than anyone else.

"And also…"

She trailed off. She'd conveyed all the necessary information.

"You done giving your last words?" White Spider readied his sniper rifle. "Thanks for that fascinating little tidbit at the end, by the way. I think we're done here."

Monika had gotten to the apartment building, but with her foes right in front of her, she couldn't take refuge there, and it didn't look like they were in the mood to let her keep running.

"*Monika…?*" Lily said through the radio. What kind of expression was she making? Monika wondered.

"And also…"

The next words she said would be her last.

The urge to silently drop the radio struck her again and again. However, it was what Grete told her that stayed her hand. That, and the want welling up inside her. She couldn't count how many times she'd feared the idea of dying without ever sharing her emotions with anyone. Her whole life had been a journey coming to terms with it.

"Hey, Lily."

Her lips parted.

"I know that me telling you probably isn't gonna do you any good..."

She felt tears start to well up in her eyes.

"And honestly, you're pretty sharp, so you might've figured out how I feel ages ago anyway..."

After she fought back the tears, a heartfelt smile spread slowly across her face as she went on.

"...but I'm in love with you."

She heard the shot and felt the shock at the same time.

White Spider's point-blank shot tore through the radio, smashing it to pieces. Monika had been holding the radio in her left hand, and both it and her ear got blasted. A thick trail of blood rolled from the side of her head down her cheek, but her hands lacked the strength to so much as press down on the wound anymore.

"You mind if I ask you something, just outta personal curiosity?" White Spider sounded like he was enjoying himself. "None of this went the way I planned it. If you'd just changed sides to Serpent for real, I was ready to spare Flower Garden's life. You could've just quit Lamplight, quit being a spy, and went and lived in peace with her. Would that really have been so bad?"

The thought had crossed Monika's mind on more than one occasion. If she sacrificed Lamplight, then she and Lily could go off and live a quiet life in some remote village. They could break ties with the entire world of espionage and simply spend their days in peace.

Depending on the choices Monika made, that was one future that might have awaited her. However, there was no way she could have ever chosen it.

"That was never an option," Monika rasped. "I'm in love with Lily, but she's not in love with me."

Upon hearing her answer, White Spider gave her a pitying look. "...I'll take that under advisement," he said, then aimed his rifle again. Beside him, Black Mantis raised his three right arms aloft.

Her time was up.

Monika sucked in a deep breath, then shot them a question. "You want me to——?"

"Huh?"

The night wind had completely drowned out the remainder of her sentence.

"C'mon, don't make me repeat myself," she said. She hoisted up her motionless right hand, then smirked as best she could to force her expression to one of pride.

"I asked if you wanted me to go easy on you shitters."

Monika saw Black Mantis's three right arms move in unison, but that was all she caught. Then a powerful impact enveloped her, and her mind went blank. Her clothes tore as her body went flying. She slammed into, then through the wooden apartment building's wall, eventually landing in someone's unit on the ground floor.

She'd arrived at her destination, but the act was meaningless. Gerde's apartment was up on the third floor. It was impossibly far away. What's more, the building had already caught fire. The Serpent duo must have set it. The flames surged in intensity as though to mock Monika's desire for respite.

Monika lay there on her side and saw the photo she'd been holding on to flutter in front of her—the photo of Lily, the one she'd taken in secret and kept hidden away for so long.

As her consciousness faded, she continued staring at her smile to the very end.

# Next Mission

The spy code named Insight looked down in silence at the city.

The entirety of Hurough was celebrating.

A heavy rain had fallen the morning after the Dock Road fire, putting out the flames and returning the city to a state of calm. The chaos in front of the station started dying down, and fewer and fewer people showed up to each protest. Criminal organizations had enjoyed a period of rapid growth recently, but thanks to a CIM crackdown, even they lost their steam.

Hearing that Prince Darryn's killer had successfully been executed brought peace of mind back to the people of Hurough.

In order to preserve their national reputation, the government celebrated the reporters from the *Conmerid Times* and other newspapers who'd published unauthorized photos of the killer as national heroes who'd fought bravely to report the truth. It was actually the Fires of War that had been behind those articles, but with the disappearance of its all-powerful leader, the group quickly collapsed.

When faced with the rumors that the assassin had been from the Galgad Empire, high-ranking Galgad officials held a press conference to unilaterally deny the allegations. "These claims have no basis in truth," they said. "Our administration wishes to express its deepest condolences for the crown prince's untimely passing. We have every desire to continue fostering bonds of cooperation with the Fend Commonwealth."

Meanwhile, antipathy toward the Empire grew stronger within the Fend populace. However, the CIM had no intention of letting the Great War's tragedies repeat themselves, and they did everything in their power to steer the public discourse. By taking advantage of the media organizations under their control, they were able to spread anti-war sentiments alongside the Anti-Imperialist tide.

Slowly but surely, things were going back to normal in the city as it woke from its long nightmare. The greatest evil had been vanquished, and now there was nothing they needed to worry about. Their smiles said as much. The people of Hurough held photos of the cerulean-haired girl in contempt, burning them as they laughed about her pathetic suicide. Then they enjoyed lovely holidays with their friends and loved ones.

A feeling of emptiness struck Insight as they looked out at the revelers.

Monika had gone and erased herself from the world.

Sorrow lingered in Insight's heart when they thought about the resolve that must have taken. They sighed, and a twinge ran through their shoulder. The wound there had fully healed, yet it throbbed with the memory of pain.

Insight was Lamplight's secret weapon.

Klaus had put the plan together shortly before leaving for Fend. He put a huge amount of trust in Insight, and Insight knew they were to be a trump card that could deceive and overcome any foe. Insight carried a heavy responsibility, but their powers were far from absolute. They had no way of operating solo.

As such, they had no choice but to wait. Wait and see what Lamplight did.

Klaus and the girls' confinement continued for three days straight.

During that time, the only event of note was Lan getting transferred to a hospital, as she'd yet to receive any sort of proper medical attention. That, and them getting word that Amelie had quietly placed the hospital room where Erna's chest wound was being treated under protection. Annette and Grete were still being treated as well, but there were no changes to speak of there.

The five of them—Klaus, Lily, Sybilla, Thea, and Sara—could do nothing but wait. It wasn't until three days later, in the morning, that Amelie came to visit them.

"Bonfire," she said matter-of-factly. Her outfit was tidy and well put together. "We've identified the CIM traitors who were working with Green Butterfly. Furthermore, the majority of our operatives believe Flash Fire, aka Monika, to have been working for the Galgad Empire. Where the CIM was once divided between Neo-Imperialists and Anti-Imperialists, we now stand to present a united Anti-Imperialist front." She gave him a small bow. "Thank you for your help. On behalf of Hide, we would like to extend you our sincerest gratitude."

For her, those were all major accomplishments. Her voice brimmed with pride at a job well done.

Klaus, on the other hand, was less thrilled. Saving the Commonwealth had never ranked high on his list of priorities. "I would've been fine either way," he replied. "If I had to kill you all and hijack the CIM, it wouldn't have been any skin off my back."

"If we had fought, both the CIM and Lamplight would have lost good people. There would be no meaning to the conflict—isn't that what drove Monika?"

Hearing Monika's name sent a ripple through Klaus's heart. They still had no news about whether she'd survived. Klaus still believed she would make it back to them alive, but at the end of the day...

He pulled himself together before Amelie could notice how shaken he was.

"There was a mastermind who engineered the Commonwealth's nightmare," Amelie went on. "We would welcome your assistance in capturing White Spider."

Klaus saw a hint of relief in her face. The only reason the Fend Commonwealth and Din Republic had been at odds was because Green Butterfly had been using her position in CIM leadership to spread misinformation about a Din spy having been the one to kill Prince Darryn. Now, though, Monika had pinned that crime on herself under the guise of being a Galgad spy, and on top of that, she'd personally put Green Butterfly out of commission. Now Fend and Din could finally work together in earnest, and it was all thanks to her.

However, there was still an elephant in the room.

"If that's the case," Klaus said, "then what's with the blatant hostility?"

There were over a dozen agents standing at the ready behind Amelie, all staring daggers at Klaus and the girls.

"Hide's orders," Amelie replied with conviction. "Surely you understand? You know Serpent well, and we want to work with you. However, you're too dangerous to be turned loose. We can't trust you, at least not running around freely."

There was a quiet certainty in her expression.

"The CIM is going to have to take Bonfire and Dreamspeaker into custody."

Klaus had been prepared for this. "Flash Fire" Monika had been one of his own subordinates, and Thea had been in charge of the criminal organization the Fires of War. From the CIM's perspective, locking them up was the only reasonable option. On this side of the world, betrayal was a constant. There was no way the CIM was ever going to give them its unconditional trust. Furthermore, resisting wasn't an option. If he tried to refuse, it would just end up sparking another useless fight with the CIM.

Grim expressions spread across the girls' faces as Amelie snapped a pair of handcuffs around Klaus's wrists. They'd been built sturdy, so he wouldn't be slipping out of them easily. Thea was restrained in much the same manner.

It looked as though their days in confinement would be continuing until the situation reached its conclusion.

"Teach…" "Boss…"

Behind him, he heard Lily's and Sybilla's voices. They sounded like they were on the verge of tears.

The nightmare Serpent had created continued.

"Forgetter" Annette had been hospitalized with a series of broken ribs.

"Daughter Dearest" Grete needed to recuperate after her prolonged imprisonment.

"Fool" Erna had been hospitalized after the CIM shot her in the side.

It was unclear whether "Glint" Monika was even still alive.

And "Bonfire" Klaus and "Dreamspeaker" Thea had been detained by the CIM.

With so many of its members out of commission, Lamplight was no longer functional. They needed to verify Monika's status as soon as possible, but they lacked the active personnel to do even that.

It was time for a different girl's story to begin.

Up until then, other people had always been protecting her, and during their missions, she'd been relegated to supporting roles. During their first Impossible Mission, the Abyss Doll bioweapon retrieval, she didn't accomplish anything of note. During the Corpse mission, her participation had been minimal at best. And things had played out the exact same way during the fight against Purple Ant in Mitario, the fight against Avian in Longchon, and the fight against Belias in Fend.

She had been trying her best. However, it was impossible to deny how much her achievements paled in comparison to the other girls'. She saw herself as the weakest member on the team, and on the whole, she wasn't wrong.

Sara quivered in the corner as Klaus and Thea got hauled away, cradling her knees with her hat pulled down low so she didn't have to face the horrible reality of their situation. She'd been sitting like that for the entire three days. Tears had been spilling down her cheeks ever since they were brought there as she fought to endure the grief welling up in her heart.

*Miss Monika...*

The odds she'd survived were slim. They all knew it. Monika was a problem for Serpent, and they had no reason to spare her life.

Each time Sara thought about the fact that Monika might very well be dead, the tears started pouring all over again. Monika had been like a second teacher to her. Sara often needed specific guidance that Klaus wasn't equipped to offer her, and Monika was always the one who'd picked up Klaus's slack there.

At one point, Sara asked Monika why she did so much for her. *"I've been wondering about it a lot,"* she admitted embarrassedly.

*"Look, you remember back when we visited Inferno's grave and told them Lamplight was getting back together?"* Monika had replied. *"How one by one, everyone said they chose to stay on the team?"*

Sara did remember. Everyone had given their answers without hesitating. Sybilla was in it for the money; Thea, out of admiration; Erna, for the sake of her dream; Annette, because she enjoyed being around them; Grete, out of love; and Lily, to live up to her ideals.

*"You and me were the only ones who didn't say anything."*

She was right. Sara had simply stood there in awkward silence.

Monika smiled. *"I hope we both find something—some reason to stick around in the world of espionage."*

Looking back now, Sara understood. Monika *had* fought it. She'd found something worth fighting for, a motive so powerful she had no choice but to turn the world on its head.

Sara wished she could have talked with Monika more. She wished she could have heard Monika say it in her own words.

As soon as she recognized that wish for what it was, she wiped away her tears.

*A reason to stick around in the world of espionage...*

She put her strength back into her legs.

*Can't my teammates on Lamplight be that for me?*

People might scold her for that and call it a cop-out. *"That's* what you're taking up arms for?" they would cry. However, that was fine. They could reprimand her all they liked. The only thing Sara wanted to hear in all the world was Monika admonishing her with that mix of exasperation and kindness in her voice.

She rose to her feet.

Monika had to be alive. This was *Monika* they were talking about. Sara had faith that Monika could overcome any crisis the world threw at her. Surely, she had survived and was hiding away somewhere. Klaus himself had said it, hadn't he? "Monika's alive. I know she is." Those were his very words.

In order to save her, though, there was one man they were going to have no choice but to face.

The thing was, *White Spider knew where Monika was.*

Maybe he'd kidnapped her. Maybe she'd escaped his grasp. Either way, he was the only one who had the info. He was the architect behind Fend's nightmare, he was Lamplight's archnemesis who killed their brothers- and sisters-in-arms, and he was the only way they could rescue Monika.

Sara clenched her fists tightly and turned toward the entrance. The Belias agents were hauling Klaus away, and Lily and Sybilla were simply staring, helpless to do anything about it.

"BOSS!!" Sara called after him.

Klaus looked back in surprise. "Sara...?"

She knew what she was about to say was preposterous.

"Ah..."

She bit down hard on her trembling lips, then bit down again, and then again.

"I..."

The sheer lunacy of what she was proposing caused tears to well up in her eyes all over again.

"I-I'm..."

She sounded pathetic, and tears were still on her cheeks. In the end, though, she managed to get the words out firmly and clearly.

"I'm going to defeat White Spider!!"

She was going to do it. Her resolve was steeled. She and the others were going to catch a Serpent member all on their own. They were going to drag Monika's whereabouts out of him and find her, no matter what it took. They were going to make him tell them why he killed Prince Darryn, why he destroyed Avian, and everything else they wanted to know, and in doing so, they would bring their mission there in Fend to its completion.

Right now there was only one thing Sara wanted—to get them all home to Heat Haze Palace without letting anyone else get hurt.

# *Afterword*

I know the Volume 7 afterword isn't the greatest place for it, but I hope you don't mind if I take a moment to talk about my writing process for Volume 6.

I'm pretty sure it'll be announced by the time this goes on sale, but *Spy Classroom* is getting an anime adaptation. How cool is that?! And it's all thanks to you readers. Thank you all so much.

Now, I'm sure a lot of you are wondering, *How are you going to pull off the twist from Volume 1?* and as far as that goes, the people involved in the anime's production came up with a really good idea. It won't be exactly same as it was in the novel, but they're treating the material with a lot of respect. I'm incredibly grateful. There are tons of people doing some amazing work on the project, and it's packed with little touches that made me go "Wow, you're really going to that level of polish?" in amazement. More news will be coming soon, so make sure you check out the official Twitter account.

I attended each and every one of the script meetings, and while the latter half were mostly online due to the COVID situation, the ones during the period when the infection rate was low took place in a conference room where I got the chance to talk to loads of different people about *Spy Classroom*. I was writing Volume 6 at the time, and during those conversations, something caught my attention.

*Wait… Is it just me, or is Monika crazy popular?*

I didn't go around asking people to fill out a survey or anything, but it surprised me just how many people I spotted saying, "Oh man, I love Monika." I mean, she hadn't even had her spotlight volume yet. Now that I think about it, though, I see a lot of people echoing that sentiment on Twitter and in the fan mail I get.

I really appreciated it, don't get me wrong, but at the same time, I felt the pressure of their expectations weighing down on my shoulders.

*...I have to make sure I really nail the Monika volume.*

Now, here it is. How did you like it? It's a good bit longer than usual.

At this point, I have some people I'd like to thank. Tomari, thank you for continuing to bless the books with your wonderful illustrations. Every time I hear about the schedule they have you on for the anime project, I shudder. *Tomari's got so much to do!!* I think. Make sure you're taking care of yourself.

I'd also like to extend a special thank-you to M, whose help was invaluable on this volume. Look, M, I finished it.

Last up, I have a preview of what's to come. The next book is the final volume of the second season, and it should go without saying who the focal girl will be. This time around, the girls who got left out of the main Corpse mission—the unchosen squad—will be going up against the big bad. This is where Lily, Sybilla, and Sara begin their counterattack. Them, and one other person who didn't get to strut her stuff this time around. Until then, that's all from me.

*Takemachi*